GREEN
PEELER

Also by lizzie Qnert

POWER SURGE
CRACKSHELL
(1st book in Rock Narrows Series)

lizzie Qnert

GREEN PEELER

Rock Narrows Suspense Series
book 2

Nordhoff
publishing

ISBN: 9798987197745 (paperback)
ISBN: 9798987197752 (ebook)

lizzieQnert.com

Printed in the United States of America

To my friends & family on the Eastern Shore. Thanks for welcoming this chicken necker into your lives.

2019   SYDNEY—May 21

Eddie's body is slumped across the table, the empty syringe still in his arm. A row of crumpled beer cans wreathes his head like a halo and empty bottles of Jack Daniels litter the floor. His breaths are irregular and slow, more than a minute apart. If he doesn't hurry up and die, I'll have to give him another dose.

My breasts are full and ache. It's time to nurse Helly. Maggie's babysitting my little parasite. I told her I needed a night out. It wasn't a complete lie. Motherhood has obliterated my alone time. A little peace and quiet would be welcome, but it's not on the agenda tonight. Tonight, I have to rid the world of an evil bastard.

I considered Maggie my sister long before I married her brother Jake, and no wife-beating monster is going to terrorize a member of my family. Eddie's increasingly violent harassment stops now.

His skin and fingernails are a ghoulish shade of blue. It shouldn't be much longer. I bend my cheek in front of his nose and mouth. Dammit! There's still a slight exhale.

My breasts leak through my shirt and are really starting to hurt. I should've expected Eddie to be too difficult to go easily. I wish I would've brought my pump. I gave Maggie plenty of breast milk, so Helly will be well fed. I, however, might end up with mastitis if he doesn't die soon.

When I realized Eddie would never stop tormenting Maggie, I hatched my plan. Eddie's whiskey breakfast and beer lunch, followed by dinner at the local crack house, makes him easy pickings. Without fail, he's passed out across his table by 9 p.m., slack-jawed face resting in a puddle of drool. As a true-crime novelist, I've learned all kinds of useful things, like a warm compress will make veins easier to access, and a 500 mg dose of heroin will kill even a longtime addict.

Jake's at the Annapolis Boat Show until tomorrow. Other than during show season, he rarely leaves Rock Narrows, so I knew I had to take advantage of the opportunity. Around eight, after settling Helly in with Maggie, I went to Dollie's. As usual, the bar was full of weather-hardened watermen, still wearing their white rubber boots and salt-splattered shirts, reeking of fish and eel.

I shot a game of Cutthroat with Snooks, the local pool shark, and Skip, one of Jake's co-workers. As expected, Snooks took me and Skip for five dollars apiece and then called it a night. Eight's late to be out in a watermen's town. Their work day starts before dawn. Anyone left in the bar much later than that is three sheets to the wind. Perfect for me. They'll remember seeing me, but won't have a clue as to when.

Around nine fifteen I came here, to Eddie's house, and found him exactly as expected—passed out drunk. I used his own stash of heroin to shoot him up with what I'm hoping is a lethal dose. Eddie's drinking and drug use has escalated since his divorce from Maggie, so no one will be surprised when he's found dead of an overdose.

I check my watch. It's been at least five minutes since his last breath. I pace around the house. It's a pig sty: black rings in the toilet, sweat-stained bed sheets, molding food in the fridge, and crusty dishes in the sink. Without realizing it, I've wiped the crumbs off the counter, thrown the funky dish towel into the washer, and folded the tea towel and hung it on the stove. I resist the urge to tidy anything else.

I take off my rubber gloves, shove them in my pocket, and hold my fingers under his nose—nothing. He's dead.

Even though this repulsive, vile man had no remorse for beating the baby out of his wife, I feel a twinge of regret over ending his life. But I am steadfast. I won't shy away from a difficult task. It needed to be done, and God gifted me with the strength and resolve to do it. Maggie has suffered too much; she does not deserve to live with the constant threat of violence. And now, I am proud to say, I've set her free.

MAGGIE—May 21

Ruby, my black Lab, growls at the back door. I look out the kitchen window and see movement. Someone is out there.

I turn off the kitchen light and lay a sleepy Helly in her playpen. Ruby bares her teeth. I bet it's Eddie. He nearly killed her once. That's when I divorced him. I could take his punches, but I damn well couldn't sit by and let him beat my dog.

I thought the divorce would be the end of it, but that son-of-a-bitch just won't leave me alone. Just in the past two months, he's messed with my bait, cut my trotline, dumped a bucket of rotten fish on the driver's seat of my truck and added water to my gas tank.

I grab Swannee's shotgun from the hall closet. We just got 'em back from the cops—almost two years since they confiscated them. It ain't loaded, but Eddie don't need to know that.

I open the back door and step out on the stoop, gun pointed at the man sneaking around my back yard.

"Jesus Christ, Nails! Don't shoot. It's me, Whitey."

I flip on the outside light. With his pale skin he looks like a ghost.

"Whitey, why the fuck are you prowlin' around here? Good way to get yourself shot."

He's so drunk he can barely stand up. "Looking for Jake."

"He ain't here."

"Bev kicked me out again."

"Wonder why."

He holds onto my truck to steady hisself. "I know. I know."

I look out the driveway and don't see his rusted-out junker. "Where's your truck?"

"Bev took my keys."

Smart woman.

I lean against the doorjamb. "Well, how'd you get here?"

"Walked."

As bad as he's staggerin', it hadda take him hours. Bev's house is a few miles out the road, a couple doors down from Eddie's house.

"How long it take ya?"

He holds up an empty bottle of vodka. "Long as it took me to drink this."

Headlights flash across the driveway and Whitey throws his arm up to cover his eyes. Syd's CRV pulls into the lane. She must spot the shotgun, 'cause she throws her car into park and jumps out.

"Maggie, what the hell is going on?"

"Nothing to worry 'bout. Whitey's drunk—again—and Bev kicked him out."

He staggers towards Syd. "What bug's up your ass? Why didn't you pick me up on the road by my house. You hadda see me hitchhiking."

"Why was you out by his house? I thought you went to Dollie's," I say to Syd.

Her cheeks get redder than an orangutan's ass and the black part of her eyes is huge.

Her laugh is weird. "Whitey, you didn't see me. I just left Dollie's."

When he swings his arm to point at her car, he trips over his own feet and lands in the dirt. "That's the car I saw. And you was in it."

Syd helps him up. "You're drunk."

"I may be drunk, but I ain't blind. Next time you need something, don't ask me for help. All I wanted was a goddamn ride."

She rolls her eyes and pats his arm. "Okay. Okay. Whatever you say. So, why are you here?"

"Bev kicked me out. Told me it's for good this time."

I hope he don't think he's stayin' here. "And?"

"And, I was gonna get a few bucks and a ride from Jake. My buddy PeeWee's up in Maine until the end of summer. Said I can crash on his Chris-Craft till he gets back."

"Where's his boat?" Syd asks.

"He rents a slip from some lawyer named Bergmann down near Hooper's Point."

"No rich lawyer is gonna want your sorry ass sleeping in a boat on his property. You just better get your shit together and move back in with Bev."

"She don't want me. Besides, the lawyer ain't around. He's in the middle of some big court case."

Syd rubs her face. "Tell you what. After I check the crab pens and pump, I'll run you out to your friend's boat."

He turns his back on us and pisses on a bush. "You got any cash on ya?"

I dig two twenties outta my pocket. Whitey staggers and falls on the ground.

He spreads his arms out wide. "Fuck it. I'll just sleep here, under the stars."

"The hell you will." I walk out to the yard. "Help me get him in your car. You better run him out the road now, before he's out cold. Helly's asleep and I'll check the pens for you. Can't do nothing for your tits, though."

Whitey gets a sloppy grin on his face. "I can."

Syd digs her foot into his side. "Don't be gross. Get up."

Me and Syd haul his ass up.

"Will you check the slough box, too?" she asks.

I nod and help Whitey stagger to the passenger side of Syd's car. I dump him in the seat. When Syd reaches across him to snap his seatbelt, a rubber glove falls out of her pocket.

I pick it up. "What's this for?"

She snatches it outta my hand, her body tightens up, and her face turns almost as white as Whitey's. She stutters, "They're for. . .

I uh, I use them for . . . um, chopping eel. The salt's been burning my cuticles and messing with my nails."

"I ain't seen you wearin' gloves when you chop the bait."

She stuffs it back in her pocket. "I was embarrassed to use them, okay? I figured you'd call me a wimp."

"Well, you is," I say, teasin' her.

Her shoulders relax. "See. Knew you would."

She slams the car door. "Be back as quick as I can."

"No hurry."

"My boobs say otherwise."

She drives out the lane and I walk to the front of my house. The moon's almost full. It shines so bright across the crick it lights up the wharf. The only thing I see on the water is the moonlight. Not a sailboat in sight. Damn shame we got less than a week before the boaters roll in for the season and spoil it.

Daisy, Syd's Basset Hound, must hear me and Ruby 'cause she starts howlin'. I walk over to Jake's and let her out. After Swannee hung hisself in jail, Jake gave up his share of the family house, making it all mine. It wasn't fair, but he wouldn't take no for an answer.

When Syd got knocked up, I ponied up a down payment on the Maxwell's house, two doors down from me. That's where Jake, Syd, and Helly live. I'm glad another generation of Swanns is gonna grow up on this crick.

The dogs follow me out the dock to the pens. Jake and Syd love the softshell business. I never much cared for it. Takes too much patience—which ain't my strong suit.

I check the pens There's a couple crackshells in the water, but it'll be an hour or so before they're free from their shells and ready to come out. I lean over the side of the dock and pull the slough box up outta the water to see if any peelers are ready to be added to the pens.

They ain't ripe unless the ring around their backfin is blood red. I check real careful. Ain't none ready. Green peelers are killers. If one gets tossed in the pen, they'll tear the defenseless softshells to shreds and eat 'em up in no time.

SYDNEY—May 21

"Where's Jake?" Whitey slurs from the passenger seat.

"At a boat show."

A perfect night got complicated. I have to hope Whitey blacks out and forgets or I have to convince him he's confused and never saw me near Eddie's. I can't have him blabbing all over town. When Eddie's body is found, folks might put two and two together. It's bad enough he told Maggie; though I'm pretty sure she chalked it up to drunken confusion.

He slaps his hand across his mouth. "I'm gonna puke."

I pull onto the shoulder and he opens the door and tumbles out, heaving into the thick grass lining the road. What if I ran over him? That would keep him quiet. But I wonder if the police can match tire tracks from a dead body.

Headlights coming towards me puts an immediate end to that possibility. Toothpick, an unnaturally skinny kid that pumps gas at Jake's marina, pulls up beside me.

"You okay, Miss Sydney?"

I hitch my thumb towards Whitey vomiting on the side of the road. "Yeah, just giving him a ride."

He looks at Whitey and shakes his head. "You need help with him?"

"Nah, I got him, but thanks."

By the time Toothpick's taillights fade in the distance, Whitey's wiping his mouth on his arm. "Where the hell am I?"

His memory loss is a positive sign.

"I'm taking you to your friend PeeWee's boat. Remember?"

"Oh, yeah, right." He falls back into the passenger seat.

When I slam the door shut, he lolls his head against the window. Slobber drips out of his open, snoring mouth. I hope I can get him on the boat.

Or maybe I don't.

Maybe an accident will befall my drunk friend. I rifle through a myriad of ideas, but ultimately discard each one. Two "accidental" deaths in one night aren't prudent.

The landscape changes from open fields to pine forests. The houses on the road leading to Hooper's Point are all enormous mansions with long swaths of land and private waterfronts, sporting pretentious names like Knightley Manor and Robeson Landing.

I punch Whitey's shoulder. "Hey, wake up."

He lifts his head and looks at me. "What?"

"Which estate?"

He rubs his eyes and points to the gravel road. "Turn here."

A mile in we come to a decorative locked gate with the name Barlow Estate scrolled in an iron arch above it.

Whitey closes one eye. His head sways as he tries to read the sign. "This ain't it."

My breasts feel like they're on fire and milk leaks onto my shirt. My car smells like a combination of stale beer and vomit. And my patience is gone. I backhand his face.

He rubs his cheek. "What the hell did you do that for?"

"To wake you up. I don't want to be out here all night. Tell me where to go."

"You can go to hell, for all I care."

"Dammit, Whitey. Which place?"

His head droops forward and he falls sideways across the seat. His cheek is smashed into my armrest. I do a U-turn and drive back out to the main road. Whitey said the lawyer's name is Bergmann. I'll look for that.

I am almost out of road when I finally see Bergmann on a stone pillar marking a long, tree-lined dirt lane. Maybe this hellish excursion with Whitey is nearing an end. My CRV kicks up a cloud of dust as it bumps along. After a mile or so, an unassuming country home comes into view. No cars are in the driveway and the house is completely dark.

I follow the circular drive to the front of the house. Trees on both sides of the property obscure the view of any neighbors. I position my car to light the dock. A boat—presumably PeeWee's—is tied at the end.

I shake Whitey roughly. "We're here. Wake up."

He lifts his hand to swat me away. Getting out of the car, I walk around to the passenger side, open the door, and try to yank him out. After three attempts he sits up.

"What the fuck?"

"We're here."

"Here where? Why am I with you? What the hell is going on?"

"You're sleeping on your friend PeeWee's boat. I'll help you down the dock."

"PeeWee who?"

If he can't remember his friend, he won't remember seeing me on Eddie's road.

Whitey somersaults out of my car onto the ground and passes out. I try to get him up, but he's dead weight. I hop back into my car and ease back out onto the road.

It's a warm night. He'll be fine. And with his inevitable black out, I will be, too.

JAKE—May 22

I'm bone-tired. Last night, after twelve hours of tellin' boat owners why my marina'd be the best place to rent a slip, and then two hours of tearin' down my booth, it hit me; I forgot to make hotel reservations. I ended up sleepin' in an honest-to-God roach infested motel. Then I hadda drag my ass outta bed at five this morning to make it to the marina by seven and put in another full day of work.

At 7 p.m., when I finally turn down the lane, the crunch of the oyster shells under my tires welcomes me home. For a long time after my older brother killed Mom, that sound triggered nothin' but bad memories: lights flashing, cops swarming all over the house, and an empty blood-splattered bedroom where my mom shoulda been.

Sydney changed all that.

I'm barely outta my pickup and Daisy's whinin' at my feet. Syd leans against the door jamb, baby on her hip. She's wearin' a puke-stained T-shirt and a droopy pair of my sweatpants with the legs rolled up to fit her four-feet-ten-inch frame. Her eyes have puffy, purple bags under them, and her red hair is a rat's nest of curls. She ain't never looked better. Being in love's like wearing permanent beer goggles.

"Hey." She stands on her tiptoes to give me a kiss. "I'm glad you're home."

I give both her and Helly a peck. "Oh yeah? You missin' your man?"

"Of course," she says headin' into the house. "Somebody's got to take out the trash."

I give her ass a little smack and she laughs. "What'd you and Helly get up to while I was gone?"

"The usual. Nursed the baby. Rocked the baby. Changed the baby's diapers."

I think the fuzzy mommy-hormones are wearing off and Syd's getting antsy to write. I'm not looking forward to her and Helly being gone while Syd does her research.

"I heard you went out last night. Skip said you two lost Cutthroat to Snooks."

"Yeah. No surprise. I doubt I'll ever beat him."

I sit down on the new sand-colored couch and Syd hands me the baby. I smell her tiny head. The finest perfume don't even compare. It was Syd's idea to name the baby after my mom. But Helen's such a grown-up name, so we decided to call her Helly.

Sydney grabs me a beer and fixes herself a cup of tea. "It was great to get out and feel like something other than Helly's cow." She sits down beside me and tucks her feet under her. "How was the boat show?"

"Tiring, but good. I got at least four new slip holders. Oh shit, that reminds me. Deacon Marine's bringing in a Sea Ray tomorrow. I gotta arrange a ride back to Annapolis for their man."

"Are they leaving it to get painted?" she asks.

"No. Someone rented it for the whole summer and they're gonna tie it up with us."

"Who rented a boat for the whole summer? Isn't that unusual?"

I shrug. I ain't been a marina manager long enough to know what's usual. "I don't know who the slip holder is. Technically, Deacon's rented the slip from us. Listen babe." I stand and hand Helly to her. "I gotta get this figured out. Everyone got a tight schedule tomorrow. I don't know who can spare three hours."

"You want me and Helly to do it? We could lunch in Annapolis."

I lean in and kiss her. Helly giggles. "You're sweet, but I can't take you up on it—insurance."

I'm a lucky man. Syd always puts family first.

SYDNEY—May 23

Last night, Helly slept, Jake tended the pens, and I got a glorious six straight hours of sleep. I needed it. The crash after the adrenaline rush from killing Eddie was epic, and then I had to deal with Whitey. I was utterly exhausted.

The darkness of night transforms into a shadowy pink. I adjust the clamp light to shine across the pens. After checking the hoses to ensure the water is circulating properly, I pull out the half-full tray of crabs from the rusty, rattling dock fridge. If we have another high profit season, a new fridge for the crabs will be our next investment.

I only need six more softshells to fill the tray, and there's at least that many busters ready to be pulled out. I slide on my protective gloves and get to work.

The pre-dawn silence is punctured by Ruby's nails clicking down the dock. She jumps into Maggie's bateau and settles herself beside the line barrel in the bow. Maggie lags behind, lugging her cooler in one hand and empty bushel baskets in the other. Her sun-streaked blonde hair is tied in a messy bun and she's got dark circles under her eyes. She looks more disheveled than normal with a stained hoodie thrown over her men's white T-shirt and her baggy jeans tucked haphazardly into her white watermen's boots.

"Rough night?" I ask.

"Yeah. I dreamt Eddie was beside my bed, glarin' down at me. Half his head was blown off, and he had parts of his brain in one hand and a bat in the other. He got a sick grin on his face, like he used to get when he was knockin' me around. And he said, 'I ain't done with you yet.' Scared the livin' shit outta me. Woke up sweatin' like a pig and couldn't get back to sleep."

I swallow wrong and start coughing. I wish I could tell her she'll never be bothered by him again.

"You okay?" Maggie grabs a bottle of water out of her cooler. "Here." She hands it to me.

I take a few sips and sputter, "Thanks. I'm good now."

"You and Helly wanna take a coupla runs with me in an hour or so?"

The gentle rock of the boat soothes me like a mother comforting her child. Sounds like exactly what I need. Until Eddie's body is found, I'll be on pins and needles.

"You bet," I answer. "We'll be at the end of the dock at seven."

A woman of little words, Maggie nods her head in agreement. After she arranges her gear in the bateau, she casts off her lines and putters out to her lay before the sun comes up. There's no official spot where she's allowed to lay her trotline but, out of courtesy, commercial watermen respect each other's claim to an area. Weekend crabbers, on the other hand, throw their lines and pots wherever they want. Their interference with the waterman's ability to earn a living understandably fuels the locals' resentment of "chicken neckers."

I slide the filled tray of soft crabs back into the fridge. The buyer will come later today. Before I head up to the house, I look across the water and inhale. The brine of the brackish water mingles with the earthy marsh to create a distinct bay scent.

A tear of gratitude slides down my cheek. After I killed Paul and Dad was incarcerated, I wasn't sure I'd ever be happy again. But now, I can honestly say I am grateful for all the horrendous tragedies I endured. After all, they led me to Jake and Maggie.

Helly's whimpers register on the baby monitor, interrupting my musings. I hurry inside to catch her before her whimpers turn to wails and she wakes her dad. As I'm heading to the nursery, I'm accosted by a warm, wet, wonderful man. Jake's blonde hair is freshly washed and dripping puddles onto the wooden floor.

"Morning beautiful." He twists my curls around his fingers and kisses me with more passion than expected at dawn. "How 'bout a quickie?"

Helly's wail answers that question. After I change her diaper, I join Jake in our kitchen/dining room/living room and nurse Helly on the rocker Millie gave me for my baby shower. Its overstuffed cushions and padded arms are a godsend. Helly and I have slept in it many nights over the past three months.

Jake's on his second cup of coffee and has the newspaper spread out across our reclaimed-wood farm table. "What're you up to today?"

"Helly and I are crabbing with Maggie at seven and then I don't know."

"Hey, hit her up for a bushel of crabs for Sunday. I wanna have a Memorial Day party."

I laugh. "You're poking the bear asking her for crabs for this weekend."

With crabs in such high demand on holiday weekends, the watermen—or women—can get top dollar for their catch.

He pretends to shake in his boots. "I ain't scared of her."

"Who do you want to invite?"

"The usuals. Millie and Harry. Skip and Deena." Jake notices my grimace and adds, "I know Deena can be a bitch, but Skip's my best friend."

Bitch is an understatement. From the day I met her, Deena has been a thorn in my side. I have no doubt she'll eventually push me too far.

I paste on a convincing smile. "Of course, you should invite them. Don't worry, I'll be the perfect hostess."

Jake kisses the top of my head. "You're gonna be such a good example for Helly."

Helly's fallen back to sleep. I point at her angelic little face. "What time do you have to leave for work?"

He looks hopeful. "6:30."

"About that quickie . . ."

MAGGIE—May 24

I'm alone on the crick today. The way I like it. Yesterday Syd was so damn jittery she made me nervous. If I didn't know better, I woulda thought she was hopped up on something.

The sun's hot, but the breeze keeps it from bitin' my skin. I guzzle a tea and watch an osprey snatch a fish outta the water while I putter back to the start of my line. The crabs is really on today. I'm catchin' a dozen or so every run.

I lift my line up to the ringer arm and start my run. Three baits in I got a big black crab. I sink my net under him and get ready to dip him up. My phone rings and I knock him off the line.

"Son-of-a-bitch!" Cell phones are a pain in my ass. I answer before I even look to see who's calling. "Yeah?"

"Margaret Craill?"

The wind blows across the crick and I get the shivers. It's my cousin Curt. He's a deputy, and when he calls me Margaret, you can bet your ass someone's dead.

"Spit it out, Curt. Don't make me wait."

"Sheriff told me to call you. Eddie's dead."

I lift the trotline off the roller arm and float. "Christ. When? How?"

"Looks like an overdose. Best we can tell, about three days ago."

I think back three days. That's the night I watched Helly.

"Listen, I know he ain't your husband no more," Curt says. "But he got no next of kin, so unless you make funeral arrangements, he's gonna go to the State Anatomy Board. Sheriff said after the autopsy we can only hold him seventy-two hours, so you gotta decide."

"Shit."

"Yeah, it ain't right. I don't blame you if you let him rot."

"Okay, Curt. I'll call you." I hang up.

I float, waitin' to see what I'm gonna feel. Pretty much nothin'. I put the bateau in gear and steer back to the start of the line. I lift it up on the ringer. Three crabs go by before it hits me, I ain't dippin'.

I splash some bay water on my face and try to get my head in the game. I dip for a big black crab and miss it. Damn. My reactions are too slow. I gotta focus.

A speedboater zooms by and rocks the bateau, making it hard to see the crabs. I flip him the bird and he laughs. Asshole.

Eddie's dead. The motherfucker who made my life a livin' hell is worm food, and I'm supposed to decide what to do with him. Don't seem right.

I run the line again and miss half the crabs.

I did love him once. Before his demons made him mean.

Two more big ones drop off the line before I can net 'em. Ain't no point in being out here, if I can't do the job. I throw a drag bucket out to slow the bateau down, so I can bait the line while I pull it up.

I take the half-eaten baits off and replace them with new pieces of eel, then snake the freshly baited line into the barrel. The gulls caw and flap all around my boat hopin' for some scraps. I chuck the pieces of eel in the air and they fight over them.

I know where I gotta go to decide what I'm gonna do about Eddie. Al-Anon.

Even though it takes me almost an hour to bait the line, I'm pulling back into shore at noon. Sydney's on the wharf, checking the pens.

I back the bateau into the slip and she throws me a line. Once I'm tied up, I heave the bushel of crabs onto the dock and climb outta the bateau.

"Good catch?" she asks.

"Eddie's dead."

Her mouth drops open. "What?"

"Yep. Drug overdose."

"Wow. How do you feel?"

That's Sydney. First question outta her mouth is always "How do you feel?"

I shrug my shoulders. "Not mucha nothing."

She gives me a hug, but I don't hug back.

"I gotta decide if I'm gonna give him a funeral or let the state have him."

"Why do you have to decide?"

"He got no family."

She scrunches her face up. "That really sucks. I'm sorry you have to make that decision."

"Yeah. It does suck." I swing the bushel of crabs into the dock cart. "He's dead and I'm still tangled up with the motherfucker."

SYDNEY—May 24

Eddie's been found. The deputy told Maggie he died from an overdose. I should be in the clear.

Maggie seemed numb. I'm sure once she's had to digest the news, she'll be relieved. It's inhumane that she's been tasked with deciding the fate of his body. If you ask me, he's not even worthy enough to be crab bait.

I'm itching to get to Millie's Place and hear what's being said, but first I have to change Helly. Her onesie is wet with spit up and her diaper oozes poop from the leg holes. I lay her on the changing table—again—and begin the mind-numbing chore, as my intelligence dissolves into a morass of breast milk and baby shit.

Once she's clean and dry, I strap her into her baby carrier, load up the diaper bag, and head out. I detour down Shore Drive for a quick stop at the post office to retrieve my mail. The spot in front of the post office is taken, so I park at the end of the street where the houses are painted in beachy colors, mimicking the covers of Coastal Living. The families that occupy these gentrified homes aren't locals. They're affluent retirees from corporate city life who snapped up Rock Narrows' properties in a frenzy for bayside, small-town living. Another source of resentment for the locals.

Leaving Helly in the car as an excuse for a quick get-away, I run in.

"Oh Sydney," Sandy, the postal worker, says as she flips through my mail." You've got lots of mail today. There's a letter

from your dad and the Delmarva Power bill, and a magazine
subscription offer, and . . ."

"Sorry Sandy, I've got to run." I grab my mail out of her hand.
"Helly's in the car."

"Oh goody." She claps her hands in delight. "I've been
waiting to see the little sugarplum Millie can't stop gaga-ing over!"

As she follows me out to the car, I take a resigned breath.
Nothing in small-town life is fast, not even a trip to the post office.
After what seems like twenty minutes of fawning, I can finally be on
my way.

I pull into the diner's crowded parking lot. Millie claims her
décor is "work with what you got," but it's an unintended
celebration of retro. The walls are lined with classic diner booths,
and oval dinette sets fill the center space. The eat-at counter with
vinyl topped swivel stools is my favorite spot and luckily, despite
the unusually large crowd, there are two empty stools.

I settle Helly's carrier on one and sit between her and Buffalo.
Almost everyone's got a nickname in Rock Narrows. Buffalo's
came from his appearance—disproportionately large head, covered
in brown shaggy hair.

When Millie sees us, she rushes right over and peppers Helly's
face with kisses. Her maternal nurturing has been a blessing, not
only to Jake and Maggie, but to Helly and me too. A dead mom and
an incarcerated dad leave me sorely lacking in family relationships.

She gives me a quick hug, grabs a pitcher of unsweetened iced
tea, and pours me a glass. "You want the usual, Sydney?"

What I want is to hear the scuttlebutt about Eddie, but I nod
and smile. "Yes, please."

My neighbor, Miss Rhonda, brings her bill up to the counter to
pay Millie. I'm sure she'll have something to say about Eddie's
death.

"Hi Sydney, I'm glad to see you." She roots around in her
purse and pulls out a Ziploc bag full of photos. "I thought you might
like to have these." She hands them to me. "I collected them after
Helen's memorial and tucked them away. I found them a few weeks
ago and have been meaning to return them."

21

I tamp down my impatience and leaf through the photos. Rhonda stops me at one of Helen and Jake in his Navy Whites.

"Dear Lord, look how handsome he is in his uniform. The girls around here used to swoon every time he came home on leave."

Millie laughs and takes a second to peek her head over the counter and look at the photo. "Like a young Robert Redford. He had a gal in every port."

I swallow my irritation. Tales of his many conquests rub me the wrong way. I flip to the next photo. It's baby Maggie in her christening gown.

Rhonda takes the photo from my hand. "Helly looks just like Nails."

Everyone but family calls Maggie Nails.

Rhonda returns the photo. Her brows furrow. "How *is* Nails?" "Is she taking the news about Eddie okay?"

Finally what I came for.

I press my lips together and nod. "It was a shock, of course, but she's okay."

"They don't call her Nails for nothing," Millie says. "That girl's made of iron."

Rhonda raises her hand to her heart. "Bless her heart. It's such a shame, but since the divorce he was going downhill fast. It was only a matter of time."

So far, so good. As I expected it seems his overdose is not being questioned.

Ned—farmer and self-appointed town crier—adds his two cents from the other end of the counter. "That's the honest to God truth. I saw his truck at the crack house at least three days a week. That man was full of demons. Maybe now he's at peace."

I hope not. He does not deserve peace after his treatment of Maggie.

Millie chimes in, "Well, I say good riddance, after what he did to—" She throws her hand up and covers her mouth to keep from blurting out Maggie's name.

Ned busies himself with his meal and Rhonda coos at Helly, pretending they don't know what Millie was about to say. Eddie's abuse of Maggie was just one more of the widely known, but never addressed, secrets in the Rock Narrows community. Millie hurries off to help another customer. She has a great heart, but a big mouth.

Helly wriggles in her seat. Her discontent gives me an opportunity to eavesdrop on the patrons' conversations. I lift her out of her seat and lay her belly against my chest. Rhonda squeezes her tiny fingers and says her goodbyes. Patting Helly's back, I pace around the crowded diner.

"The stench was god-awful. I knew something was dead. He had to be rotting for days."

"The cruisers were there for over three hours, probably tossin' the house to find all the drugs."

"How many overdoses does that make so far this year?"

"It's a shame, but ain't no surprise. With as much shit as he was shootin' it was only a matter of time."

"Ain't that much of a shame. Eddie wasn't good for much of nothing."

With each comment I hear, I breathe easier. Even with my meticulous planning, there was always a small chance of being discovered. But obviously, the benefits far outweighed the risks. It's a fact that half of all women murdered are killed by former partners. There was no way I was going to allow Maggie to become a statistic.

Satisfied with the community's reaction to Eddie's death, I decide to grab my lunch to-go. I still need the buy the supplies for the Memorial Day picnic.

Bayside Foods, our mini-mart-size grocery store, is also crowded. I'm forced to park at the far end of the lot. As I'm unhooking Helly from her car seat, a dented pick-up wheels in beside me. It's Whitey.

"Hey Sydney. What's up?"

If I lit a match his breath would go up in flames.

"Hi Whitey. Just doing some grocery shopping."

He runs his tobacco-stained fingers through his white hair. "Some shit about Eddie, ain't it?"

I perch Helly on my hip and grab my purse from the passenger seat.

He lights up a cigarette and exhales the smoke into the air. "They're saying he died the night Bev kicked me out."

Interesting. I hadn't heard they established a timeline. "Oh?"

He twists his ever-present anchor necklace. "Yep. I saw you that night."

I can feel my pulse in my throat. "You did. I took you to your friend's boat. Remember?"

"Oh, I remember. I remember I was hitchhiking and you didn't bother to pick me up. I also remember I saw you come out of Eddie's house."

Dammit! This is bad. Really bad. I was really hoping he was drunk enough to forget he saw me at all.

Sweat puddles in my bra. "Whitey, I don't know what you're talking about. You were very drunk that night. You must be confused. I was at Dollie's and then I went home where I found you begging for a ride and some money. I did take you to the boat out near Hooper's Point."

"I know that. I'm still staying there 'cause Bev said we're done. But I know what I saw, and I want to know what you were doing at Eddie's that night."

My mouth goes dry. "Whitey, really, you're confused."

"I ain't, and I tell you one damn thing, even though Eddie's dead, if I find out you's been steppin' out on Jake, I ain't gonna keep my mouth shut."

Dear god, Whitey actually believes I would cheat on Jake with that detestable bastard. I almost laugh in his face, but stop. My attempts to convince him that his memory is faulty aren't working. I need to buy myself a little time to get a plan in place. If he really does think I cheated, maybe I can use that in my favor.

I force tears into my eyes and grab Whitey's hand. "Please Whitey, don't say anything. I went there that night to break it off. I hate myself. I never wanted to hurt Jake."

Whitey rips his hand from mine and spits on the ground. "There's a special place in hell for bitches likc you."

"I know. I know. I'm disgusted with myself." Even though it's bs, I really do feel nauseous owning up to something as heinous as sleeping with Eddie. "But Whitey, why hurt Jake? Eddie's dead and I've learned my lesson. I swear to you, it will never happen again."

He flicks his cigarette butt on the ground. "It goddamn better not. I'll be watchin' you. I mean it, Sydney, one too-friendly smile and I'm tellin' Jake what you done. You got me?"

I give Whitey a one-armed hug. "I do. I do. Oh, thank you so much. I won't forget your kindness. In fact, let me bring dinner to the boat one night. I'm sure you could use a home-cooked meal. Jake will be swamped at the marina on Memorial Day. How about I bring you a meal to thank you?"

"Yeah. Fine. Food would be good, and maybe some Bloody Marys." He pulls the lining out of his empty jeans pocket. "And I could use a few bucks."

I pull a twenty from my wallet and hand it to him. "Thanks again, Whitey. I'll see you on Monday."

Whitey has left me no choice. I'm not foolish enough to believe he'll keep quiet for long; this gossip is too juicy not to share. Me being at Eddie's the night he died—no matter the reason—will raise questions. I have to shut Whitey up permanently.

DEENA—May 24

After pouring her a sweet tea, I settle Miss Mary, a client for over ten years, in my chair and drape the cape around her. She was my first customer when I started at Peggy and Renee's fresh out of cosmetology school. I wanted to go to the University of Maryland for marine biology. I got accepted, but my grades weren't good enough to get any scholarships. Mom sure didn't have any money to help me, and I was too afraid to go neck deep in debt, so I settled for being a stylist.

Miss Doris, the local realtor, is in Peggy's chair. They schedule their hair appointments for the same time to gossip their way through them.

"Well, have you heard the latest news?" Miss Mary asks.

I bet she's praying we haven't, so she can inform us. She's married to Joe, the local sheriff, and loves to fill us in on Rock Narrows' latest arrests. Working at the salon keeps me up to date on *everything* happening in this town.

Not to be one-upped in the rumor department, Miss Doris says, "You mean about Eddie's overdose?" She rolls her eyes. "I heard that first thing this morning."

It isn't shocking Eddie overdosed. I saw his truck at the crack house almost every day on my way to the salon. My dad lost his battle with drugs and died when I was ten, so I have a soft spot for addicts, but not for Eddie. Eddie was cruel. What he did to Nails, and the string of girlfriends that came after her, was sickening.

Miss Mary looks like the cat who ate the canary. "No, everyone's heard Eddie's dead, but how he died is up for debate."

She has our attention.

"What?" Peggy says.

Miss Doris leans forward in her seat. "Well, tell us."

Miss Mary's smile is smug. "I overheard Joe talking to his deputy. They haven't ruled Eddie's death accidental."

I stop cutting Miss Mary's hair. "You mean not accidental as in suicide?"

Miss Mary turns her seat to face Miss Doris. With drama she says to the three of us, "No, as in murder."

We all look back and forth at each other, not sure what to say.

My shoulders tense and my chest tightens. The anxiety that's always buzzing in the back of my mind rears its ugly head. I try to talk myself down before it flares into a panic attack. Stay calm. Even if Eddie was murdered, I'm not in danger. There's no random serial killer on the loose.

I take slow deep breaths. Plenty of people would have a motive to kill Eddie. Nails, of course, but even Jake. After years of watching Eddie beat the crap out of his sister, it's not that far-fetched to think he might snap.

Happy that she's got our undivided attention, Miss Mary continues, "A witness saw someone coming out of Eddie's house and driving away the night he died."

Miss Doris is almost out of breath with excitement. "Who was the witness?"

Miss Mary sighs. "Well, unfortunately, that's the problem. It was Mrs. Ennis."

Miss Doris flops back in her seat. "Oh, for Pete's sake, Mary. Mrs. Ennis is pushing ninety and is nearly deaf and blind. Who knows what she saw."

My body relaxes. There was no murder. This is just Miss Mary trying to keep the spotlight.

Miss Mary crosses her arms and snaps at Miss Doris. "Well, she knows she saw a person. She thinks it was a woman, but isn't sure, and she said the car looked like a RAV4 or a Blazer and was dark colored—green or black, or maybe even blue."

Peggy and I go back to cutting the women's hair. Miss Mary's hair is a silvery gray and she prefers a simple short, layered bob. Miss Doris's hair is straight from the eighties. She has it bleached yellow-blonde and wants it teased within an inch of its life.

Miss Doris waves away Miss Mary's story. "A woman at Eddie's isn't unusual. He had a parade of bimbos in and out of that house."

"True. But maybe he was beating up on one of them like he did Nails, and they got sick of it," Miss Mary says.

Having finished the cut, Peggy's moves onto drying Miss Doris's hair with a giant round brush to give it extra volume.

Miss Doris raises her voice to be heard over the dryer. "That doesn't make any sense. Won't the autopsy show if he died from drugs?"

"Of course." Now, Miss Mary rolls her eyes at Miss Doris. "But, if his dealer was in his house that night, the police might try to pin it on him for supplying the drugs."

I can tell Miss Doris is annoyed at Miss Mary's exaggeration of the situation. "So, the police aren't considering murder, in the sense of someone deliberately killing him?"

"Well." She struggles to save face. "Probably not, but who knows? Maybe his drug dealer killed him for not paying."

"That makes even less sense." Miss Doris shakes her head. "Then he'd never get his money."

Apparently irked by the humdrum response to her gossip, Miss Mary opens a magazine and buries her nose in it. Miss Doris sniffs in response to the snub, and scrolls through her phone. Me and Peggy give each other a look, holding back our smiles. Same shit, different day. This is how Miss Doris and Miss Mary's hair appointments always end.

MAGGIE—May 24

Before I head to my Al-Anon meetin', I go to Eddie's house—our house. When we first moved in, I was fulla ideas 'bout casseroles and baby cribs. That didn't last long.

I park in the driveway. The yard's got more dandelions than grass. A shutter on the front window's half-hanging off the house. The wind musta knocked the rocker over and Eddie ain't bothered to pick it up. Maybe he was already dead when it happened.

The screen door flaps open and shut. I walk up on the porch to latch it and the smell damn near knocks me over. Christ, didn't know three days of rot could be so bad. I hope something'll get the stink out or I won't be able to sell the house. I still own half. I guess now I own it all.

On the porch, I wait to see if any tears are gonna come. Nothin'. I'm gettin' better at lettin' myself cry, but I guess I just ain't that sad.

I lift the rocker up and pull the shutter off to lay it on the porch. Shoving the key in the lock, I open the door. Two steps in and I gag. I run and puke in the toilet. It's bad. I ain't never smelled nothin' like it. I root around in the medicine cabinet for some Vicks. I saw cops use it to deal with dead bodies on TV. I find some and smear a glob under my nose. It helps enough that the heavin' stops.

I open all the windows. The stench is worst in the dining room. There's only one chair at the table. No doubt he smashed the rest since he ain't got me to punch. I don't see no drug stuff layin' around—cops musta took it—but there's plenty of empty beer cans and booze bottles.

I go in the kitchen to grab a trash bag. There's dirty dishes piled up in the sink and dried-up spaghetti sauce in a cast iron pan on the stove. On the oven door handle, there's a tea towel, folded into thirds and hung so the back and front edges are exactly even. Eddie ain't never folded or hung a tea towel in his life. Musta been one of his sluts.

I open the fridge. Plates of food sit uncovered on the shelves, growing all colors of nasty-ass mold. I scrape the food into the garbage bag. This whole place smells like rot.

You know what? Fuck this. I kick the fridge door shut and leave the garbage bag layin' on the kitchen floor. I walk through the house, close all the windows, and slam and lock the front door. I'll pay someone to come in and deal with this filth—'cause I'm goddamn done cleanin' up after Eddie.

I pull into the parking lot of the church ten minutes late for my meetin' and walk down the steps to the basement. The folding chairs are set up in a circle. All but two are full. I sit beside Myra.

Two of the fluorescent lights are burnt out and another one's makin' that god-awful buzzin' sound that means it's ready to go. A new guy is talkin'.

"I hit the trifecta. I go to AA, NA, and now here." He rubs his hand together like he's washin' them.

He got slicked-back dark hair with gray streaks and a clean shave—looks like a banker. He's a first-timer in Al-Anon.

"Hi, my name is Mitch. I was released from jail a little over a week ago. That's no place I want to see the inside of again, but it did get me clean and sober." He holds up a chip. "Five years. It's a lot easier to get straight when you're locked away." He runs his fingers through his hair all nervous. "I know you're here because you've been hurt by alcoholics and I am one. I'm not making excuses for all the horrible things I've done, but I need this program too. My family, especially my dad, was f'ed up. I know that's a big part of why I ended up a drunk. I need some help to get healthy. Is it okay if I keep coming to this meeting?"

Everyone nods yes or says welcome. Al-Anon don't judge. If someone's boozin' fucked you up, you can be here.

"Thanks. That's all I got."

"Thanks for sharing," everyone says.

Mitch looks like he got money, but fancy clothes or a good job don't save you from the demons. In these rooms, we're all dealin' with the same shit.

It's Myra's turn. "Hi, I'm Myra."

"Hi Myra," we all say.

She looks at Mitch. "Let me first say newcomers are always welcome. You are the lifeblood of our meetings, reminding us all where we started and how far we've come. You bring new wisdom and hope just by being here. Keep coming back." She smiles at Mitch and he nods. "Tonight, I want to talk about forgiveness," she says. "A lot of us used to believe that forgiveness was for the person who harmed us. It absolutely is not. It's for us. It doesn't excuse or justify the crime. It only means you're no longer willing to be a victim."

I needed this. You know, I had all this shit figured out with Swannee. If I stayed mad, I only hurt me. It's the same with Eddie. I gotta let go of the pissed-off to move on. I know what I gotta do with his body.

Myra stops talkin' and a couple more people share. I don't. I ain't big on talkin' in a group, so I only share when something's festering.

When the meetin's over, a lotta people stay for coffee. I don't. I ain't big on small talk. I get my books and head out to the truck. Mitch is five steps ahead. Bet he don't like gabbin' neither. He's parked beside me. He got one of those fancy cars with the four circles on the grill. His is silver.

He sees me coming and waits at his car. "Good meeting."

"Yep."

"You been coming long?"

"Couple years."

His eyes are green like a cat.

"I think it's going to be good for me. I joined AA and NA a week after I started my sentence and they got me where I am now,

31

but I need Al-Anon to take me the rest of the way. I've got more baggage to deal with than a luggage handler." He laughs.

I laugh too. He's funny and ain't stuck up like I thought. "Yeah, I ain't never gonna be done unpacking."

"I didn't catch your name in the meeting."

"Nail . . . Maggie. I'm Maggie."

"Nice to meet you, Maggie. I hope to see you next week."

I like how he says my name. He reaches out his hand to shake. He got clean fingernails and smooth hands. Mine are rough with calluses and broken nails, but he don't seem to mind.

DEENA—May 26

Jake and Sydney have their eight-foot picnic table covered in butcher paper. I can smell the Old Bay as Nails steams the crabs and corn. Jake's been a solid friend to me and Skip, and there's nothing better than a crab feast, but I didn't want to come. I don't like Sydney. She thinks she's better than me, and I don't trust her.

Nails sets a tray full of hot, steamed crabs and corn in the center of the table. I sit our son, Davey, between me and Skip. Nails slides in beside me. Sydney pours out little cups of vinegar for the ones who want it.

"Who needs a beer?" Sydney asks.

"Me," Harry says, from the end of the table. His normal drink is whiskey, but everyone drinks beer with crabs.

Skip raises his empty in the air. "Me too."

Sydney grabs the beers and sits between Millie and Jake, across from me. Jake cracks open a claw with his teeth. The juice runs down his face.

He wipes the juice with the back of his hand. "Damn, there ain't nothin' like Maryland blue crab."

Jake is one of those men who gets better with age. After his break-up with Cammie, we had a few dates. I was ready for it to be more, but he wasn't interested in a relationship. Oh well. Life works out like it's supposed to. I lean over and kiss Skip and the top of Davey's head.

Skip cracks a claw open for Davey. He loves them. Calls them lollipops. Nails's dog loves them too, and snatches it right out of Davey's hand. He's not happy and lets out a loud wail. His crying makes Daisy howl and then Helly starts crying. I climb off the bench and pick Davey up. Millie rushes to Helly's blanket. Sydney keeps eating, barely blinking at her daughter's cries. As soon as Millie picks Helly up, she quiets. Skip cracks open another claw and gives it to Davey. Now he's happy.

"You're so lucky that Helly can be comforted by other people. Davey only wants me," I say to Sydney.

"Oh, that's unfortunate," Sydney says, being catty. "It's so important for children to feel comfortable in a variety of situations. I hope he becomes more secure as he gets older."

She knows exactly what buttons to push to make me feel bad about myself.

Millie tries to ease the tension. "Both of your kids are amazing. Boys mature slower than girls. Look at all these fools." She points to the men. "They're barely out of diapers."

Everyone laughs and gets back to eating. Nails steamed the corn with the crabs. I pick up an ear, pull the husk back and smear on the butter until it's dripping off the kernels. I grab a pinch of Old Bay and sprinkle it on top. This is my favorite way to eat corn.

Sydney eyes my corn. "Mmm, butter. I had to give it up if I wanted to get back to pre-baby weight."

I hand my calorie-covered corn to Davey.

"I heard you and Sydney got your asses beat in Cutthroat the other night," Nails says to Skip between bites of crab.

"Yeah." He laughs. "And I shot a game after Sydney left and lost another five. Good thing Deena wants me home by nine or I would've lost a lot more."

"Nine?" Maggie asks Sydney. "You didn't get home till ten. Where'd you go when you left Dollie's?"

The vein in Sydney's temple pulses and she squeezes her eyebrows together. "Nowhere. Skip, you must've gotten home later because I didn't go anywhere else."

Skip looks at me like *did I?* I think back. That's the evening me and Connie Smith took our kids down to the public beach to make sand castles, splash in the water, and have a picnic. Come to think of it, that's also the night Eddie died. I passed his house around seven, when I took Connie home. I flash to Miss Mary's story about a dark, SUV. I only recall seeing Eddie's truck in his driveway.

"No," I say. "He was home by nine."

Why would Sydney lie about the timing unless she's hiding something? What if she's cheating on Jake? I know he was at the boat show that night.

Sydney looks off into space and then snaps her finger. "That's right. I did leave before Skip." She taps her forehead with her palm and smiles. "Me and my mommy brain. I was almost home and realized I had left my jacket so I went back to get it. Skip was gone by the time I got back. I ended up playing a few rounds of Liar's Poker."

Sounds plausible, except it was almost seventy-five degrees that night. Me, Connie, and the kids were still sweating at dusk. Why would she have had a jacket? Something doesn't add up.

"Did you win?" Jake asks, smiling at Sydney.

"With this poker face?" She points to her cheeks. "I always win."

JAKE—May 26

I look around the table of friends and family and feel like I'm the winner. Life was pretty fucking bleak for too many years. We stopped having parties when Mom got sick 'cause she didn't want no one to know she had Alzheimer's, and then Swannee shot her—like she begged him to do—then hung himself 'cause he couldn't live with the guilt. Dark days. But look at us now.

Sydney scrapes a pile of shells into the garbage can to make room and Maggie dumps two more dozen crabs on the table. She bitched plenty, but saved a bushel of papershells for the party. I prefer papershells, especially right outta the steamer. They're juicy and easy to pick.

Millie bounces Helly on her knee. Sydney don't mind sharing the baby. She wants a "grandma" for Helly 'cause that ain't nothin' she ever had.

Harry points his chin in Millie's direction. "Your little girl is the light of her life."

Harry's gruff, but his eyes get all soft when he looks at Millie. They been married longer than they can remember, but never had kids of their own. I think they tried for a long time. He acts like Millie's the only one to fuss over Helly, but I seen him tickle her nose and make goo-goo eyes at her.

"We count you and Millie as her grandparents. Helly needs that kinda spoilin'."

His face turns red and he coughs to hide his teared-up eyes. He slides off the bench. "I could use another beer. Anyone else?"

Maggie gets up from the table and stretches. "Yeah, I'll have one." She rinses off her hands with the hose and takes the beer from Harry.

Helly fusses on Millie's lap. "I think this sweetie pie is hungry."

Sydney drags the garbage can of crab shells halfway down the dock so it don't draw the flies around us, rinses her hands, and takes Helly inside to nurse. I can tell she ain't happy to have to leave the party. I keep reminding her it'll get better when Helly's done breast feeding.

After Deena settles Davey on a blanket with some toys and the dogs, she scoots in on the bench beside Skip. Daisy lets Davey play with her ears. Ruby ignores him. Millie and Maggie pull up chairs and join us at our table. We all take a break from eating.

I take another swig of beer. "Summer's here."

"Don't remind me," Maggie grumps. "The chicken neckers'll be as thick as ants on a dropped hot dog. No offense, Millie."

Millie's lived in Rock Narrows for over thirty years and still ain't considered a local. If you ain't born here, you ain't local.

"None taken," she laughs. "But you know, your niece is half-Pennsylvanian."

"And your best friend is one-hundred percent chicken necker," I chime in.

Maggie rolls her eyes, throws her hands up and laughs. "Fine, fine. Y'all win. I ain't sayin' they're all bad . . . just most of them."

Deena jumps on the PA-haters bandwagon. "I hate how they think they're better than us just because they got more money and use proper grammar. When I used to waitress down at Bayside Crabhouse, they acted like they owned me for the night. '*I need this. I want this. Why don't I have this*' They'd barely look at me, just boss me around, never saying please or thank you. And they'd always leave a helluva mess, giving no thought to the person who's got to clean it up. Dirty napkins all over the deck. Spilled beers. Knives thrown in with the empty crab shells so I had to pick through the mess. Very annoying."

"Yeah, some of them definitely got an attitude, but without tourists a lot of us would be out of a job," I say.

Maggie hits me on the shoulder. "Your opinion don't count. You're a traitor. You married one of 'em!"

Everyone is laughing when Sydney returns with Helly. I grab a chair for her and the baby and pull it into the circle.

"You guys are having too much fun without me," she says.

"What does that tell you?" Deena says, being bitchy. Everyone holds their breath for a beat before she adds, "Kidding, just kidding."

By the red around Sydney's neck, I can tell she didn't take kindly to Deena's dig. It *was* kinda mean. To Syd's credit, she ignores it and talks to Millie.

*****

By nine, the crabs are gone, the cooler's empty and everyone's heading home.

"Thanks for the crabs, Maggie. It was a great party," I say.

She drains the water from the cooler. "It was. It's been too long since we had people over."

Me and Maggie finish cleaning up outside, while Sydney gets Helly settled in her crib.

"Did you decide about Eddie?" I ask Maggie.

When she told me he was dead, I had to stop myself from cheering. That sick motherfucker tortured my sister for years. Overdose was too easy a death for that piece of shit. I sure as hell hope she lets the state take his worthless body.

"I did."

"Well?"

She wraps up the crab shells in the brown butcher paper and throws the whole wad into the garbage can. "Well, I know it ain't what you want, but I'm gonna bury him beside his mom and pop."

I scrub the steamer pot harder. "Why the hell would you do anything for that no-good cock-sucker? You don't owe him shit."

"It ain't for him. It's for me. Resentment just keeps me knotted up with him and messes with my happiness. Burying him is my way to finally get him the fuck outta my life."

I fling two bags of trash into the bed of my pick-up. I'll run 'em out to the dump on the way to work tomorrow. "He never was good enough for you and he don't deserve it, but do what you gotta do. I can tell you one fucking thing, I ain't gonna be there."

"Be where?" Sydney asks, joining us, baby monitor in hand.

"At Eddie's funeral," Maggie answers for me.

Maggie grabs the hose. Sydney sets the monitor on the arm of the Adirondack chair and grabs the dish soap and a scrub brush from the sink on the wharf.

Syd squirts the soap on top of the picnic table. "So, you've decided to give him a funeral."

"Yep." Maggie waits for Sydney to scrub the soap around before she rinses it down.

"I applaud you," Sydney says. "Only the strong can forgive. When will the funeral be?"

Maggie wraps the hose around the holder and Sydney wipes the pools of water off the table.

"I ain't planned it yet, but I'm doin' it alone."

"You don't gotta worry about that," I tell her. "Ain't no one in this town gonna show up to mourn that cock-sucker."

People 'round here don't like smart asses or lazy bastards; he was both. If Maggie hadn't taken up working on the water, they woulda starved.

"Can you tell? Jake ain't happy with my decision." Maggie is talkin' to Syd, but glaring at me.

"No, I ain't."

"Oh Jake," Sydney says in her shrink voice. "You must see this is absolutely what Maggie needs to do. Forgiveness is freedom."

I don't say a word 'cause she's probably right. Just like she was right about forgiving Swannee. But her and Maggie get there faster than me. I felt so goddamn helpless all the years Eddie was bustin' Maggie up; I wanna wallow in pissed off a little longer.

39

SYDNEY—Memorial Day

After spending the morning planning Whitey's unfortunate accident, I want to destress. It's a gorgeous day to be at the marina pool. The sky is cloudless and the sun is hot, but the humidity of summer has not yet arrived.

I'm applying Helly's sunscreen, when I notice Deena at the entrance. She's juggling a beach bag, a cooler and a squirming Davey, while filling out paperwork for a season pass. I haven't forgotten her bad behavior. Far from it. I'm already pondering her punishment. But let no one think I lack basic courtesy.

I hurry to the entrance. "You poor thing. You've got your hands full. Let me take Davey while you settle up."

"Would you?" She seems surprised, but grateful. "That would be a huge help."

I take his hand and guide him to my lounge chair. He peers in at Helly and laughs when she smiles at him. Such a sweet little boy.

I hope he acquires better manners than his mother, and maybe learns more quickly too. Despite suffering the unpleasant effects of her past rudeness, she continues to insult me. Her abuse of my hospitality at the picnic was unacceptable. This time the consequences will be more extreme.

Deena drops her load on a lounge chair on the other side of the pool and tucks her chestnut hair behind her ears. She comes to collect Davey who's contentedly wiggling Helly's toes. "You're a peach," she says. "Did you get a season pass too?"

"Yep. It's one of the perks of Jake's new job."

"I can only come mornings because I have to be at the salon by noon, but it suits me. It's empty and quiet before all the chicken neckers roll off their boats and swarm." Apparently, she notices the tightening of my lips because she continues. "Oh, I'm sorry. I didn't mean to offend you. I forget you're from Pennsylvania. I count you as one of us."

They're nice words, but her saccharine delivery reveals her insincerity. A person can only tolerate so much disrespect.

I put a deliberately open smile on my face and chuckle. "No worries, sometimes I even call them chicken neckers."

She picks up Helly's sunscreen. "You use zinc based for Helly too. I only use Banana Boat coconut scented for me, but I wouldn't dare put it on Davey. He's had enough toxic chemicals in his body for a lifetime. I'm actually almost out. Can I use some of yours?"

"Of course."

Davey got lead poisoning from Skip's paint-dust-covered clothing. Most older boats have lead-based paints on the bottom. The chelation treatments were costly, and they were already in debt from his complicated birth. Jake couldn't stand to see Skip struggling to find enough money to get treatment for his son so he gave him the money. That's Jake in a nutshell.

Deena drops the bottle of sunscreen back into my bag. "Thanks."

Davey's slathered in sunscreen, his dimpled cheeks an alien-esque white. He plants a cute little peck on Helly's forehead with an exaggerated smack and waves bye as he and his mother make their way to their lounge chair. She pulls her cover up off and her sunscreen out. In a bathing suit, it's obvious she's struggled to get the baby weight off. She coats herself in sunscreen and pops on a sunhat.

My wheels are spinning. A plan is starting to jell and a summer full of mornings with Deena gives karma plenty of time to exact its due.

*****

41

Deena was right about one thing, as morning wanes the pool fills up. Boaters—in various stages of hangover—stumble in, exhausted by the heroic effort of walking the hundred yards from their dock to the pool. Some jump in, needing the bracing shock of the ice-cold water to revive them. Others flop on the lounge chair, covering their heads with beach towels to block out the cruel light of the sun.

At 11:45 Deena waves a goodbye as she heads out. Fifteen minutes later Jake stops in for a quick visit during his lunch hour. Between his glacier-blue eyes and the Elvis-Presley-curl to his lip, he's irresistible.

"Hi gorgeous." He leans in for a kiss. "And how's my sweetie pie?" he coos to Helly as he lifts her out of her bouncy seat.

"She's happy as a clam. Apparently lounging poolside agrees with her."

"It agrees with her mommy too." He winks. "And seeing you in that bikini agrees with me!" Jake moves closer to whisper in my ear, "I'd like to see you out of it."

Unlike Deena, my body is almost back to pre-baby. I'm grateful that's one thing that wasn't permanently changed by Helly's arrival. No woman can fully comprehend the immense sacrifice you make to become a mother until it happens.

His lusty murmurings are interrupted by a leggy blonde. "Hi Mr. Swann. Thanks for all your help this morning."

"Oh, hey there," he stutters. He's probably embarrassed to be caught flirting with me at work. "Call me Jake. Glad to help. Tierney this is my wife, Sydney, and daughter, Helly. Syd, this is Tierney. She's the new slip holder I told you about the other night. The one that got the rental for the whole summer."

Tierney's twenty at most. Her straight long hair frames ice-blue eyes, almost as light as Jake and Maggie's.

She extends a graceful hand with bubblegum pink fingernails. "Nice to meet you. Mr. Swann, I mean Jake, helped me figure out my electric." She has the slightest southern lilt. "Silly me, I had no idea you had to plug a giant cord in to get power to the boat."

More unprepared than silly.

"Are you new to boating?" I ask.

"Yep! This is my high school graduation present—a summer on a boat. I'm so excited. I've waited my whole life to be here," she says, with what appears to be genuine enthusiasm.

I can understand being excited about summering on a boat, but to dock it in Rock Narrows? Peculiar. Ocean City maybe, but not a teeny-tiny watermen's town.

"Well ladies," Jake interjects. "Some of us gotta work." He settles Helly back into her bouncy seat. "Syd, I won't be home till nine or later. I got a staff meetin' at seven to wrap up the holiday weekend."

Exactly what I was counting on. Nine gives me plenty of time to deal with Whitey.

Jake gives me a quick kiss and turns to Tierney. "And as for you, I'll check your lines before my meetin' to make sure you ain't floatin' down the river by morning."

"Super," she gushes. "What would I do without you?"

Maybe do some damn research before you plan to live on a boat.

"You're in good hands. Jake'll help you get your sea legs in no time," I say sweetly.

"Mind if I sit here?"

I shake my head and she spreads her striped beach towel on the lounge beside me. "Your daughter's adorable." She tickles Helly under her chin. "She looks like you and her daddy."

She found my soft spot.

"I agree, but I'm hardly impartial." I laugh. "So, what on earth made you want to spend a summer in Rock Narrows?"

"Quiet. Between work and school, I need a break. I want to do nothing. Since you're a new mom, I bet that sounds whiny to you."

"Luxurious. I'm quite jealous. Got room on the boat for one more?"

"Well, the table does convert to a bed," she jokes. "But seriously, I'm from Norfolk. There are people, noise, and activity everywhere. Plus, I've got a beach town practically in my backyard. I don't need more action."

"You've come to the right place. I can guarantee there's no action."

Helly fusses. Her diaper's wet and it's lunch time. I lift her out of the seat and lay her on the lounge to change her. She screams bloody murder. Tierney tries to distract her. She reaches her finger out to hold Helly's chubby little hand and clicks her tongue to get her attention. Helly stops wailing and grabs her finger.

"She's strong. And such a cutie. I could stare at her for days."

After snapping Helly's onesie, I drape the towel over us and relax into the lounge chair to nurse her. Tierney stares at us so intently it's unsettling.

"When you're done feeding her, may I hold her?"

A prickle raises the hairs on the back of my neck. Through experience, I've learned to listen to my body's signals, but I also know my see-sawing hormones have thrown my radar out of whack. I conclude my unease is due to a mother's overprotectiveness. Plus, I'm sweaty and I'd love to take a dip.

"You bet. It seems like you really like kids."

"Especially this one." She reaches out to stroke Helly's arm.

I stiffen at Tierney's response and warning bells ring. What exactly does she mean by that?

She notices my tension and pulls her hand back. A tinge of pink sneaks into her cheeks like she's been caught doing something inappropriate.

"I'm sorry for invading your space. That was pushy. I get baby brain when I see their little faces and chubby hands. And Helly is just so cute."

I chide myself for being an alarmist. Helly *is* adorable. Fawning over her is an entirely normal reaction.

Tierney laughs self-consciously. "It's probably because I'm an only child."

"Maybe."

I can't relate. I'm an only child and babies never excited me. Of course, Helly's different. We've been wired to fall head over heels in love with our children and give our life to protect them. That's how our species survives.

Helly's sated. I tug and twist to get my suit top back in place, before letting the towel drop.

"Do you want to burp her?" I ask Tierney.

"Could I?" She's clearly delighted by my offer. "That would be awesome!"

Once the burping towel covers her shoulder, I hand her Helly. Tierney's beaming. She gently rests my baby's head on her shoulder and rhythmically pats her back. Tierney snuggles her nose into Helly's neck and inhales her scent, almost like a mother meeting her infant for the first time.

Helly's burp is loud; too big for such a little body. Tierney and I both laugh.

"I'll keep holding her if you want to swim," Tierney offers.

I hesitate for a moment, but nursing Helly made me hot and sticky. Besides, I'm only going to be twenty feet away from Helly at the most. What can happen?

I smile and stand. "I'll take you up on that."

I dive in, allowing the frigid water to temporarily wash away the heavy responsibilities of being a friend, a wife, and a mother.

JAKE—Memorial Day

Memorial Day Weekend's like the Super Bowl for marinas. I got six docks packed with boats and every slip holder is here. Most for the first time this season. And they always got a thousand things wrong. "My electric doesn't work." "There's a loose board on my catwalk." "My cleats need to be secured."

I been runnin' non-stop since Friday. I'm damn glad the weekend's almost over. Being the marina manager is a lot bigger job than I wanted, but you do what you gotta do. Syd wanted a house and babies are expensive.

I check the time; twenty of seven. I wanna check Tierney's lines before the meetin'. Can't have her boat break free tonight. She's on C Dock. The marina keeps the powerboaters separate from the sailboaters. The constant clang of sailboat riggings slappin' against the mast might be music to them, but it drives the rest of us fucking nuts.

Tierney's on her back deck wearing a see-through cover-up over her bikini. Her nose is in a book and drink's in her hand. She's a pretty thing. Woulda been my type before Sydney—young, blonde, leggy. Smart too. Talks a lot like Sydney.

She rented a decent boat—30' Sea Ray. More power than she needs since she ain't takin' it outta the slip. It's got a V-berth, a couch you can make into bunks and a table that converts to a bed. Her bathroom's small. The shower's just a curtain that wraps around the toilet and the floor in front of it, but she can use the marina bathhouse for showering. Overall, plenty of room for one person.

"Hey, I'm here to check your lines," I call out.

She jumps at my voice. "Oh hey. You startled me." She stands up and welcomes me on board. "Thanks for doing this."

She flits around behind me while I make the changes to her lines, like somehow that helps. "You're set," I tell her. "You ain't floatin' away tonight."

"Super. I'd offer you a beer, but I'm not old enough to buy it." She flutters her eyelashes at me, hintin' she wants me to buy her some booze. Seems like a sure-fire way to lose my job.

"That's okay. I don't need a beer."

"I've got orange mint tea. I made it today."

I check my phone. I still got time. "Yeah, sounds good."

She pours me a cup of tea, then hops up sideways on the captain's chair. Her long, tan legs dangle from the seat. I sit on the stern bench.

"I got to hold your baby girl today. She's so cute."

"Yeah, that little gal's got me wrapped. But I ain't got the hard job. Until Helly is done nursing, it's like Syd's on call all the time. She ain't used to being tied down. It takes some gettin' used to. And she ain't been able to get back to work with a baby interrupting her all the time. I'll be glad when Syd gets back to her normal self."

I don't know why I said all that. Ain't like me to tell my stuff to no one.

Tierney swings her legs in circles. "What does Sydney do?"

"She's a writer."

"Oh my God, that's so cool. I'll have to buy her books."

"She writes under a pen name, Sylvia Clint."

"Ooh. I can't wait to read them. I'd love to be a writer, or maybe a journalist, but I don't think I've got the guts to pursue it. It seems too iffy."

"Nothin' wrong with wanting something stable." This girl's got a good head on her shoulders.

"You know, maybe I could watch Helly at your house for a couple of hours a day. It'd be great. The pool is going to get boring, and maybe I could pick Sydney's brain. Plus, she could work. What do you say?"

"That's Sydney's department. I got no say in that. Run it by her next time she's at the pool."

"Okay, I will." She smiles at her idea.

"Thanks for the tea, Tierney." I set the empty glass on the deck. Her name is so familiar to me, but I can't place where I heard it. "See ya round."

I stand to leave and she jumps off her seat and catches me off guard with a hug. "Thanks for helping me. It means a lot to know you're watching out for me."

I don't hug back. Seems like a slippery slope

SYDNEY—Memorial Day

If Whitey wants Bloody Marys, he'll get them. Using gloves, I lace the spicy tomato juice with crushed Benadryl. A cocktail of vodka and antihistamine should make him groggy enough for me to enact my plan. I'll leave the partially used packet of pills in his friend's boat, so if the police bother to do an autopsy—when and if they find his body—they'll expect to see it in his system.

Though I'll try to minimize any evidence of me being on the boat, since Maggie knows I dropped Whitey off on the twenty-first, if any of my prints or DNA are found, there is a logical explanation.

I drive forty minutes to a seafood market in Weston and pick up a shrimp boil; shrimp, sausage, red potatoes, corn, and lemon wedges, steamed together and seasoned with Old Bay. It's a fifty-dollar splurge, but it is, after all, his last supper.

Hooper's Point is between Weston and Rock Narrows, and I arrive around six. My timing, as usual, is impeccable. The holiday weekend has drawn to a close and I don't see a single car on the lane leading to the Bergmann property.

As I drive around to the front of the house, I scout for security cameras and see none. Whitey's lounging in a hammock strung between two massive oak trees. Six crushed beer cans litter the grass under him. He rolls out of the hammock and lands on the ground when he hears my car.

"Never could get out of those damn things," he grumbles as he brushes grass from his ripped, jean shorts.

The sleeves of his cotton, plaid shirt have been cut-off, and the loose threads trail down his tattooed arms. The shirt is unbuttoned and his anchor necklace rests in a mat of white chest hair. He rubs his red-rimmed eyes. "Did you bring the Bloody Marys?"

I nod. "Sure did."

Helly's sleeping peacefully so I lift her seat from my CRV and set it in the shade of the tree. I grab the supplies from the car and spread a paper table cloth over the picnic table.

Whitey looks like a stork as he clomps over to the table in his rubber watermen's boots and plops down on the bench seat. He smells like sweat and his eyes are already glassy from the beer. Once he downs my special drink, I bet I won't have to wait too long.

I pour him a drug-laced drink, going heavy on the vodka, then unload the meal.

"Damn. Nice spread. You wanna make damn sure I keep quiet, don't you."

I smile as I fix his plate. "I want to show you how much I appreciate you giving me a second chance."

He slurps down his cocktail. "Join me. I hate drinkin' alone."

The empty beer cans refute his claim.

I pour him another. "I would, but I'm still nursing Helly. Wouldn't be good for her."

He shrugs. "Oh well, more for me."

Diving into the food like an animal, he doesn't bother to use the plastic utensils. Shrimp juice runs down his arm, adding more stains to his shirt. "You know, Eddie was such a goddamn loser. He don't seem like the type of man you'd fuck."

I shake my head, presumably in shame. "It was the biggest mistake of my life and I'd rather not talk about it ever again."

He burps and holds out his Solo cup for a refill. "I got to thinkin'. I ain't so sure you cheated. And since you won't even drink, I doubt you went to his place for drugs. You killed him, didn't ya?"

My stomach drops. This might make things more difficult. If Whitey thinks I'm capable of killing Eddie, he might be more vigilant, making it harder to enact my plan.

I widen my eyes and drop my jaw. "What? That's crazy. You can't really believe that."

When he lifts his leg over the bench, swinging around to face me, he almost topples over. The booze and Benadryl are working.

"I'm sure by now you know what he did to Nails, and she's your best friend. You sure as shit ain't gonna sleep with him. So why else would you go there?"

I sigh. "Whitey, don't be ridiculous."

"Listen." His words are slurring and his eyes look heavy. "I'm happy you did it. And I'd damn sure bet Swannee was smilin' down when you did it. He wanted to kill that motherfucker hisself. Christ, half the town'd be happy you offed him."

And no doubt half the town would hear about it if I let Whitey live. I have to get him in position before he gets too drowsy to walk.

"C'mon. Fess up. I ain't gonna tell no one. He deserved it. You did it didn't you?"

Whitey'll be dead soon, so I decide to lean into it. I smile and shrug my shoulders coyly.

"Goddammit! I knew it! Son-of-a-bitch. Tell me how you did it. I hope that bastard suffered."

"Tell you what, let me use your bathroom first and I'll tell you everything."

Whitey looks like a little kid waiting his turn for a ride on a roller-coaster. "Holy shit. Does Nails know? Did she put you up to it? How about Jake?"

I laugh. "C'mon Whitey. Let me pee."

"Yeah, okay. C'mon." He grabs the half-empty bottle of vodka and stumbles towards the dock.

As I check to make sure Helly is still sound asleep, I slide my rubber gloves and the box of Benadryl from under her bottom. Whitey staggers down the dock, using the pilings to steady himself. I hurry to catch up to him.

"Christ, I'm fucked up." He takes another slug of vodka.

When we reach the Chris-Craft, he flops his arm towards the boat and says, "Hop on. Head's to the left. I gotta take a leak."

When he turns his back on me, I quickly scan the opposite shore for witnesses. Seeing no one, I shove Whitey. His forehead hits the cleat on the back of the boat and cracks wide-open. His body twists mid-air and the back of his head slams against the swim platform before he splashes into the murky water.

He doesn't flail as he sinks. His snow-white hair fans out from his head like translucent tentacles. The blow must've knocked him unconscious. I hop onto the swim platform, waiting to push him back down if he surfaces, but he never comes up.

I slide out my phone and set a timer. As I wait, I again search the summer homes within view; all closed-up for the week. After ten minutes, I'm confident he's dead. His rubber boots would've filled with water, serving as weight to keep him down. It could be weeks, or even months, before his body surfaces.

Whitey said the boat owner isn't coming back from Maine until the end of summer, and Mr. Bergmann is involved in a court case. When Bev kicks him out, Whitey's been known to skip town. Though Maggie is aware he was coming to stay on this boat, she has no reason to check on him.

I should be good. I inhale deeply and exhale slowly, stabilizing the adrenaline coursing through me. The only thing left to do is plant the Benadryl. I slip on the gloves and jump into the boat. Taking the foil packet of antihistamines from the box, I tuck it in his Dopp kit between his toothbrush and a baggy of marijuana.

As I'm leaving the boat, a glint catches my eye. Whitey's anchor chain hangs from the cleat. It must've gotten hung up in the fall. I untangle it and slide it in my pocket as a memento.

MAGGIE—May 29

When I pull into the church parking lot for my Al-Anon meetin', I see Mitch's silver car. Not that I was lookin' for it. It just stands out against all the pick-ups.

A woman with super-short hair and a ring in her nose holds the door to the church open for me. She smells like lilacs.

When I pass her, she says, "Hey, Nails. Good to see you."

I stop and look. I ain't got a clue who it is.

"It's me, Shelby."

"Shelby-from-Rock-Narrows, Shelby?"

"Yeah." She laughs. "Don't look the same, do I?"

"You sure as shit don't."

The last time I saw Shelby she was so skinny her bones poked outta her skin, her hair was long and greasy, and she was missin' half her teeth. This woman's pretty.

She waves her hands from her toes to her head. "This is what nine months in jail, two years sober, and a good dentist will do for you."

She musta been in the AA meeting. It meets right before Al-Anon.

"You look healthy. Glad to see it."

She smiles. Straight, white teeth shine out at me. "I am. I got a good job at a bistro here in town. I got a decent apartment with a sober roommate and I'm happy. For the first time in my life."

She used to be a helluva mess. She was shacked up with JJ, the biggest drug dealer in Rock Narrows. They lived in a trailer with no electric and stayed fucked up most of the time. Shelby and Jake's ex, Cammie, had a long runnin' feud. One night Shelby beat the shit outta Cammie. Nearly killed her. That's what landed Shelby in jail.

"Well good for you," I say.

"Hey, tell Jake I said hi. And tell Sydney I said thanks. You know what, just tell her I said hi. I need to thank her in person. I'll look her up soon."

I didn't know Shelby and Sydney knew each other. I check my phone. I'm gonna be late. "Will do."

I head down the concrete stairs to the basement. The room ain't welcoming—the linoleum floor is baby-shit green and the fluorescent lights are too bright—but the people are. Cookies is spread out on a table on the back wall, beside the coffee and a rack of Al-Anon pamphlets. The foldin' chairs are set up in a circle in the center of the room. Plenty are empty. I take one between JohnyJoe and Myra. Both of them been comin' to Al-Anon a long time. We all stand, hold hands, and say the openin' prayer. Then it's Myra's turn to share.

"Hi, I'm Myra."

"Hi Myra," we all say.

"Tonight, I want to share about trust, not just trusting other people, but even myself. When I first started coming to Al-Anon, all the lies, betrayals, and secrets left my heart broken and hard. Having a safe space to share my deep-dark life is transforming. I no longer have to carry the darkness inside of me. When I reveal my secrets to the light of day, the pain lessens. Thanks for listening."

"Thanks for sharing," we answer.

Myra always says somethin' good. And she's right. Secrets eat you up.

I ain't shared all mine. I still got a real biggie. But I'm an old dog; I need some time to learn a new trick. Momma expected us to keep a lotta secrets. She said no one needs to know our black eyes and busted lips were from the old man. And she made me, Jake, and Swannee swear to keep her Alzheimer's quiet. If like Al-Anon says, "you're only as sick as your secrets," we was on our fucking death bed.

GREEN PEELER

JohnyJoe's chair scrapes the floor when he gets up to fix hisself a cup a coffee. Myra turns her chair to face Mitch. It's his turn to share. He looks like a sailboater tonight: pink polo shirt, canvas belt with whales on it, and khaki pants.

"I think my dad's the root of all my secrets and shame." He rubs his face and then kinda hunches over. He got his elbows on his knees and his chin leans on his clasped hands. "I stuffed down who I wanted be to make him proud. He paraded me around like a trophy—his golden boy. He'd take me to golf outings, hunting camps, fishing trips, and would always encourage me to drink, like one of the boys. As soon as I was tall enough to sit at the bar, he'd have the bartenders slip a shot of rum into my coke. I guess he was trying to make me into his kind of man. Instead, he made me a drunk . . . before my thirteenth birthday." His eyes get wet. Mitch pinches his nose. "That's all I got."

"Thanks for sharing," we say.

Mitch looks worn out. Sometimes meetin's are hard. A couple more people share before it ends. I check my phone. I gotta roll. I told Jake and Syd I'd watch Helly tonight so they can shoot some pool. I take the steps to the first floor two at a time and head out into the parking lot. I hear someone behind me. It's Mitch.

"Hey Maggie, wait up."

I stop. "Yeah?"

"I'm glad you were here tonight."

Damn, it's sticky out here. My face feels hot.

"Okay." I ain't sure what else to say to that.

"You want to grab something to eat? I'm starving."

Sweat drips between my tits and my hands are slick. Whew, I need a cold drink.

"Nah, I gotta watch my brother's kid tonight."

"Okay then. Another time." He walks to my truck with me, and closes my door once I'm in.

Now my whole body's sweatin'. I crank up the AC, but it spouts out hot air. Mitch waves and smiles before he gets in his car. My gut flutters. Must be hungry.

DEENA—May 31

For days, I've been tearing my house apart for to find Davey's lovey. It's a stuffed puppy dog head with a silky blanket for a body, and Davey has been miserable without it. When I'm driving to Bayside Foods it hits me—I must've left it at the picnic. Hopefully, Jake or Sydney found it when they cleaned up Helly's toys.

Their house is only a mile away, so I decide to swing by and see if they have it. My car clock says it's four. I'm sure Jake's not home from work yet. Hopefully Sydney's there. I can't take another night of cranky Davey.

The dogs bark when the tires of my hatchback crunch over the driveway's shells. I pull in front of Sydney's house. Nails comes out on her porch. She sees me, waves, then whistles for Ruby, taking her into her house. When I step out of my car, Daisy jumps up and knocks me back onto my seat.

"Daisy," Sydney yells from her front door. "Come." Daisy looks at her and walks down to the shoreline. Sydney shrugs her shoulders. "Stubborn dog. So, Deena, to what do I owe this unexpected pleasure?"

Her words sound sarcastic and my neck heats up. "I'm sorry to just drop by. I guess I should've called first."

She raises her eyebrows and it feels like a slap on the wrist. "It's fine. I've got something on the stove, but come on in."

GREEN PEELER

I get Davey out of his car seat and climb the three stairs to her porch. I've never been in her house. This is the first time I've been invited. At the picnic we used Nails's bathroom.

She flips an omelet. "Sorry. I skipped lunch and have got to eat now! If I had known you were coming, I would've made one for you."

I cringe at my lack of manners. "Please. Don't worry about me. I just showed up on your doorstop without calling. I'm the one who should be sorry."

"You can put Davey in the playpen with Helly if you want."

Her kitchen, dining room, and living room flow together in one open space. The playpen's near the couch. I settle Davey in with Helly and look around. The house has good bones, but overall, her style is too minimal for me. It feels cold.

There are a few things I like. Her coffee table's made from reclaimed wood and has black industrial wheels, and above the couch there's a huge canvas print of a photo. It's a black and white of Sydney and Jake, sitting side by side at the end of their dock, heads and hands touching. It's from behind, so you don't see their faces. It's really cool.

I point at the photo. "Did you have that made?"

"I did. And it wasn't that expensive. You can use any photo. I'll give you the company's information. Do you want something to drink?"

"That'd be great."

"Tea okay?"

"Perfect," I say.

"It's unsweetened. I don't like to drink calories during the day. Do you want sugar?"

"Please." I feel every bit of the twenty pounds I want to lose, and take the sugar anyway.

She pours us both a tea, adding sugar to mine. Her glasses look like blue mason jars with handles. She plates her omelet and brings everything to her farm table. Davey and Helly are completely content, so I join her at the table.

"Listen, I'm really sorry to barge in on you like this, but I think I left Davey's lovey here the other night."

"Hmm. I don't remember seeing anything new, but it could've been gathered up from the yard with Helly's stuff. What's it look like?"

"A little brown puppy head and a light blue blanket body."

She takes another bite of food and a sip of tea. "I'll look when I'm finished eating."

We sit there quiet, me watching her eat her food. When I'm uncomfortable, I'm really good at sticking my foot in my mouth. I usually say the exact thing I keep telling myself not to say. Today's no exception.

"So, doesn't Jake mind you going out with guys when he's away?"

She stops eating and looks at me like I grew another head. "Why would he?"

"I don't know. I mean, after what Cammie did . . ."

"I'm not Cammie."

"I know, but I don't think Skip would like it if I went out without him."

"Jake trusts me."

I can tell she's annoyed. She slugs back the rest of her tea and puts her dirty dishes in the sink.

"I'll go look for Davey's thing," she says.

She walks back the hall and I mosey around her living room. There's a few more family photos scattered around and a rustic wood bookshelf in the corner. It's filled with thrillers by Patricia Cornwell, Gillian Flynn, and Tami Hoag. And, there are four books by Sylvia Clint. I've never heard of her.

I pull out *A Father's Mistake* and flip to the back. My mouth falls open. A younger Sydney looks out at me from the book jacket. Damn, she really is a writer. I never quite believed it.

I skim the book summary. This is her first book and it's about her father. Holy shit! He's serving life for murder. I pull out the next title, *Mean Girl*. It's a true story about a seventeen-year-old who murdered and scalped a classmate. My stomach flips and my mouth

58

goes dry. I grab the next novel, *Black Leather*. It's another true-crime story about a biker who shot a young boy. My head spins and my hand begins to shake. I pull out her final book, *The Journals*. Before I can read the jacket, I hear Sydney clearing her throat.

"Are you finding what you're looking for?" she says in a creepy voice.

My heart starts pumping really fast. I'm actually scared. "So, uh, you really are a writer."

Shit! Why did I say that? Once again, open mouth, insert foot.

Anger flashes across her face. She walks towards me and I reflexively take a step back. Her eyes are black, sending a shiver down my spine.

The vein on her temple throbs. "I thought I cleared up your doubts about my writing years ago when you tried to embarrass me at the church fish fry, but apparently not." She reaches out, takes the book from my hand, and replaces it on the shelf.

"I didn't mean . . . I uh, I just never got to read your books. . ." I let my words trail off, desperate not to say anything else stupid.

She lifts her arm. She's gripping Davey's lovey, tight around its furry neck. "Is this it?"

I nod and lick my lips nervously. "Yep. Thanks." I try to take it from her but she holds on for a few seconds before letting go. It feels like a threat.

She drops her hand. Her smile goosebumps my arms.

"Glad it was here. Wouldn't want Davey to lose something so precious to him."

Now I know that's a threat, and all I want to do is get the hell out of there. I mean she's clearly obsessed with murder. She hangs out with actual killers. Her own father *is* a convicted murderer. I'm totally freaked out.

I back away from her. "So, I uh, I'm gonna get going. I'm sorry about the writing comment. I didn't mean anything. It's just, I uh, never met a real author—"

She holds up her hand. "Deena, say no more. I know you didn't mean anything by it. I shouldn't have let it ruffle my feathers."

I'm not buying this act, but I force a laugh. "You know me, always saying something dumb." I snatch Davey up and wave as I'm walking out the door. "See ya. Thanks."

"You're welcome. Stop by anytime."

Like hell I will. Sweat dampens the straps on Davey's car seat as I buckle him in as fast as I can. My chest feels tight and I'm panting.

What does Sydney do? Scour the news for gruesome stories and ambulance chase them? I had no fricking idea her dad is a murderer, or that her job is to get into the brain of killers. And now I've pissed her off.

Oh my God. What if she's like one of those fireman guys who start fires so they can put them out? What if she conspires with people to murder so she can write about them? Or maybe she's some kind of death-cult leader like Manson. I jump into the driver's seat, slam the car in gear, and fly out of the driveway.

As soon as the shells under my tires changes to pavement, I stop spiraling and start to calm down. I take a few deep breaths and try to think more rationally. By the time I hit Main Street, I'm laughing at myself. I'm not in danger. She may be annoyed, but she's not going to hurt me because years ago I doubted she was a writer. Sydney's not a cult leader. She's not inciting murders. Yes, she writes about gruesome stuff, but she's an author, nothing more. Once again, I let my anxiety get the best of me.

But in my defense, I was right about her shadiness. I always knew she had ulterior motives when she came to Rock Narrows. It's clear she came here to write about Jake and Nails. I tried to warn Jake she wasn't what she seemed, but he fell for her hook, line, and sinker.

What I don't understand is why the hell she's still in their lives? They have to know by now what she writes. They have to know she came here to write about their mom's murder. I don't get it. Something is very wrong with this picture.

SYDNEY—June 1

Deena's comment rankled me, but it also inspired me. I think maybe I feel like I've lost myself because I haven't been working. Writers need to write.

After she left, I read over *Swann Song*, my manuscript about Helen's murder. It's good. In fact, I think it's the best book I've written so far. It's time I get Jake and Maggie to agree to let me publish it and it's time I find a new story. But like the Al-Anon slogan says, "first things first."

Helly and I are in Bakerstown. The quaint village seems like a vibrant metropolis in comparison to Rock Narrows. There are at least fifteen stores, a few cafes, numerous bars, and a downtown that's several blocks wide. It provides a soupçon of the hustle and bustle I'm missing.

I wish I could enjoy a leisurely lunch or browse the indie bookstore, but I'm on a mission. First stop is the local drug store where I pick up diapers, baby wash, and a bottle of Banana Boat coconut-scented sunscreen.

Next stop ACE Hardware. I grab a pair of rubber gloves, a disposable dust mask, and a small box of TSP. Not only is Trisodium Phosphate a heavy-duty cleaner, it has the added function of neutralizing lead dust. It's also a significant skin irritant.

After one last stop at Woody's to pick up a part for Maggie's bateau, we're on our way home. Maggie turns down the lane right after I do.

She rolls down her window and yells, "Bring Helly over here. I ain't seen her in two days."

Nothing has done more to solidify my place in Maggie's life than Helly's birth. I guess it's as close as she'll ever get to having her own baby. Eddie made sure of that.

"You bet," I call back. "See you in a few."

As I grab a blanket for Helly, I notice the answering machine is flashing. I know it's Dad without listening. The landline is only for his calls. I'm sure he's badgering me to visit. It's sad how small and monotonous his life is, but his poor choices landed him there.

It *has* been over seven months since I've seen him, but I was heavily pregnant for four of them and adjusting to having a newborn for the rest. I let the answering machine flash. I'll deal with it later.

Maggie's changed out of her work clothes and is waiting for me in the yard. I'm still ten feet away when she reaches out her arms for Helly. "Hand her over." She cuddles her close and gives her kisses all over her whole face. She motions her head to the porch steps. "There's a beer for you. Grab me one too."

I spread the blanket across the grass, grab the beers from the porch, and crack them open.

Maggie lounges beside Helly. I hand her a beer and sit down on the edge of the quilt beside her. Helly is content and Maggie is smiling and calm. It seems like an opportune time to broach the subject of *Swann Song*.

I let out a dramatic sigh. "Jeez. What a hard day."

"Why?" she asks, as I hoped she would.

"Jake doesn't even know this yet. I got a call from my publisher. If I don't get a manuscript to them by June 30, they're going to sue me."

Appealing to her desire to help me is the fastest way to get Maggie on board with publishing their story, so this is a necessary white lie.

"What the fuck? That ain't right! What are you gonna do? You can't write a book in a month."

"Exactly. I'm in an impossible situation. I have a manuscript ready and could avoid financial ruin by sending it but . . . ." I trail off, sigh again, and cast my eyes downward.

"But what? Send the motherfucker."

"No." I shake my head dejectedly. "Unfortunately, it's just not an option."

"Why the hell not?"

"Oh Maggie, I can't," I whine, with as much regret as I can muster. "It's the book based on you and Jake. I know how you feel about having it in print."

"Shit."

I just nod my head and sit glumly drinking my beer. I need to give her time to mull over the possible ramifications if I don't send the story.

"Aw hell, Syd. For me it ain't never been about havin' the story out there. The gossip's probably worse. I was pissed 'cause you lied about why you was here. But Jake's a different story. He ain't gonna be happy if you get it printed. He thought you was past all that."

"I know. And that's why I haven't told him yet. Oh Maggie, I don't know what to do. I don't want to risk losing our house, but I also don't want to upset Jake." I summon a few tears and let them spill down my cheek.

"Well, he'll get over it. You ain't got no choice."

Bingo! I've persuaded Maggie.

I lean over and give her a quick hug. "Thank you for understanding the impossible situation I'm in. Will you read it before I send it to make sure you're okay with it?"

"Yeah. All right."

I suppress a satisfied smile. Not only have I convinced her to allow me to publish my best work to date, I've also guaranteed that she'll read my book, which after all was the original goal.

"Will you help me sway Jake?"

"Christ, it's a good thing I like you. Yeah, I'll help, but I ain't looking forward to it. He'll be madder than a hornet in a coke can."

I chuckle. Maggie comes up with the most colorful expressions. "You're probably right about that. Let's all have dinner tonight and I'll tell him after. I'll run out and get some of Millie's crab soup to soften him up. And I'll see if Ned's got any fresh corn. Can you think of anything else?"

"Make sure you got plenty of beer!" She tickles Helly's belly. "And I'll keep this little dough ball. You don't need to drag her all over hell and creation. She already been on the road with you half the day."

"Suits me. She might get hungry while I'm gone. There's breast milk in the freezer. I'll also stop at the marina and let Jake know our dinner plans. I'll be back in an hour or so."

"No hurry." She strokes Helly's hair. "Me and this little lard biscuit got plenty to do."

JAKE—June 1

"**J**ake! Wait!" Tierney calls across the parking lot. She's just leaving the pool. She jogs over to me and Skip. "I'm sorry to be so needy, but I have a favor to ask."

"Whatcha need?" I ask.

"What the hell, man? Don't you got no manners? Introduce us." Skip chimes in before Tierney can answer.

"Skip, this is Tierney. She's a slip holder here for the summer. Tierney, this is asshole—I mean Skip. He's a co-worker."

Skip's eyes damn near bug outta his head staring at Tierney's tits. I think she sees where he's looking 'cause she drapes her beach towel over her chest.

"Hi, Skip. Nice to meet you."

"So, what's the favor?" I ask Tierney.

"Some kind of alarm keeps going off on my boat and I have no idea what it is. It kind of has me freaked out, like I might explode or something. Would you mind taking a look at it?"

"Not a problem. I only got one more thing to take care of and I'll be over. See you in a few."

"Great, thanks." She lays her hand on my arm before she walks away. Skip sees it and raises his eyebrows at me.

"What?" I laugh. "I didn't do shit. I know better."

"Man, I don't know what it is about you that gets girls creaming their jeans." His eyes are glued to her ass swayin' down the dock. "Mmm, mmm, mmm. That's a tight ass. Wouldn't mind a piece of that myself."

"Don't be a dick. She ain't even old enough to drink. Besides if Deena found out she'd cut your cock off."

"Ain't that the truth. But Sydney'd do the same to you, so you better watch yourself."

"You know it, brother! Let's get back to work so we can get home to our pretty wives. The generator on the 50' Hinckley is on the fritz. Owners are coming down next weekend and want it in top shape. Can you fit it into the schedule for tomorrow?"

"You bet. We got a light load." He writes the order.

"Okay. That's it for today. Get home to your boy. I ain't gonna be far behind you."

I do one last test on the pool water, log the results, and lock up the office. I'll help out Tierney and then I'm done for the day. It'll be nice to get home early.

I hear the alarm going off as soon as I hit the end of Tierney's dock.

She flaps around like a nervous goose. "See, see. It keeps going off. I don't know what I'm doing wrong."

I jump onto her boat and flip on the bilge pump. The alarm stops.

"You're a magician. What did you do?"

"The alarm's for your bilge. It means you got water in the bottom of the boat." I show her the switch. "This is the bilge pump. When you turn it on it pumps out the water. That's why the alarm stopped."

"Water? Is the boat sinking?"

I shake my hand and laugh. "Nope. I'll check your bilge, but if the alarm goes on and off it's either broke or there can't be much water." I move the deck chair outta the way and pull up the engine hatch. I gotta lay across the deck to hang my head down into the opening. "Looks dry. I think you got a problem with the alarm. I'll see if Skip can take a look at it tomorrow. If it goes off before he looks at it, hit the pump switch and that should shut it off." By the time I got the cover on and the deck chair back in place she's already poured me an iced tea.

She hands it to me. "To thank you. Boats are complicated. Without your help I probably would've packed up and gone home. I really appreciate it." She pours herself a tea and sits beside me on the bench seat. Her long, tan leg brushes against mine. "I haven't seen Sydney at the pool lately. I really want to babysit. Will you let her know?"

"Yeah, if I remember. Work keeps me here so much we barely got time to talk."

"And then I add to your load."

I shrug my shoulders. "No problem. That's my job."

"So is Helly your only kid?"

"Yep. I'd like more, but I'm off to a late start being a dad so we'll see."

Tierney smiles at my answer and then the alarm goes off again. She jumps and her tea sloshes onto the deck. She gets a rag from the cabin to clean up her mess.

While she wipes the deck, her tits strain against her bikini top. "So, you were saying you want more kids . . ."

"Yeah, I want more, but I ain't sure Syd does."

She rinses out the rag in the galley sink and lays it over the side rail to dry. "I'd love to pick Sydney's brain. I'm planning to major in English in college so I'm sure she could give me a lot of advice."

"Oh yeah? What college?"

"William & Mary. With in-state tuition and some scholarships, I should be able to afford it."

"Damn, you must be smart. That ain't an easy school to get into. One of my dates for the Navy Ball went there. She was a brainiac."

Her cheeks turn a cute shade of pink. "I was my high school valedictorian, so I guess you can describe me as smart."

"Don't be shy about it. Be proud. Ain't too many people got that claim to fame. I bet your mom and dad were proud as peacocks."

"Mom was. She cried so much she went through a whole box of tissues at graduation. I didn't know my dad."

"I'm sorry. That must suck."

She shrugs her shoulders like no big deal, but I see a little wetness in the corner of her eyes.

"What about you? You were in the Navy. If you had a date from William & Mary, my guess is you were stationed in Norfolk."

"Yep."

"That's my hometown."

"How 'bout that. Small world. I ain't been there in years. I raised a lotta hell on those streets. I remember one night I drank a halfa bottle of whiskey and . . ."

"You corrupting this young lady?" Sydney asks.

Me and Tierney was so busy talking we didn't see her coming.

"Hi Sydney." Tierney jumps up from her seat. "Jake fixed my alarm and I was thanking him with a cup of tea. Do you want some? Fresh brewed."

Sydney raises one eyebrow at me and says, "Tea? I didn't think you like tea."

"Course I do. I just like beer better."

"No thank you, Tierney. Jake, can you make it home for dinner tonight? Obviously, you're swamped with work, but I planned a little something special for you with Maggie." Her tone is sharp. She ain't happy with me. I guess it does look bad.

"I sure can." I gulp down my tea. "Tierney's alarm was the last thing on my list. I can follow you home now." I hand my empty glass to Tierney. "Now remember, push this switch if the alarm goes off, and Skip'll come by tomorrow to look it over. Thanks for the tea."

"Thanks Jake. Y'all have a great night!" Tierney waves.

I brace myself to get yelled at. Me and Syd hold hands walking to the parking lot and she don't say a thing.

"Where's Helly?" I ask.

"Maggie kidnapped her." She laughs. "She can't get enough of her. It's so adorable. Listen, I have one more errand to run. Go home, get yourself a shower, and relax with a beer. I'll be home in a jiffy."

What the fuck happened to my pissed off wife?

SYDNEY—June 2

The morning sky has lightened to a purple grey and the world waits quietly, holding its breath for the arrival of the sun. I hum a happy tune as I put on a pot of coffee. Everything is falling into place. Eddie's death has been accepted as an overdose, and I've heard no mention of Whitey. My plans are in place for Deena, and last night's dinner was a success. After Jake reads it, *Swann Song* will finally go to my publisher. Of course, catching him in a flirtation with Tierney made persuading him a little easier.

I head out to the check the pens while the coffee brews.

Tierney's coquetry is a wake-up call. I trust Jake as much as I trust anyone, but I don't leave things to chance. Statistically more men cheat in the first year after childbirth than at any other time.

It's obvious why. Men are nothing more than overgrown children. The birth of a baby takes an inordinate amount of the new mother's time and dads feel abandoned. So, not only is the new mother required to sacrifice all of her time and identity to the baby, she's also supposed to worry about dad's feelings. It's ridiculously unfair. Railing against it, however, doesn't change it. I plan to pay more attention to Jake, and put Tierney at the top of my watchlist.

Ruby bounds through the yard greeting a new day. Maggie's not far behind.

"Gonna be a scorcher." She pulls her sweat dampened hair up into a haphazard pony tail.

She's right. It's only five and the air is heavy with heat.

She tosses her cooler into the bateau and whistles. Ruby hops in and Maggie casts off, tossing me her lines. Her boat putters into the shadowy light of dawn.

Finished with the pens, I head back in the house for coffee. I hear Jake stirring and peek into the bedroom. He's leaning against the headboard, arms spread in a big yawn. His abs tighten as he stretches, highlighting his six-pack. His surfer hair is rumpled, calling out for fingers to run through it, and his lazy smile curls his lip enticingly. I can't resist. I strip off my clothes and crawl in bed beside him running my hands up his muscled chest and through his sexy bedhead.

My arousal is strong. I straddle him and, right on cue, Helly cries. My breasts spray milk all over us, giving added meaning to the expression wet blanket. Sure, moms are cleared to have sex six weeks after childbirth, but this is the reality. Jake jumps in the shower frustrated and I feed Helly.

Twenty minutes later Helly's rolling around with Daisy on the floor and Jake and I are eating scrambled eggs. It's pretty much all I cook.

I lean in and nuzzle his neck. "Get home early tonight and we can finish what we started. I'll ask Maggie to watch Helly."

I want to ensure he'll be thinking about me all day.

"Done. Speaking of Helly. Tierney offered to watch her a few hours a day so you can get back to work. Whaddya think?"

I think, *that's intriguing and I'll have to ponder her motivations.* I say, "I'll think about it. I'm not sure I'd be comfortable with such a young girl watching our child. Tierney's barely past puberty."

He shrugs. "Whatever you decide. Are you comin' to the pool today?"

I answer noncommittally "Maybe. Or I might stay home and do some research to find a new project. We'll see."

He picks Helly up for a snuggle and kiss before he leaves. She gurgles and smiles, wrapping him more tightly around her finger. After he hands her to me, I get a brotherly peck on the cheek. So much for foreplay.

"See you tonight," he calls, as the door closes.

When I no longer hear his tires on the driveway, I spring into action. I need to get to the pool when it opens. I want to arrive when Deena does.

I collect my supplies: Banana Boat sunscreen, TSP, mask, and gloves. After emptying out about half of the sunscreen, I put on my protective gear. I use a chopstick to stir a hefty dose of TSP into the sunscreen, making sure no powder is visible in the lotion. When I'm finished, I slide the bottle of coconut-scented retribution into my beach bag.

On my way to the marina, I swing past the dumpster behind Bayside Foods and dispose of my supplies. My timing is excellent. I pull into the parking lot a few minutes before ten and Deena shows a minute later. I dawdle just long enough to make sure I am right behind her. She's got Davey on her hip and her beach bag slung over her shoulder. Her sunscreen bottle peeks over the edge of her bag. It's an easy swap. Deena doesn't even notice me until we stop at the gate to show our passes.

She looks over her shoulder and flinches when she sees me. "Oh hey." She pulls Davey tighter against her. "I didn't see you standing there."

"Hey," I reply casually, even though my heart is pumping with anticipation. "Have fun."

She walks to the far side of the pool. I choose a lounge chair on the other side, but directly across from her. I want front row seats to the show. She settles Davey on a towel beside her with a bucket of water and a few fish toys. I drape a towel over Helly's seat to protect her from the sun, then pull out a book and pretend to be absorbed. Deena reaches for her beach bag and my heart skips a beat.

Damn, it's Davey's sunscreen. She slathers it all over him, even through his hair, making a greasy Mohawk. I hope she uses hers as copiously.

Five minutes pass, then ten. What's that old saying? A watched pot never boils? I yell across the pool to her, "Would you keep an eye on Helly for a sec while I use the restroom?"

"Yep."

We may not be friends, but we're both moms. It's kind of an unwritten code—moms help moms—especially when it comes to peeing.

I take my time, letting the sun bake Deena. When I return, Helly hasn't moved an inch, but Davey's getting sweaty and fussy. Deena slips swimmies onto his arms and takes him in the pool. He's delighted. He smacks the water, belly-laughing when it splashes his face. She plays peek-a-boo with him, ducking her head under the water and popping up.

I drape the towel over me to feed Helly and try to tamp down my impatience. Refreshed, Deena and Davey get out of the pool. Deena reapplies Davey's sunscreen and sits him on his towel with a bowl of cheerios. I switch Helly to my other breast.

Deena grabs her sunscreen. This is it. I can barely contain myself.

She squirts out a thick line on her arms, chest, and legs and rubs it in. She squeezes out another handful and massages it into her face, neck and belly. I burp Helly.

A few minutes pass and Helly's head lolls against my shoulder. She's asleep. As I'm laying her into her chair, I surreptitiously glance at Deena. She's wiping her skin with a towel, gently at first, but then more vigorously. She's turning red, purple red, like raw liver. She jumps up frantic.

"Help me," she cries out to no one in particular. Her face winces in pain. "I'm burning up!" She grasps her throat as if it hurts to breathe.

Hmm, I wonder if skin absorption of TSP could cause her throat to constrict. Most likely not.

Davey looks up from his towel, curious.

"Oh my God!" she yells. "It's getting worse." Blisters are forming on her arms, face and chest. "Aiyeeee!" she screams.

She's frightened Davey and he begins to cry. The pimply faced kid in the gate office hears all the commotion and comes running into the pool. Deena gets ready to jump into the water.

"STOP!" I yell at her. "The chlorine might make it worse. Take a shower. I'll watch Davey. And you," I say, pointing to the teen. "Call an ambulance."

If it does affect her breathing, we'll need it.

When Deena and acne boy are out of sight, I switch out the sunscreen bottles, and take a moment to congratulate myself on a job well done. People must experience the consequences of their actions and words to grow.

As soon as I pick Davey up, he settles, snuggling his head into the crook of my neck. I hear the ambulance siren in the distance. Deena sulks out of the bathhouse, hair dripping wet and skin so raw it looks flayed. Apparently, after calling EMS, the teenager found Jake and told him what was happening. He and Skip barrel through the pool gate like rodeo bulls released from the chute.

When Skip sees Deena, he falls to his knees. "Oh my God babe. What the hell happened?"

Deena's too traumatized to answer. She stands stone-still, arms out and legs spread, so no skin is touching skin.

"I think she had a reaction to the sunscreen," I volunteer. "Her skin started burning a few minutes after she put it on. It was awful." I try to sound appropriately distraught. "I didn't know how to help her."

Skip runs over and grabs the sunscreen out of her beach bag. "This is the kind she always uses. Why would it mess her up now?"

Deena's lips quiver and her whole body is trembling. I think she may be going into shock. "Deena," I say, as soothingly as possible. "Please lie down until the ambulance gets here."

She walks with arms outstretched like Frankenstein and gently lowers herself onto the lounge. Other than the top of her shoulders, her back is unmarred. Skip kneels at her side.

"I'll take Davey home with me," I offer, charitably. "He can stay as long as you need. Skip, give me your house key, I'll run by your house to get him some pj's and clean clothes."

"No," Deena croaks. "Skip, you take Davey. It's . . . I uh . . ."

I hold my hand up to stop her protests. "Really, it's no problem. Skip needs to focus on you."

Skip looks relieved. "She's right honey. We need to get you to the hospital. Sydney will take good care of him."

Skip digs his key out of his pocket, and gives it to me, hands shaking.

"Please take care of him," Deena whispers hoarsely. A few tears roll silently down her blistered cheek. I bend Davey down to her face so she can kiss him. She looks at me with a mix of pain, wariness, and maybe a little gratitude.

I hope Deena's learned her lesson because if her behavior doesn't improve, my next punishment won't be as kind.

MAGGIE—June 5

Sydney's had Davey for three days and she's damn near ready to pull her hair out. After I rode my catch out to JimBob, I told her to come over. Thought I could help her out for a couple hours. We ain't had a minute to relax since she got here.

Helly's fussy, switchin' between whines and cries. And Davey shoves everything he can get his hands on into his mouth. Sydney puts Helly on her hip and bounces her and I take the TV remote out of Davey's mouth.

"It's nice of you to help Deena out. I know you two ain't really friends."

Helly wails and it starts Davey cryin'. I jingle his tambourine and tap his drum to quiet him. Sydney tries to nurse Helly but she throws a tantrum and flips her head from side-to-side.

"No, we aren't friends, but I don't hold grudges," Syd says. "Helly, for God's sake, latch on and stop squirming." She's still tryin' to get Helly to cooperate when she says, "Deena got what she deserved, so I can let it go."

Damn! I can't believe she said that. It ain't like Syd to be nasty. "Shit, Syd. That's fucking harsh. Why would she deserve to get burnt up? 'Cause she dissed you?"

Her face turns white and she looks up at me. "Oh, Maggie, that was horrible. I don't even know what I'm saying. I'm so frazzled having two kids, I'm just babbling."

She bends forward to grab a pencil out of Davey's mouth and squishes Helly's head into her chest. Helly lets out a mad wail. "See.

My mind is scattered. Of course I don't think she deserved what happened. It was brutal."

Deena only stayed overnight in the hospital, but she's in so much pain, she can't hold Davey. That's why Syd still got him.

"When's he going home?" I ask.

"As soon as she can hold him for more than a few minutes."

"Can't one of Deena's relatives take him?"

"I'm sure they would, but they don't live in town so she wouldn't get to see him as much. I can take him to visit her every day, so it's better for me to do it."

Now that's more like Sydney—ready to fix everything. If you don't want help, Sydney can be annoyin' as fuck, but you gotta take the good with the bad. She done a lot for us. She cared for Ruby after Eddie beat the hell out of her. She helped me and Jake deal with Momma's death and Swannee's suicide, and got me movin' in a new direction with Al-Anon. Without her, my life wouldn't be half as good.

Sydney pulls her bra over her tit, smooths her shirt down, and stands up. "Can you burp her, I've got to pee."

"Sure." I reach for Helly and Syd scoots to the bathroom.

In the half-second I take my eyes off Davey, he climbs up on the bench at the farm table. I jump over his toys and catch him with my free arm just before he falls. Both kids start cryin' and my head feels like it's gonna explode. No wonder Sydney ain't thinkin' straight; kids'll drive you nuts.

*****

Finally, Syd and the kids are gone and the house is quiet. I pour myself a shot of elderberry wine—Momma's remedy for jangled nerves. I'm gonna drink it and soak in a tub. I dump half a bag of Epsom salts into the tub and run the hot water, then throw a load of wet wash into the dryer and grab clean clothes from my bedroom while it fills.

The water steams. It's so hot I gotta scratch my ass and legs till they get used to the temperature. I lean my head back, lay my cheek on the cold porcelain, and close my eyes. When the wine's gone and water's cold, I stand up and grab for a towel. Three towels hang on the rack, folded into thirds and hung so the back and front edges are exactly even. Other than me, Sydney's the only person who been in my house today, and I sure as hell didn't hang my towels that way.

The tea towel on Eddie's stove flashes into my mind. Was Sydney in Eddie's house? For what? What reason would she have to be there?

A chill runs up my back. She wouldna . . .

Ruby barks and I pull my brain outta my ass. I'm sure plenty of people fold towels that way.

SYDNEY—June 6

Four days with Davey has confirmed that I don't want a second child. He's sweet, but kids are vampires, sucking out all energy and intellectual acuity and leaving a mindless, exhausted husk named Mom. I'm at the marina pool, straining to juggle two kids and a beach bag when Tierney comes to my aid.

"Let me help you." She grabs the beach bag and Davey's hand and heads to the lounge chair beside hers. "This okay?"

"Yep." I'm out of breath from the exertion. I swear Helly's seat weighs fifty pounds. I create a little tent with a towel spread between two chairs and sit Helly's chair under it.

"Should I put sunscreen on Davey?" Tierney asks.

"Please." I'm truly appreciative. The baby-safe zinc sunscreen has the consistency of toothpaste. Trying to spread it on a squirming child is no easy feat. "It's in the beach bag. Be sure you use the one with zinc."

"Yeah, especially after what happened to his mom. I heard it was horrific. I'll never use Banana Boat brand again—just in case."

"It was pretty bad. How'd you hear about it?"

"Oh, Jeremiah told me."

"Who's Jeremiah?" I ask.

"You know. The tall, cute guy that checks us into the pool. He said he's the one who called the ambulance."

Oh, pimple boy. Right on cue, Jeremiah comes into the pool area.

"Hi Mrs. Swann," he says. "Tierney, you forgot your change."
He hands her two dollars with a shy smile. Clearly, he's got a crush.

She tucks it into her beach bag. "Oh thanks, Jeremiah. I was
just telling Sydney that you were the one who filled me in on the
accident with Davey's mom."

He nods his head. "You really saved her, Mrs. Swann. The
paramedic said jumping into chlorine water would've made it a
million times worse."

I shrug. It would be unseemly to toot my own horn.

Tierney's finished applying Davey's sunblock and hands me
the tube. She grabs her own sunscreen from her beach bag and offers
it to Jeremiah. "Can you do my back?"

His Adam's apple bobs nervously. "Sure." His voice cracks
when he answers.

A boater rings the call bell at the entrance wanting admittance
to the pool and Jeremiah looks crushed. "Oh man, I gotta go."

I grab the sunscreen from her hand. "I'll do it."

Tierney gives Jeremiah a flirty wave, apparently her go-to
behavior with men. "Thanks anyway."

I rub a thin layer on sunscreen on her back. "He's handsome."

She blushes. "Isn't he?" Davey pulls on her arm, wanting to
get in the pool. "If you're okay with it, I'll take him in."

I could use a break from him. "That'd be wonderful."

I lay back and close my eyes, reveling in a moment of calm. I
miss being able to think. I miss being able to work. I miss me.

A few drops of icy water drip on my toes. Tierney's made a
soggy burrito out of toddler and towel. Davey's lip quivers with
cold. He sticks his tongue out to catch the droplets running down his
face from his sopping wet hair and belly laughs every time he snags
one. I rub him to dry him off and slip his T-shirt over his head. He
cuddles beside Helly and I cover him with a dry towel. It's naptime.
I bet he'll be asleep in minutes. Helly's content to gurgle beside
him.

"Thanks," I say to Tierney. "I needed a few minutes of peace.
It's been hectic."

"I bet. Have you had him all this time?"

"Yep."

She sprays a detangler on her head and combs through her wet hair. "You're really nice. Taking on another kid is a big deal."

I shrug again. "Neighbors help neighbors."

She slides her legs over the side of the lounge and sits up. "Speaking of helping, did Jake mention me babysitting Helly?"

"He did."

She rambles a mile a minute. "I absolutely love kids and have tons of experience babysitting. Helly is the cutest baby on earth and I adore her. And I know I said I wanted a chance to do nothing, but I'm kind of going stir crazy lounging at the pool every day. I'm not used to just sitting around. And Jake mentioned you're a writer and might be ready to get back to work. So, full disclosure, I'm hoping to somehow make a living with words and I'd love to pick your brain."

I throw my hands up. "Take a breath, Tierney. You had me at *I love kids*."

She claps her hands in delight. "When can I start?"

I think she's genuinely excited. Tierney's a tough read. I thought I was dealing with a crush on Jake, but she's also interested in Jeremiah. And now, it seems she's equally enamored with Helly and intrigued by me. You know the old saying, "Keep your friends close, but your enemies closer." Having her at my house a few hours a day seems like a wise decision.

"How about Monday morning. Eight till noon? Davey will be back at home by then so it will be less chaotic."

"I can do that. What murder are you working on now?" she asks.

Her question shocks me. I've kept the subject matters of my books under wraps; I don't need to rev up the Rock Narrows rumor mill. Would Jake have told her? Maggie certainly wouldn't have. I remember the shock on Deena's face when she found my books on the shelf. Could she be spreading spiteful gossip? I certainly hope not. I'd hate for her to have another accident.

"Tierney, how do you know what I write about?"

"I read your books."

"You did?" I ask skeptically. I make a living writing, but my books are by no means best sellers.

She stutters. "I, uh, yeah, I um, I ordered them the day Jake told me you're a writer." She regains her composure. "To have the privilege of meeting a successful author and not reading her books would be sacrilege."

Her ego stroking is pleasant, but doesn't diminish my skepticism. "I use a pen name. How did you find them?" I ask.

She fidgets with her fingers. "Jake told me your pen name because I told him I wanted to order your books."

Hmm. Jake's typically not forthcoming about books. He knows tongues will wag if the Rock Narrows community finds out what I write.

She pulls a book out of her beach bag. It's *I am not a Serial Killer* by Dan Wells. "This is what I'm reading now. I like books from the murderer's point of view, but yours are so different. I love how you set me up to want to hate the killer by starting with the graphic details of the murder, but the story doesn't allow it. It's brilliant! It kneads and tugs your heartstrings until you're rooting for the murderer."

So, she did read them.

"That's the whole point," I say. I have to admit, it's nice being able to discuss my work with someone. "I want to help the families of murderers find solace by showing them their loved one isn't a monster."

"You really accomplish that! By the end, the villain is the circumstances that led to the crime, not the person who committed it."

Not only did she read them—she gets it. She fricking gets it. She swings her legs back up onto the lounge chair and sits cross-legged. After staring off into space for a few minutes she asks, "That's how you met Jake, right? You came to write his story?"

Now I'm suspicious. Clearly, if you know what I write about, and you know about Helen's murder, it's completely logical to assume that's why I came here, but why is she aware of Helen's murder. It happened almost two years ago. My profession requires

81

me to take note of unusual murders, but a sixteen-year-old? A state away? Seems unlikely.

"You know about their story?" I ask.

Her cheeks pinken and she ducks her head, picking imaginary lint from her beach towel. She stumbles over her words, "Well, um, yeah, I mean it was national news. I mean matricide in a small town is a front-page headline . . ." She pauses as if she's searching for a more reasonable explanation. "And you know by then I was already planning my graduation trip to Rock Narrows so I took notice." She blinks back tears.

"Are you okay?"

She nods and sniffs. "It was just so sad."

I suppose her explanation is feasible.

"It was really sad, indeed."

She drinks a few sips of water. "Why can't I find it? I tried to order it. I'd really like to read it."

The set up is all I could hope for. Rock Narrows is an insular community. These folks protect their own. I have to control the narrative regarding the writing and release of *Swann Song*. In this instance, I'm hoping Tierney has a loose tongue.

"I came here to write Jake's and Maggie's story. To help them through the unimaginable horror of your brother murdering your mother. The story is written, but I'm waiting for Jake and Maggie give me the go ahead. It's their story. For me to publish before they're ready to see it in print would be disrespectful."

My explanation is brilliant, but it's a load of crap. I know that Jake and Maggie's healing would've been much faster if I had published it two years ago, but they're stubborn. The only way to get back into their life was to shelve the book, so that's what I did.

"Can I read it?" She puts her palms together in prayer position.

"You mean before it's in print?"

"Yes! And I'm bursting with questions! What made you pick Jake's story to write about? What was he like right after the murder? Did you meet his brother? Has he talked about his mom? What was she like? Did he share any childhood stories? How about his Navy days? I just want to crawl into your brain and get all the answers."

"Whoa!" I laugh. "You need to rein it in."

She blushes. "I'm sorry. Having access to a published author is so cool. I got carried away."

She's like an eager puppy and I'm her new bone. Though I'm flattered by her adoration, I can't let it cloud my judgment. "No worries. It makes sense. You want to pick the brain of someone who's achieved your career goals. I won't let you read the manuscript until Jake and Maggie have given the project the go-ahead, but I'll give you thirty minutes of writing questions on the days you watch Helly. Sound fair?"

"Oh my God, yes! That's so awesome. Thank you!"

While I'll be glad to be able to keep a close eye on Tierney, I'm also a champion of paying it forward, and mentoring Tierney is just one more way I can give back.

MAGGIE—June 6

I walk down the basement stairs to the Al-Anon meetin'. I'm damn near blinded. They fixed all the fluorescent lights and now it's bright as the sun. There's a bunch of empty chairs. I sit in one across from Mitch. He's beside Myra. I look around the room at everyone. It's weird. These people know a lotta deep shit 'bout me, but I don't even know their last names. Tonight's meetin' is about grieving, and it ain't just about the dead.

After Myra opens, she shares. "My husband is an alcoholic. I had to grieve the loss of my dreams of happiness and till-death-do-us-part love. Only after I processed the grief could I let those expectations go and find the happiness in my actual reality. My husband's still a drunk, but at my core I am happy. Thanks for listening."

We all say, "Thanks for sharin'."

To me they ain't just words. I mean it. These people showed me how to change my shitstained life into something worth living.

It's Mitch's turn to share. "Hi, I'm Mitch."

The group says, "Hi Mitch."

"I can relate to what's been said about letting go of what we wanted reality to be and accepting what is." He takes a big breath and leans back in his chair. "My dad was my hero. I wanted to be him. Every sport I joined, every girl I dated, every book I read was chosen to make him proud." He gets quiet and drops his face in his hands like he don't wanna see what he's rememberin'. When he talks again, his voice cracks. "And then I saw who he really was." His shoulders shake.

Nobody moves. Nobody talks. We all give him a minute to cry.

He sits back up and wipes his eyes with his forearm. "When I realized the man I emulated was a monster, I was devastated. That's when I started using oxy. The booze wasn't enough to numb the pain." He gets choked up again. "That's all I got."

"Thanks for sharin'," we all say.

It's my turn. I almost pass, but decide I got something to say. "I know what it feels like to find out your hero's just a regular person. For me, it was my momma. She was the world to me and what she said was gospel. But really it was bullshit. Bullshit heaped on fear. Momma wasn't no god; she was just a beat-down woman tryin' to survive. She gave me a lotta bad advice, and then she died before I could tell her how pissed I was at her. I had to make my peace at her grave." I stop talkin'.

The group waits to see if I got more before saying, "Thanks for sharing."

A few more people share, but I don't hear 'em. I'm stuck in my head, thinkin' about all the times Momma told me to keep quiet. Don't say nothin' about Pop or Eddie or Jed.

Secrets are like cancer. And I still got one eatin' me up inside.

Chairs scrape on the linoleum and get my attention. It's over. We all stand for the endprayer. Myra, JohnyJoe, and the others gather around the table for cookies and coffee. I clean up the books and fold up the chairs. Mitch comes over to help me. He don't say nothin', just stacks chairs. That suits me. When the job's done I wave goodbye and head out to the truck. Mitch follows me out.

"Hey Maggie, wait up. Thanks for sharing your story. It made me think about resolving my issues with my father, before I'm standing on his grave."

"Yeah. It ain't easy. Took me a long time to get there with my momma."

"I'm sorry you lost your mom. I'm sure she wasn't perfect. Who is? But she raised a wonderful person."

My face gets hot. I ain't good at taking compliments. "Thanks, I miss her."

I start towards my truck.

"Any kids to watch tonight?" he asks.

I'm quiet for a second. If I say no, I know the next question. My heart beats faster. I swallow. Here goes nothin'.

"Nope."

"Then how about that dinner?"

My palms is sweaty. "Okay, but no yuppie veggie bullshit. I want some real food."

Christ, he gives me the thumbs up. I try hard not to roll my eyes. For a minute I think about backin' out, but Sydney does dumb-ass shit like giving thumbs up and I still like her.

"Pizza? Burgers?" he asks.

"Burgers and beer sounds good."

"I don't drink. Remember. I'm an alcoholic too."

I'm an asshole for forgetting. "No problem." I try to joke it away. "I'll drink enough for both of us."

He laughs. "DJ's it is. I'll meet you there." He closes my truck door and gets in his fancy car and pulls out.

My hands shake like I got palsy and I think I might puke. I'm goin' on a date. My first since High School. I'm scared shitless.

Five minutes later, we slide into a booth and both order burgers and fries. I get a pitcher of beer and Mitch gets a soda. He sits back against the pleather bench-seat and rests his arm across the top. He looks cool as a cucumber. I ain't. My gut flops and sweat dribbles down between my tits.

"So, how did you end up being a waterman, I mean woman? What's the right word?" he asks.

I shrug. "Ain't thought about it, but waterwoman don't sound right."

The pimply high-schooler brings our drinks. Mitch pours me a glass of beer and I slug it down in three gulps. He pours me another.

"Okay, so how did you start working on the water? See how I did that?" he says, proud of hisself. He takes a swig of his soda.

I smile. "I work on the water 'cause I gotta pay the bills."

The server brings our food. I squirt ketchup over my fries and take a bite of burger.

"I get that, but why not work as a teacher, or a doctor, or any other job. What made you pick the water?"

Like I coulda been a teacher or doctor. I ain't that smart. "I ain't picked it. It's just what I know."

He chomps on his sandwich and waits for me to say more. I don't. My hands is slimy with sweat and I can't think of a damn thing to say.

When I stay quiet, he rescues me. "Correct me if I'm wrong, but isn't it unusual for a woman to work the water?"

"Yeah, so?" Christ, I bet he's just another chauvinistic pig thinkin' women ain't strong enough to be on the bay.

He wipes his mouth and takes a gulp of soda. "So, I think you're amazing. It must've taken a lot of guts to buck the system. I can't imagine the men were thrilled to have you join their ranks."

I laugh out loud. "You got that right. They hazed me like a runt in gym class. They cut my floats so I couldn't find my line. They pulled the lid off my bait barrel so it'd rot. They even cut holes in my dip net."

"Damn," he says. "That's rough. Did you ever report it to the police?"

"Hell no! That woulda made it a million times worse. I just kept at it. I worked harder and longer than any of 'em. JimBob— that's my buyer—learned he could count on me to get crabs when he was hard up. I'd stay out ten, twelve hours till I caught what he needed."

"So that was enough to earn their respect?" he asks.

"That and I helped one of 'em out when he hurt his back."

The high-schooler comes over and clears our empty plates. "Another pitcher? Dessert?" he asks.

I wanna stay, but I can't drink more and drive.

"How about dessert?" Mitch asks me. "I'm not ready to leave."

"Yeah, okay. Watcha got?" I ask the kid.

"Cherry or banana pie. Ice Cream. Smith Island Cake . . ."

"Cherry pie," me and Mitch say at the same time and laugh. The kid goes off to get our pie.

"So, you helped him how?" Mitch asks gettin' back to what we was talkin' about.

"All we talked about is me." My life ain't special enough to take up the whole damn night. "What about you?"

"I like talking about you. You're interesting. Tell me the story. I'll fill you in on me on our next date."

I choke on my beer. "You assumin' there's a next date?"

"I'm hoping."

I know I'm blushin'. The kid brings our pies, and I share the story.

"You know watermen don't got no disability fund and can't claim unemployment. If we don't bring in a catch, we don't get paid. Simple as that. So, when I found out Snooks—that's the guy who hurt his back—was gonna be off the water for at least six weeks, I caught an extra bushel of crabs a couple days a week and told JimBob to give Snooks the money anonymously. I know damn well he wouldn't wanna take it from no woman."

"Was he one of the guys who hazed you?" Mitch asks.

"Yeah, one of the worst."

"Maggie, I'm going to say it again, you're amazing. Most people would've said 'served him right' after the way he treated you."

"He had a pregnant wife and a toddler that was gonna suffer if he didn't have money comin' in. My momma taught me to help your neighbor."

"Neighbors yes, but assholes? I doubt I would've been so kind."

"Anyway," I say. "Somehow Snooks musta found out the money was comin' from me, 'cause, not too long after he was better, he bought me a beer and I ain't been messed with since."

I take the last bite of my pie. The kid clears the table and hands Mitch the bill. I dig out a twenty for my half, but he waves it away.

"I asked you to dinner, so it's my treat."

He throws the money on the table. We head out to the parking lot and he walks me to my truck.

"I meant it about a second date. Will you have dinner with me next week, before the meeting? If the weather's good, I'll pick up take-out and we can eat at Simmon's Pier. If it's rainy we can go to DJ's again."

I feel shyer than a schoolgirl. "Yeah, okay."

He takes hold of my hand and I feel like a fool 'cause it's wet with sweat. He don't seem to care.

"Can I kiss you?" he asks.

My mouth falls open and I must get a weird look on my face 'cause right away he says, "That's okay. No rush. I mean I want to kiss you, but I don't want you to feel hurried. It's all up to you. I would never, I mean, uh. You let me know when you're ready. I mean if ever, I uh. Well, I hope sometime, but if not that's okay too."

This is the first time in my life that a man gives a fuck if I am ready for somethin'. Sweat pops out on Mitch's forehead and his hand gets wet too. He might be more nervous than me. I smile before I lean in to save him by givin' him a kiss. It's short and sweet, not much more than a friendly peck, but I feel it in my toes.

JAKE—June 7

I had a line of slip holders waiting at my office door when I rolled in this morning. Joe, the Jersey stockbroker with the half-million-dollar cigarette boat, and his drunk-ass crew got rowdy again last night, settin' off M-80s at three in the morning.

I walk down to the end of C-dock. Joe's on his catwalk with a cup of coffee in his hand.

"Hey man," I say. "You and your boys gotta keep it down tonight."

I hate babysittin' a buncha grown ass men, but I gotta keep the masses happy.

Joe dumps his coffee dregs in the water. "Christ dude. What the hell am I paying $4500 a year for? Am I docking my boat in a fucking nursing home? I work hard and I play hard. I deserve to cut loose on the weekends."

I gotta bite my tongue. Does he think he's the only one who works hard? It ain't no cake walk suckin' up to a buncha asshole boaters like him. I take a breath and do my job.

"I hear ya. I like a good party myself, but some people come here for peace and quiet." I shrug my shoulders like I don't understand them. "Hell, I'd be right here partyin' with you, but it's my job to keep everyone happy. So, you gotta shut it down by eleven. And man, I gotta write it up as your second warning."

Joe looks at me like are you fucking kiddin' me?

I tell him, "You know I'd let it slide, but the big boss heard the complaints so my hands is tied. One more write-up and I gotta kick ya out. So, keep it chill tonight. All right?"

"Yeah okay. I feel ya, dude. You're just doing your job. Eleven p.m. chill out. Gotcha."

Went better than I thought. Usually, the ones with the loudest boats got the loudest mouths.

I pass Tierney's boat and she yells from the cabin, "Hey Jake, hold up a minute."

Her bikini top ain't much bigger than a couple Band-Aids. I try not to stare, but it ain't easy.

"Whatcha need?" I stay on the dock and keep it professional.

She hops off her boat and hugs me. "Thank you so much!"

I try not to notice her warm tan skin pressing against me. "For what?"

"Sydney's going to let me watch Helly."

"*That's* what you're all pumped up about?"

"No, I mean yes. I mean . . ."

She's cute when she's flustered.

"Yes, I mean I'm happy to watch Helly, but I'm really excited because Sydney is going to give me the inside scoop on being a writer."

She's still got a hold on my arms. She gives me another squeeze, then bounces up and down. "I start on Monday!"

My dick's caught her excitement. I bite down on my tongue till I taste blood. Ain't no time to get a hard-on.

"Cool." I walk away from her to check the electric cord on the boat next to hers. "Well, I gotta get back at it," I yell over my shoulder, keeping my distance.

"Sure. okay." She jumps back into her boat. "I guess I'll see you tomorrow." She waves.

"Yep, see ya 'round." I get my ass off the dock before anything pops up.

Skip's standing where the pavement meets the dock. "What the hell was that?"

"What?" I snap.

"You two look pretty friendly."

"I got work to do." I walk past Skip, through the parking lot to the office. Skip follows me. I pull out the work orders and flip through them.

"Watch yourself, man. You know you're a sucker for a pretty blonde."

I'm gettin' damn irritated with him. I look up from the papers. "You need something?"

"Yeah. I wanted to know if it's okay if I run home for lunch. I wanna check on Deena."

"Go, just leave me the hell alone."

"Don't be mad at me." Skip throws his hands up and takes a few steps back. "You're the one skating on thin ice."

He's right. I ain't mad at him. I'm mad at my two-timing dick.

DEENA—June 8

Sydney just left after bringing Davey by for his daily visit. She rebandaged my healing skin, did some laundry and the dishes, tidied up the bathroom and made me lunch, and I feel like an absolute bitch. Since she came to town two years ago, I've been nothing but nasty, doubting her at every turn. I was so wrong. She is selfless and I am ashamed at my behavior. I'm really going to have to figure out how to make it up to her.

The screen door in the kitchen bangs open.

"Sydney is that you? Did you forget something?"

"No, it's me," Skip yells. "I came to check on you."

He strolls into the living room and bends down to give me a gentle kiss, being careful not to hit the right side of my cheek. I still have a raw spot there. The doctor doesn't think the scarring will be too bad, but right now I look like a skinned rabbit.

"You look better every day." Skip tries to be reassuring. He knows how self-conscious I am about my looks.

He eases down on the couch beside me. "I can't stay too long, Jake's already pissed at me so, I don't want to be late."

I reach out to hold his hand. "I'm sorry you're having a rough day, babe. Why's Jake mad?"

He shrugs. "Guy shit."

"What kind of guy shit?"

"I probably shouldn't have said nothing." He turns and leans back onto the arm of the couch so he's facing me.

This is typical Skip. Any time something's bugging him he makes me dig it out in bits and pieces.

"Well, you did, so now you can't leave me hanging," I say.

"We got this new slip holder at the marina."

"Uh-huh."

"She's a pretty, young blonde."

Jake's weakness is blondes.

"Oh no. Please don't tell me . . ."

He leans forwards and shakes his head and hands. "No, no, no. Nothing happened, yet. At least I don't think so."

"Well, then what?"

"He and Tierney, that's her name, seem a little too friendly. I called him on it and he ain't happy with me."

I think back to two years ago when I found the disgusting crotch shots and dirty texts on Skip's phone. I felt like my world collapsed. Luckily it wasn't what it looked like. They were sent to his phone by mistake—a wrong number. There were no texts before the dirty one. And none since—I still check his phone regularly—but for those few days, when I thought he had cheated, I wanted to die. I don't want Sydney to go through that.

"Well, you had to call him on it. Sydney would be devastated if he strayed, and after all she's done for us, I don't want to see her hurt."

"Yeah, you're right. I had to say it. I'll try to keep him on the straight and narrow. Shit," he says, looking at the time. "I gotta roll."

He jumps up and gives me one more gentle kiss before he leaves. He's a good man.

MAGGIE—June 10

I ain't workin' today. Can't remember the last time I took off. Swannee's funeral?

Now it's Eddie's. I can almost feel sorry for him. He ain't never felt like he was good enough. Maybe that's why he beat me. Made him feel like a man, at least for a little.

I picked up his ashes from the coroner on Friday. They's got him in a cardboard box. Been riding with 'em strapped in my passenger seat all weekend. Worm, the grave digger, already got the hole dug and the urn vault—that cost me two hundred bucks—in place. If you ask me, it's damn stupid I gotta buy a waterproof, bug proof box. What the fuck? He's dead. Ain't nothin' left but soot. What's it matter if he gets wet or some bugs make a home outta him?

I park my truck under an old oak tree and grab the box. I pay my respects to Eddie's momma and old man. It's just me and his dead parents here to mark the end of his life. Ain't nobody but his drug dealer gonna miss him. He was a bastard.

Was. That's a good word.

I try to stuff the box of ashes into the vault. Ain't gonna fly. It's too big to shove in. I gotta take the plastic bag of ashes outta the box to make it fit. There's less left than I expected. I lift up one side of the bag and watch the ashes fall to the bottom. I do it on the other side. These five pounds of dust made my life miserable.

After shovin' the bag into the vault and closing the lid, I stand up. A little bit of ash is on my hands. I brush it on my pants. It's fuckin' over. I kick dirt on top.

Worm comes over to me. "Want me to finish?"

I shake my head, "Nah, I got it. Just leave me the shovel."

He walks over to the hole, spits tobacco juice onto Eddie, then looks at me. "Nails, you deserved better." He don't say no more, just hands me the shovel and walks away.

It ain't right he spit on a dead man. I head back to my truck to find a rag or shirt to wipe off Eddie's vault before I bury him. I see the bloodstains on my seat from when he busted my nose and I drove to Momma's house for her to patch me up. My face gets hot. Worm's right. I did deserve better. Fuck the rag.

I walk back to the hole and dump a shovelful of dirt on him. The head of the shovel hits the urn and clangs. The sound reminds me of the night he dented up the lawn mower with a hoe. It's the same night he busted two of my ribs. I kick over the urn. The lid falls off and the bag of ashes slides half way out. That motherfucker made my life a livin' hell.

I take the shovel and slam the pointed end on the bag. The plastic tears and the ashes spill onto the dirt. I throw the shovel to the side and get down on my knees. I hiss into the hole, "Rot in hell, you son-of-a-bitch."

I grab a handful of dirt and slam it as hard as I can into the hole. He couldn't break my will so he broke my bones. I slam another fistful of dirt on top. When he couldn't shut me up, he'd choke me till I'd pass out. I slam another fistful of dirt. He wanted me to hurt so he beat our baby outta me. Over and over, I keep smashing handful after handful of dirt onto him.

When the hole's filled in, I collapse back against his pop's headstone. I'm breathin' hard and my head's soaked with sweat. I can feel the mud caked on my face and my fingers are bloody, but I feel better than I have in years. I'm leavin' my hate and pain with his burnt skin and bones. I'm finally fucking free.

SYDNEY—June 10

Davey is back home with his mostly-healed mother and Tierney showed up for her first day of babysitting. She and Helly are giggling in the living room, and I'm holed up in my makeshift office, trying to reclaim parts of my pre-baby life. Despite scrolling through two hours' worth of headlines, I've struck out in the inspiration department. For me, my reaction to a true-crime story has to be visceral. When it's right it grabs hold and won't let go.

I stretch and twist out the kinks. Maybe I need to clear my head. I put Daisy in her harness and click on her leash. I pop my head into the living room. Tierney's making fish faces and Helly's waving her hands and belly laughing.

"I need some fresh air. I'm going for a walk."

"Have fun!" Tierney says. "We're all good."

I drink in the buoyancy of walking out of the door sans diaper bag and baby. Daisy strains at her leash, sensing our unusual liberation, and we take off on a run. As we pass the woods, the fresh pine scent invigorates me and I move faster, feeling lighter with every step. You don't realize how much freedom you've lost until you begin to regain it. The rhythmic slap of my shoes on the pavement is hypnotic and I lose myself in thought.

The blare of a horn jars me into the present. Maggie's truck pulls alongside of me and Daisy. Her hair is tangled with dirt, and sweat and tears have made trails through her mud-smeared face, but her eyes are clear and she looks serene.

"Hey," she says.

"Hey, yourself. How'd it go?"

"Best funeral I ever been at."

I am proud I could deliver peace to her.

"I knew his death would be good for you." The words are out of my mouth before I can consider the impression they may convey.

Maggie gives me a questioning look.

I back pedal. "I mean. Of course, I wouldn't wish death upon anyone, no matter how deserving, but once I heard he overdosed, I was certain it would be freeing for you."

To my relief she changes the subject. "Who's with Helly?"

"Tierney, the new slip holder at the marina. She loves kids and wants to be a writer so I'm trading wisdom for babysitting."

She chuckles. "You're gettin' the best end of that trade."

I stick my tongue out at her. "What are you doing with the rest of your day? It's not often you have spare time."

Maggie never rests. She's a human doing. She stays busy so she doesn't have time to think.

"I'm gonna read your damn book. It's a day to get ridda all the shit that's weighin' me down."

I'm pleasantly surprised. Even though she agreed to read it, I thought I'd have to twist her arm. "Cool!" I only allow a little of my excitement to shine through. "That'll give me time to make the adjustments you want and get it to my publisher by June 30."

Done conversing, Maggie gives me her two-finger wave and heads down the road. I indulge in a moment of celebratory self-congratulation. Not only have I released Maggie from Eddie's hold, after reading my book she'll finally get closure to her mother's murder at the hand of her beloved brother. In two years, I have completely turned her life around.

My success has me itching to find a new family to help. Back to Google. Daisy and I sprint towards home. We burst through the front door to find Tierney elbow deep in pictures and memorabilia from our curio cabinet.

Her face turns crimson and beads of sweat line her forehead. "Umm, I know this looks bad, but . . ."

Still out of breath from my run, I can barely choke out, "But what?"

"But I um, was just curious to see if Helly looks like Jake when he was a baby. I was looking for a photo album or baby photos and when I found these . . ." She waves her hands over the pile of pictures. "I got carried away." Shamefaced she continues, "I'm so sorry. I was curious, but I know I shouldn't have rooted through personal stuff."

Her explanation feels contrived. I don't speak, letting the silence rattle her.

Frantically, she picks up photos and shows them to me, jabbering to cover her embarrassment. "She really does look like her daddy. She's got the same coloring and head shape. I'm guessing this is Jake's sister?" She points to a young Maggie. "Helly looks exactly like her. And in this one you can see that all the Swann kids have exactly the same shaped eyes, just like Helly's. And is this the older brother? The one who killed their mom? He's got the same mouth as Helly. Helly doesn't have a curl to her lips, like Jake. I mean maybe she'll get that when she gets older but . . ."

I raise my hand to stop her ramblings and take the pictures from her fingers. I take a slow, deep breath and rein in my anger. "Tierney, I do believe your lack of judgment came from a place of fondness for Helly."

I don't believe this for one second. This girl is up to something. I feel like my family's being stalked. The easiest way, however, to discover her intentions is to keep her close. If I put the fear of God into her, she may become too cautious, making it more difficult for me to expose what she's up to. No, this calls for a slap on the wrist. Hopefully emboldened by "getting away with it," she'll proceed with confidence.

I continue. "I'm sure you can understand that it's upsetting to find you looking through our drawers. So, let's not let it happen again. Okay?"

She nods, too chastened to answer verbally.

"I think we should call it a day. I'm tired after my run and ready to spend some time with Helly."

Again, she nods and begins to put the photos back into the cupboard.

"Leave them. I think I'll look through them before putting them away. It is fun checking out the family resemblance." I offer her a broad smile meant to ease her discomfort. "Same time tomorrow?"

"Yes! Oh, thank you so much for still letting me come. I'm so sorry. I promise it won't happen again!" She scurries out the door like she's worried if she doesn't leave quickly, I'll change my mind.

I do look through Jake's collection of photos; dozens of shots of bare-footed, free-range children with carefree smiles concealing the reality of abuse. My favorite is gone. The one with the whole family—Helen and Bill included—gathered around their new Golden Lab puppy. It's the only photo I've ever seen of them truly happy and all together. I flip through the pile again to see if I missed it. Nope. I rifle through the drawers and shelves of the curio. It's not there. Disappeared like the moment of happiness it had captured.

I know Tierney has it, but why?

JAKE—June 12

I find a shady spot near the pool to take a fifteen-minute break. These damn boaters are runnin' me ragged. Never heard so much bitchin' in all my life. And by the time I get all their complaints taken care of, it's late and I'm dog-tired. Me and Syd barely said three words to each other lately. I crack open a cold soda and guzzle it down.

"Hi Jake." Tierney's voice startles me. Her bikini gets tinier every time I see her. This one's blue with white stars on top and red and white stripes on bottoms that ain't much more than butt floss.

"Hey there." I slug back the rest of my Mountain Dew. "Not watching Helly today?"

"Nope. Sydney was taking her visiting today, so I have the day off. Actually, do you think I could borrow your house key? I left my book there and I wanted to finish reading it while I have the time."

I dig the key out of my pocket. "Here. Just be sure to lock it when you leave."

Her fingers brush mine when she takes the key from my hand. "Will do. Thanks."

"You bet. Bring it back when you're done."

"Yepper." She rubs the house key between her fingers. "You know, I saw some photos of you as a little boy the other day. You were absolutely adorable. I mean not that you aren't now. . . I mean, obviously you're handsome, but back then . . ."

I like the pink in her cheeks, so I tease her a little. "I getcha. I was a cute kid and a damn fine-lookin' man now." I wink.

She covers her face with her hands and shakes her head. "I'm so embarrassed. I get so flustered around you. I sound like a moron."

I give in and save her. "A soon to be William & Mary student is definitely not a moron." I laugh. "I was just teasing you. I knew what you meant. Helly looks like me, doesn't she?"

"She does! And really like your sister. Are you guys close? Is she married? Does she have any kids? I really hope I get to meet your sister sometime."

What's with all the questions about Maggie? Weird.

I toss my empty can into the garbage can. "Oh, why's that?"

She turns pink again and stutters. "Um, I . . . uh, I adore Helly and feel like I should know her whole family."

"Hey boss," Skip interrupts. He stops dead and looks Tierney up and down. His mouth falls open and he forgets what he came over for.

"Whatcha need, Skip?" I ask to get his attention.

"Yeah, right. Uh, we got a problem on D-Dock. You gotta smooth some ruffled feathers."

Never-fucking-ending drama with these cry-baby chicken neckers.

"Gotta roll." I say to Tierney.

"I'll bring your house key back as soon as I'm done." She waves and heads out to her car.

"What's she going to your house for?" Skip asks, staring at her might-as-well-be-naked ass until she slides into her car.

"Left something there. She babysits for us sometimes."

He shakes his head and rubs his chin. "Shit, man. Be careful. That's just too damn tempting. I'm telling you, Jake, that's one flag you better not wave."

102

MAGGIE—June 12

Seems nuts, but things are better since I buried Eddie. Like today. The sun looks like it's dancin' on the choppy water and the riggin's clang against the fake 1768 schooner's mast sounds like a song. And Mitch's body looks damn fine when his white T-shirt pulls tight across his muscles.

He spreads a red-checked tablecloth out across one of the picnic tables on Simmons Pier and lays out the food. The closer I get to him the more my gut flips. I gotta get over the schoolgirl jitters.

"Hey," I say, when I'm close enough for him to hear me.

"Hey back." His smile takes up his whole face. He pulls me in for a hug and whispers, "I missed you this week. Seven days is too long to go without seeing you."

I hug him back. I ain't gonna say I missed him, but I did think about him a lot. 'Course on the crick you got all the time in the world to think.

"Yeah, well I'm here now."

He laughs. "I'm withholding food until you promise to let me treat you to sundaes tomorrow night."

I guess it's nice he wants to see me again so soon. "Twist my arm."

He kisses me instead.

"Okay, so feed me. I'm starved. Whaddya got?"

"A little of everything."

He ain't kiddin'. He got chicken and ribs, coleslaw and potato salad, strawberries and blueberries, carrots and celery, and a cherry pie.

"Damn. Are you feedin' an army?"

"No, just a beautiful woman who deserves to have something she likes."

This man makes me blush more than a virgin in a whore house.

He pretends not to notice, so he don't embarrass me. "Sit, sit. Let's eat."

I'm not a picky eater. I load up my plate with a taste of everything. The seagulls sneak closer to our table, hopin' we'll drop something.

"Do you want a drink?" he asks.

"Yep."

He grabs a bottle of Arizona out of his cooler.

I'm surprised. "How'd you know that's my drink?"

"I noticed an empty bottle in your truck."

Damn! He sure pays attention to the little things.

"Good catch today?" he asks.

"Great. Three bushel. I dipped so fast my arm got tired. But we ain't talkin' about me tonight. You're up."

"Okay, okay. What do you want to know?"

"Well for starters, whaddya do?"

"Sell advertising. It's soul sucking and I hate it."

"Well, why don't you do something else?"

"I guess it's like you said about your job; it's what I know." He looks out over the river at a catamaran sailing by. "I used to like it. It was kind of like a game, manipulating the customer until they said yes. Now it seems pointless. Prison and sobriety changed me."

I almost ask what he went to prison for, but I don't. When you got skeletons in your closet it ain't fun when people try to pull 'em out before you's ready.

Instead, I ask, "Well, if you could do anything, what would it be?"

"This'll probably sound like a Miss America answer, but something to help people. I've got a lot to make up for and I want the rest of my life to make a positive difference."

At least he didn't say world peace.

I take a swig of my tea. "So why don't you do it?"

"My excuse is I'm reacclimating to free living. The truth is I'm scared shitless. Bravery's not been my strongest trait."

Wow! I think that was fucking brave. The men I know don't admit when they's scared, they just get mean.

"But you know what?" He takes hold of my hands. "You inspire me."

I look away without thinkin' about it and he lets go of one hand to lift my chin.

"Really Maggie, you are one of the bravest people I've ever met. You face life with your head up and you tell it like it is. You don't hide behind social niceties. You are who you are, and the world can take it or leave it. That takes guts."

He's right. I don't hide behind niceties—just a hard shell and a mountain of secrets. Ain't it funny? I think he's brave and he thinks I am. And we's both just scared little rabbits.

Our picnic ends with a walk on the public boardwalk runnin' along the river. We stay longer than we should, and roll into our Al-Anon meetin' ten minutes late.

The group's already sharin'. Tonight is step nine. *Made direct amends to such people wherever possible, except when to do so would injure them or others.*

Myra says, "When I made the list of people I had harmed, I put myself at the top. I was so busy tending to everyone else's needs I neglected my own."

She's a fucking genius. I ain't never thought about how much I hurt myself. Sure, I got apologies to make to others. I can be a bitch. But ain't nobody I hurt more than me. I didn't do a damn thing 'bout all the bad shit that happened to me. Just kept quiet and swallowed it. Somehow, I guess I thought I deserved it. Maybe making amends to myself means callin' out the motherfuckers who hurt me. At least the one who's still alive. I ain't young and scared no more. Maybe it's time.

"Thanks for sharing," the group says when Myra's done.

It's Mitch's turn. "I know about amends. I've had some doozies to make. The screw-up that landed me in jail caused damage that I'll be atoning for my entire life. But that's not what keeps me up at night. I owe a huge amend. So huge it haunts me. But I don't know who to make it to."

What's he mean? How can you owe a sorry and not know who to say it to? Whatever it is, it got him torn up. He rubs his hands together and fights not to cry.

"I hate the spineless, pampered boy I used to be." He almost spits out the words. "A decent man would've cut ties, but I didn't." Mitch hangs his head and holds it in his hands. "I took Dad's money for college and I took the internship he got me. I played nice and kept quiet." He shakes his head and you can damn near feel his shame. "I guess that makes me as callous and culpable as he is."

JohnyJoe pats him on the shoulder and we all say, "Thanks for sharing."

It's my turn and I pass. I wanna say somethin' to make Mitch feel better, but I gotta figure out what. A few more people share and the meetin' ends. Me and Mitch help fold up the chairs, but he don't talk. He looks like a beat dog.

"You know," I say to him. "We all done bad things, but it don't make us bad people. Hell, my brother shot my momma to death and he wasn't no bad person."

He looks damn surprised, like a rooster who laid an egg. "Is, I mean, was Swannee your brother?"

"Yeah. Guess you heard 'bout the murder."

"No, I mean yes, I know about it because Swannee was in my cell block."

"He was? Holy shit!"

"He didn't say one single word the entire time he was in there. Kind of freaked us all out. We called him the zombie."

I nod. "Fits. He was the walkin' dead."

All the chairs are folded and I need some air. We wave goodbye to the rest of the people and head upstairs and out into the parking lot. I head straight for my truck. He grabs hold of my hand.

"Wait, I know you shared what happened to you to make me feel better, and I do. But now you feel worse and I'm so sorry."

He's still holdin' my hand. I lean back against the truck, and he takes my other hand too. "That must've been so hard for you, losing your mom and your brother."

"Yep."

"Don't shut down. Talk to me."

I pull my hands loose and run my fingers through my hair to clear away the flashback. "I'm okay."

He pulls me close and wraps his arms around me. I let mine hang at my side. He rubs my back like he's calmin' a baby. "You don't have to be okay. You can cry, or yell, or whatever you need to do."

I put my hands on his chest and push him away. "No, I'm good. It just shocked me is all."

I'm sure he don't wanna hang out with a murderer's sister. I'm gonna give him an out. "So now that you know about my fucked-up family . . ."

He puts his finger on my lips. "I like you even more."

SYDNEY—June 13

Mission accomplished, to quote W (except mine really is). Jake and Maggie expressed gratitude for the book. I knew all along it would offer them the clarity and closure they needed. I'm not one to say "I told you so," but life would run so much more smoothly if people stopped doubting my wisdom.

I've stopped breast-feeding and am making the necessary arrangements for a trip to the city to take my manuscript to my editor. I really wouldn't have to go, but I could use the get-away. Mommy duty is suffocating. I'll also visit Dad before I return and get him off my back.

I called Deena last night and she was thrilled to be able to pay back my excellent care of Davey by babysitting while I'm in New York. Her churlishness has peeled off like the burnt surface of her skin. Just goes to show how effective it is to let people suffer the consequences of unacceptable behavior.

Now I'm at the marina. I've been puzzling over Tierney's snooping and photo theft, and thought a girls' lunch might prove illuminating. I step out of the car and my hair whips into my face. The wind has picked up and the sky is graying. A summer storm is fast approaching. The water laps the sides of the boats and the sailboats' riggings clatter.

I hurry to get Helly out before the rain starts. Skip sees me struggling to lug Helly and her seat out of the car and rushes over.

"Hey there." He kisses me on the cheek. "Let me help you out. These car seats are so damn heavy." He grabs her seat. "Deena got herself an umbrella stroller instead of haulin' this around."

"Good idea. I think I'll do the same. I talked to Deena last night. She's going to watch Helly for me."

"Cool. It's the least she can do after all the help you gave us. You and Jake are saints. If you're headed to the pool, you might wanna change your plans." He points up. "Rain's on the way."

The clouds have darkened ominously.

"No pool. I'm going to C-Dock, Tierney's boat." He stops and a caught-with-his-hand-in-the-till look passes over his face. He breaks eye contact with me. "Oh, okay."

"What's with the weird face?"

"Nothing, I didn't know you know her is all." He moves towards the dock, walking a lot faster now.

"How do *you* know her?"

"I, uh, worked on her boat. And I see her around the marina." His cheeks redden. I wonder if he's been cheating on Deena. If he's not guilty, he sure looks the part.

Just as Skip sits Helly's seat down on the dock in front of Tierney's rented Sea Ray, Jake comes out of the cabin with Tierney close behind. His hair is mussed and his face is red from exertion. He is clearly surprised to see me. Tierney's wearing a skimpy bikini and a see-through cover-up. Skip takes one look at the situation and beats a hasty retreat. Looks like he's not the one cheating after all.

"Hey beautiful," Jake says too casually. "What a nice surprise." He climbs off her boat and hugs me. I smell sweat, but not sex. "Is that my sweet baby girl?" He coos to Helly and picks her up out of her seat.

I'm silent.

"Hi Sydney!" Tierney chimes in, wide-eyed and innocent. "It's good you're here. I was having baby withdrawal." She clambers off the boat, adding her kisses to Helly's chubby cheeks.

Thunder rumbles in the distance and the water gets choppier, rocking the boats in their slips. The air turns chilly and Tierney shivers in her flimsy cover-up.

Jake hands Helly to Tierney. "What're you doing here? I thought you was packin' for your trip."

Yes, it appears as though he assumed I'd be tied up most of the day.

"What are *you* doing here?" I ask pointedly.

"Oh, this?" He gestures towards Tierney's boat. "The macerator on her toilet didn't vent right, so she couldn't flush. I got her all fixed up."

Really? Since when did he become the marina handyman?

"Poor Jake had to squeeze into that tiny little bathroom to get it fixed. They really don't make boats for grown men," Tierney adds.

They're putting on a good show.

"Well, I was coming by to invite Tierney to lunch, but if you two are busy with repairs . . ."

Laughing, Jake puts his hand on his hips and sticks out his chest like Superman. "My work here is done. You two go have fun." He gives Helly one more kiss, pats my behind, and heads to his office. His actions seemingly guileless.

Tierney hands Helly to me. "Lunch would be awesome. Let me throw on some clothes and I'll be ready to roll."

Maybe she should have thrown on some clothes *before* having Jake in her cabin. Jake may have remained faithful—this time—but this scheming vamp doesn't seem to be giving up.

I swallow my anger and put a smile on my face. "Great, I'll meet you at the car."

Tierney's youthful naivety has her feeling bulletproof. She's anything but.

DEENA—June 13

As I back into the parking space in front of Black Dog Bistro, the first drops of rain sprinkle my head. Pulling my scarf tighter around my cheeks, I lift Davey out of his seat and scoot into the restaurant before the storm lets loose. I'm stir crazy. I haven't been out of the house since the accident? Disaster? I'm going to have to think of a name for what happened. Maybe Hell Day or Burn Bash. Anyway, I can't stare at the walls any longer.

My face and body still have raw spots and scabs, so I wasn't ready for people in Rock Narrows to see me. That's why I'm in Bakerstown; no one knows me here. I'm standing at the hostess station waiting for a table.

"Deena?"

Are you kidding me? It's Sydney, Helly, and a really pretty blonde woman. I puff the scarf up to cover the worst of the marks on my cheeks and shift Davey to my other too-big hip.

"Hey Sydney."

"It's good to see you getting out of the house. This is—"

Before Sydney can introduce her friend, the hostess returns to the station and asks, "Three and two highchairs?"

I'm already feeling self-conscious. I really don't want to eat with Sydney and a Jennifer Lawrence look-alike.

"Um, yeah sure," Sydney answers before I can say anything. "But only one highchair."

The hostess shows us to a little round table for four and brings a highchair for Davey. Sydney puts Helly's car seat on the extra chair.

"So anyway," Sydney says. "This is Tierney. She's here for the summer."

I choke on my water. Sydney mustn't have a clue Jake's been sniffing around this chippy.

"You okay?" Sydney jumps up to pat my back.

After a fit of coughing, my scarf has slipped away from my face.

"Your face looks good," Sydney says.

"Oh, you're the woman with the Banana Boat burn?" Tierney asks.

There it is, the name—Banana Boat Burn.

"I am. I guess I made a big scene at the pool."

"I wasn't there, but I heard about it. I'm so sorry you had to go through something like that. It must've been so scary. But honestly, I wouldn't have known from your face at all. I just thought you had a chemical peel."

"She did." Sydney pats my hand. "Just unintended. When it's all healed, you'll have baby smooth skin."

The waitress brings the menus and refills our waters. "I'll be back in a minute to take your orders."

"The avocado smash is my favorite," Sydney says. "I'm having that and an arugula salad."

"Ooh. Good choice. Sounds delish. I'll get that too," Tierney says.

Is Tierney brown-nosing Sydney to keep her from suspecting what's going on with Jake?

"Tierney has been doing some babysitting for me. I wanted to bring her to lunch to thank her."

"Are you kidding me? I love it," she gushes to Sydney. She turns to me and says, "And Sydney's so cool. She's giving me pointers about trying to have a career as a writer."

A chill goes up my spine and this time I almost spit out my water. They've got to stop doing this to me.

"A true-crime writer?" I ask.

"No, nothing as admirable as what Sydney does. Probably fiction."

Admirable seems like a weird word to describe what Sydney writes. "I'm curious. Why do you say admirable? I haven't had the chance to read her books yet," I ask Tierney

Sydney bows her head modestly. I hate to say it, because we've been getting along so well lately, but it looks fake, like she's trying too hard to be humble.

The waitress comes and takes our orders. I order a ham and Swiss sandwich, and Tierney and Sydney place their identical orders. Helly whimpers and Sydney lifts her out of her seat to bounce her on her lap.

"So, to answer your question, it's because of how she helps the families," Tierney explains. "She shows them how to let go of the shame and keep loving their family member even though he, or she, is a murderer. You've got to read the books. They're amazing."

Now I'm humbled. Once again, I've thought the worse of Sydney and once again, she's proved me wrong. "Is that why you came to Rock Narrows? To help Jake and Nails?"

"It is," Sydney says quietly. "But until recently they weren't ready to see their story in print. That's why it's not published."

"I can't wait to read it. It's going to give me so much insight," Tierney says, practically bouncing out of her seat.

That's another strange thing to say.

"Insight?" I ask.

Tierney's face turns pink and she folds and refolds her napkin. "Well, what I mean is—"

The waitress brings our plates and Tierney looks relieved at the interruption.

"Do you need anything else right now?" the waitress asks.

"All good," we answer.

Now composed, Tierney continues, "What I mean is insight into the creative process, from start to finish. I think I'll learn a lot about developing a story."

Doubt flashes across Sydney's face before she hides it behind a bland smile. "Well, you'll have to wait a while. It's only going to my publisher when I go to New York."

"Speaking of New York," I say. "If it's okay with you, I'll watch Helly from your house. Not only does Davey adore playing with Daisy, I think he'd like splashing around at the shoreline."

"Whatever works for you," Sydney says. "I'll give you a key and you can come and go as you please. I just appreciate the help!"

Disappointment clouds Tierney's face. "Why didn't you ask me?"

"Oh, it just seemed too much. Don't worry, I still want you to keep her while I work."

Apparently satisfied with Sydney's answer, Tierney smiles and digs into her avocado toast. I catch Sydney give Tierney a sideways glare. Maybe she's *not* blind to what's going on with Jake.

A brunette with a cute pixie cut and a little gold ring through her nose comes up to our table. "It's you," she says to Sydney.

The woman looks familiar, but I can't place her.

By Sydney's reaction, I'm sure she recognizes the woman, but she says, "I'm sorry. Do I know you?"

"Yeah. Don't you remember? I thought a lot about you in jail."

"I'm sorry, I think you have the wrong person," Sydney replies.

"No, I don't. You're Sydney, right? Jake's woman. I'm Shelby. Shelby from Rock Narrows. You came to my trailer."

Holy crap! Shelby lived a few houses down from me in a rusted-out trailer before she got tossed in jail for beating the hell out of Cammie. Sydney's face turns white.

"Shelby, it's me Deena. Oh my God, you look amazing," I say.

"That's 'cause I'm clean and sober for almost two years now." She twirls around to show off a killer body. She used to be a scrawny, greasy burn-out. "Maybe that's why you don't remember me," she says to Sydney. "I look a helluva lot different."

Sydney stutters, "I uh, maybe we uh, met in town, but I'm sure I didn't come to your trailer."

"Yeah, yeah you did. Remember. You brought food for me and my dog, Rocky. No one ever gave a shit about taking care of my dog, so it meant a lot. You said you know how it is. Your Bassett Hound, is her name Daisy?"

Sydney nods.

"You said she was your baby."

Sydney swallows and looks like a deer in the headlights. There's no denying they know each other.

"Okay, I sort of remember," Sydney admits. "That was a while ago."

"Yeah," Shelby agrees. "Two years ago. I remember it real good 'cause shortly after you came by I got nine months for beating the hell outta Cammie. I found out she was cheating with my man."

"Cammie was cheating with JJ?" I interrupt. "Are you sure?"

JJ sold Cammie's husband, Donnie, the drugs that killed him. Cammie's hated him ever since.

"Damn sure," Shelby says. Redness creeps up her neck. "I found her special-made red underwear with a big, white C sewn into them in our bed." She takes in a deep breath and lets it out slow. "But I know what I did wasn't right. You got a lot of time to think when you're locked up."

"Pull up a seat and fill us in," I say.

"I can't. I'm working as a waitress here." She puffs up like a proud peacock, then turns back to Sydney. "Sydney, I been meaning to look you up. I thought about you in the pen because you was one of the only people—in my whole life—who was nice to me without expecting a thing back. So, I wanted to say thanks and give you this."

Reaching in her pocket Shelby pulls out some kind of coin. Sydney takes the coin from Shelby. "It's my one-year chip, from AA. It's to remind you your kindness made a difference."

"No, I can't." Sydney holds it towards Shelby.

Shelby puts her hands in her pocket, refusing to take it back. "Visit me again," she says and walks away.

My head's spinning. I'm so caught up in my thoughts, the rest of lunch is a blur. We pay our bills and say our goodbyes. The storm outside has passed, but I feel like there's a tornado in my head.

I know I often jump to conclusions, but my gut is screaming that Sydney's hiding something. Situations keep coming up where I catch her shying away from the truth—like where she was the night Jake was away. I'm not buying she went back to Dollie's for a jacket. And now she tried to act like she didn't know Shelby, when it was clear she had been to her trailer. Add her strange behavior with Tierney into the mix and I'm doubly confused. I want to believe we're truly friends and she's as kind as she seems, but I've got my doubts.

MAGGIE—June 14

The sun's barely up and it's already hard to breathe. Sweat drips down my ass crack and I ain't done nothin' but lay the line. Syd's checkin' the pens. Her hair's skinned back in a straggly-ass ponytail, but it don't hide the frizz.

I chug down an Arizona tea and soak my hat with the hose. Better.

"You want a tea?" I ask Sydney.

"Yeah, please. It's too damn hot for coffee."

When Sydney won't drink coffee it's hot! I hand a cold bottle to her. She holds it against her face before she drinks it. I walk on up to the tree, and sit in the shade to try to cool off before I gotta go out for the day. Ruby pants beside me. There ain't no breeze. It's like sittin' in soup. When Syd's done, she joins me.

"You sure you don't mind tending the pens while I'm gone?" she asks.

"As long as Jake does the overnight, I'm good."

"Yeah, he will. Thanks." She finishes her tea. "Maybe check in on Helly too?"

"You know it. Who's watchin' her during the day? That girl that been helping you out?"

Her eyes scrunch up and she looks mad. "No. Not her. Deena."

"Good. Helly loves Davey. And it's only fair after all you done for her."

She shrugs her shoulders like it ain't no big deal. "Why don't you come over after work tonight? I'll pick up some of Millie's chicken salad and get some watermelon and cucumbers. It's too hot to cook or eat hot food."

"Can't," I say. "Got plans."

"Plans?" she says, all smarmy like. "What kind of plans?"

"I got a date, okay? Don't wanna hear nothin' more 'bout it."

"A date? Are you kidding me? That's big news!" She scoots forward and sits on the edge of the chair. "No way you're heading out on the bateau until you dish! Come on give me the details."

"You're a goddamn nosy pain in the ass. You know that?"

"Yes." She nods her head real fast and laughs. "Now spill it."

I can't help but smile. Sydney's pretty much the first girlfriend I ever had. And it ain't bad havin' good news to share.

"Ain't much to spill. We's goin' to Roma for pizza."

"Who is this guy? What's his name? Where did you meet him? Is this your first date?" She fires questions at me like a machine gun.

"Mitch. Met him at Al-Anon. It ain't our first date. Now chill the fuck out."

"You've had more than one date and you're only telling me now. What kind of friend are you?" She acts like I hurt her feelings.

"The keep-shit-to-myself kind."

"Fine." She pouts. "At least tell me about him."

"He ain't perfect, but he don't pretend to be. He owns up to the shit he done. I like that."

"Well, when do I get to meet him?"

"You can put a brake on that. It ain't happenin' any time soon. Enough of this bullshit. I got work to do."

"Fine. For now. I will table this discussion, but we *will* revisit it when I get back from New York."

I just give her a look. I don't need to argue; it'll happen when I'm goddamn good and ready. My doormat days is over.

I take Ruby in the house. Too damn hot for her to work with me today. I grab a couple extra bottles of tea and an extra ice pack for my cooler. By the time I come out and hop on my bateau,

Sydney's already inside her house. Guess she's pissed. Aack, she'll get over it.

I putter out to my line. The osprey caws when I pass her nest on the channel marker, warnin' me not to mess with her babies. My head's already wet with sweat and I ain't even started. I scoop up a bailer fulla water and pour it over me. Better. I'm at my float. I use my hook and lift my line up on the roller. Three baits in I got a big number one. My line's heavy with crabs. I'm dippin' so much I got three crabs in my net before I even got time to dump 'em in the basket. Damn, this day's off to a good start.

Glad the crabs are hittin' early. By lunchtime this crick'll be fulla boaters. They swarm like fucking mosquitos, buzzing all around and buggin' the shit outta me. I take a cruise back past the duck blind to give the crabs time to come on. A heron's wading near the shore, on the hunt for softshells or fish. Me, Jake, and Swannee used to tie up to the blind and make it our fort. And when Pop was especially mean, we'd hide in it and wait out his mood.

I guess that's why I put up with so much shit. Momma raised me up to think it's a woman's lot in life to take what men dish out. *She* always did, and expected me to, too. Even when I told her what that bigwig asshole did to me, she shushed me up. Told me ain't no one gonna believe a teenage girl over a powerful man and I shouldna prettied myself up so much to meet with him.

But you know what I been thinkin' about more and more? I ain't no teenage girl no more. And I found my backbone. He thinks he got away with it, but I think it's time I call him out.

MAGGIE—June 15

Last night, me and Mitch's date at Roma went good. So good he invited me to his house for dinner. I pull my truck up to the curb and check the house number Mitch gave me again. This can't be right. The house is a mansion. It's got big white columns and two concrete urns with la-di-da bushes beside the door. A fountain sprays water outta the mouth of what's supposed to be a fish, but looks more like a pukin' snake. I start to pull away.

Mitch runs out the front door and waves his arms. "Where're you going?"

I throw my truck in park and jump out. "This is *your* house?"

"Yeah?"

"How'd a jailbird end up livin' in the Taj Ma-fuckin-hal?"

He laughs. "I love how you always say what you're thinking. No filters. It's refreshing."

I shrug.

"Come in." He motions to the door. "Dinner's almost ready. I've got cold Natural Light waiting for you."

I let outta whistle. There's a big ol' staircase with a sparkly chandelier hanging over it. I'm waiting for the butler with the white gloves to come 'round the corner.

"You ain't let on you was rich."

"Comfortable. I wouldn't say rich."

Ain't nothing comfortable 'bout this. The expensive rugs and fancy vases got me too scared to move. What if I break something?

"Come on, let's head to the patio." I stick my hands in my pocket and keep my elbows tight against my side. He walks me through a hallway beside the stairs, into a kitchen that's bigger than my whole downstairs, and out onto a brick patio. He got a kick-ass view of the river. My beer's stuck in a silver bucket fulla ice.

Mitch sits it right beside my chair and pops one open for me. "Glass?"

"Nope." I guzzle half down. Steaks and zucchini sizzle on a giant stone grill. The smell makes my mouth water.

"I'm so glad you're here. I missed you."

I get jitters in my belly. "You saw me six nights in a row. How the hell you miss me?"

"Because I didn't see you all day."

More jitters. I smile but don't say nothin' else. I finish my beer and crack open another. Gotta calm my nerves. This dinner's a big step. We been goin' out for ice cream, or burgers, or pizza every night this week, but this is the first time we ain't been in a public place.

Mitch flips the steaks onto the plates with the zucchini beside them. "Order up," he jokes, and sets the plates on the table.

It smells delicious, but my gut flops around so much I don't even know if I can eat. I pound my second beer and open another to settle my nerves.

"Whoa there! You're downing those beers pretty fast."

"I'm thirsty." Ain't nothin' worse than a reformed alkie telling you to watch what you drink. I down that one in three gulps—just to spite him—and got myself a nice little buzz.

"Suit yourself." He shrugs. "I absolutely won't allow you to drive drunk, but I won't mind one bit if you end up staying the night."

I can't decide if his wink is sexy or gross. What I do know for damn sure is I ain't ready to be spendin' the night. "Well then you better pour me a glass of water."

He laughs and pours me a glass.

I normally ain't one to sit around and talk, but the three beers took the edge off. I'm blabbing away about my brothers and Sydney, and even Momma and Pop.

"So, when do I get to meet Sydney, Jake, and the cutest baby in the world?"

"I swear, you and Sydney's in cahoots. She was just buggin' me 'bout meeting you."

"Well then, we should plan it."

I nod my head 'cause my mouth's full of food. The steak's so good. Now that I'm calmed down, I'm gobblin' it up like a wild dog.

"How about tomorrow or the next day?"

I shake my head no and swallow some water to wash the food down. "Nope, won't work. Syd's got a trip to New York planned. We'll do it sometime after she gets back."

"Are you watching Helly while she's gone?"

"No, I gotta work. Deena's gonna babysit. Speakin' of Helly." I pull out my phone and scroll through the pictures. "Here she is in the little turtle outfit I bought her."

He smiles. "Can I scroll through and see more?"

"Sure, they's all Helly."

He looks through my photos and I finish my meal.

"You might be right; she is the cutest baby in the world. Do you want kids of your own?" he asks.

I get the gnawing ache in my gut that I get every time someone asks me about kids. "Ain't gonna happen."

"Why? You're not too old."

"Damn near." I clear off the table. "Besides, I can't have kids."

"Oh shit. What an ass I am. That was so insensitive. I'm sorry, Maggie."

I shrug. "I woulda liked to have kids, but even if I coulda, I wouldn't with Eddie as a daddy. How 'bout you?"

"I'd like kids, but it's not a deal breaker for sure. With the right person, I think I'd even prefer to adopt. So many kids need a loving home, it seems like a way to help."

I roll my eyes and laugh. "You and your Miss America answers."

He gives me one of those pageant waves where he holds his arm still and twists his hand side to side. I like that he can poke fun at hisself.

After he scrapes the food bits off the grill, we move to the couch. I curl up beside him and rest my head on his shoulder. It feels damn good. We talk more about happy memories from when we was kids, and he asks a million questions 'bout trotlinin'.

"It's hard to believe I was born and bred on the Eastern Shore and have never been crabbing."

"Well then, you's past due. Come with me." Christ, I don't know why I said that. I hate showin' newbies. Beer musta gone to my head.

"Yeah?"

I nod.

"I'd love to. When?"

"Pick the day. You gotta be at the wharf by 5 a.m."

"That's ungodly! Is that really what time you start work?"

"Every day."

"And I bitched about a 6 a.m. wake-up in prison."

"How'd a pretty-boy like you manage in there?"

His mouth falls open. "Don't hold back."

My face gets hot—half from mad, half from embarrassed. "Look, I probably shouldna said that, but I been shushed all my life and that shit's over. I get it if I'm too rough around the edges, and you wanna cut bait."

"Maggie." He takes my face in his hands. "Don't ever think that. You are perfect exactly the way you are. Yes, sometimes you shock me, like a bracing wind. That's just another reason I want to be with you. I don't need another kiss-ass in my life. People have always kowtowed to me because of who I am. Hell, even the prison guards gave me special treatment. Probably how this 'pretty boy' made it through."

"So, who are you? I don't even know your last name."

He looks at me and sits quiet for a minute.

"I know this is asking a lot, but can we keep that for later? I like that you're getting to know me out from under the shadow of my name."

"What, are you a Dupont?" I'm only half-jokin'. He could be. That family got a buncha waterfront estates around here.

He laughs. "Far from it."

I get it. Eddie was such a fuck-up, I hated tellin' people my married name. And then when Swannee shot momma, my maiden name wasn't much better.

"Yeah, all right. Tell me when you're ready."

His eyes get gooey and he puts his hand on my cheek. He leans close and whispers, "You're amazing."

When he kisses me soft and slow, I get tingles in places I thought were long dead.

DEENA—June 20

Sydney's in New York and I'm at her house watching Helly. This morning, I found a locked trunk in the far back corner of Sydney's closet when I was hunting for clean sheets for Helly's crib. It's been taunting me ever since.

Sydney's hiding something. I'm sure of it. At lunch, she pretended not to know Shelby when it was clear she went to her trailer. She claimed to stay late at Dollie's the night Eddie died. And, she took the girl who's been flirting with her husband under her wing. None of it adds up.

I try to resist opening the trunk, but it really could contain all the answers. As the kids eat their lunch, I watch three internet videos on how to pick padlocks. When their bellies are full, their little eyelids droop. Nap time.

Once they're both asleep, I get to work. I find a box of paperclips on Sydney's desk. Now for needle nose pliers. I dig through the kitchen drawers and the cupboard in the mudroom with no luck. Maybe the basement.

The rickety steps are closer to a ladder then stairs and creak with each step down. Their basement has a dirt floor and smells musty. A jumble of yoga mats, dog toys, decoys, and floats sit on wooden shelves. Under the last shelf I see a Craftsman toolbox. I drag it out from under the shelf and open it. The needle nose plier is right on top. I climb up the stairs and get to work.

I bend the paperclips into picks and a tension wrench. Tools made, I try my hand at the lockpicking. Sitting down on the floor beside the trunk, I slide the tension wrench into the lock. Then I slip in the pick and jiggle. Up and down, side to side; it looks a lot easier on the video. I scoot my butt to the other side of the lock and try again. No dice. I adjust the pick with the pliers and try again. I'm making progress when Helly lets out a huge scream. I jump and the pick drops out of the lock.

I check my phone. Two hours have flown by. Helly's cries get louder and I try to reach her before she wakes Davey. I lift her from the crib. Her bottom's wet. When I change her diaper, her wails wake Davey. Grumpy with having his nap cut short, he rubs his eyes. His cheeks are red and his forehead is warm. Holding Helly on one hip, I balance Davey on the other. Daisy whines at the front door to be let out. When I lay Helly in the playpen so I can open the front door, she screams.

Davey covers his ears and yells, "No, no, no, no, no."

Davey, Helly, Daisy—nobody is happy. It's total chaos. I thought I was ready for a second child—I'm not.

Letting Helly scream for a minute, I let Daisy out then settle Davey on a blanket. He sneezes and snot comes out of his nose. I wipe his face and give him his lovey. He pops his thumb in his mouth and lays down with his toy. I think he's getting sick.

I lift an unhappy Helly out of the playpen and bounce her on my hip, while I warm her bottle. After she's fed and burped, she's content to play in her her playpen. When I let Daisy in, she runs right over to Davey and licks his face. He giggles and grabs hold of her ears. She flops over beside him. It's adorable. I snap a few photos and text them to Skip.

Finally, at four o'clock I have another chance to try the lock. I give Davey a bowl full of cheerios and put PBS Kids on the TV. After thirty minutes of trying, it clicks open. I'm so proud of myself!

As I lift the lid, I can see it's jammed pack with a weird assortment of things. Before touching anything, I snap a photo, so I can put it all back exactly how it was. Then I pull out a pair of scuffed, black-leather biker boots. Tucked inside the boots is a stack of letters from Frackville State Prison. Maybe these are from her dad. I flip through a few of them. No, not her dad, a man named Mark. Jeez, she knows a lot of people in prison.

From the letters, I learn he's serving life for murder, and was a subject of one of her books. From the boots, I'm going to guess it is *Black Leather*. It's hard to believe he's in jail for murder, because from his letters he sounds like a big teddy bear. It's clear he loves Sydney like a sister and is grateful she wrote the book.

After tucking the letters back into the boots, I dig out the next piece of memorabilia. It's a rubber-banded stack of journals with the name Abbott on the front. I read a few entries in the first one. The pages are filled with the ramblings of an obviously deranged man. I put them aside, they're too disturbing.

Next there's a green, velvet jewelry box on top of a crumpled photo and another stack of letters. The photo is of Jake, Swannee, and Nails. I open the jewelry box and find a tiny gold cross on a delicate chain.

I flip through the stack of letters. These are from different people and places. I open one from the McCune's. It's a handwritten note thanking Sydney for writing the book about their daughter. *"What Kylie did was monstrous, but your words helped us find our little girl again."*

Each letter is a thank-you to Sydney for her work. The one from Abbott's family was especially interesting. *"You showed us how to love the man and hate his disease."* I guess what Tierney said is true, Sydney's work is admirable.

Davey coughs. I run out to take a quick peek. Helly's fallen asleep and Davey's still happily watching his shows. I feel a pang of guilt; for not paying attention to the kids, and for digging through Sydney's things. I'll read a few extra stories to Davey tonight. As for the digging, I'll have to live with the guilt. Having these doubts about her is driving me crazy.

I get back to snooping. The next layer of stuff is what you might expect to find in a trunk: Sydney's yearbooks, birthday cards from her dad, a program from her mom's funeral, childhood photos, and a baby blanket.

As I get deeper, the stuff gets creepier. There's a ragged piece of an oriental rug with what I swear is blood caked into it. A switchblade is tucked in the corner, beside an empty bag of peanuts, and there's a set of chopsticks poking above a pair of rubber gloves. Under the gloves is a laminated article. It's about a man named Rob, who fell from a third-floor balcony because of a loose railing. Across his picture, KARMA is scrawled in red. The hairs on the back of my neck raise. Whoever wrote that—and I'm guessing it's Sydney—*really* didn't like that guy.

In the back corner of the trunk, I find an anchor necklace. It seems familiar, but I can't place it. It's tangled in a four-inch piece of net. The net pricks at a memory. I run it between my fingers trying to dredge it up.

Oh. My. God. Cammie.

Cammie mends nets for all the watermen. A few years back, shortly after Sydney came to town, every net in Cammie's barn was cut. She lost a month's worth of work and had to buy some of the men new nets. Did Sydney do that?

Fear slithers up my spine and my hands tremble. What else am I going to find?

A scrap of black silk is tucked inside a Valentine's Day card from Jake. I pull it out. It's a pair of thong underwear with a red C embroidered on the front. I guess it could be for Clint—Sydney's pen name—but I think about what Shelby found in her trailer and shiver.

I'm afraid to keep looking, but I'm afraid not to.

I find another article, folded, and tucked under a cheap, flip phone. I carefully unfold it. The headline reads *Catfight Ends in Bloodshed*. Under the headline is a photo of Shelby and Cammie. I swallow hard. Sydney set the whole thing up.

I want to grab Davey and run, but there's no turning back. I lift the phone out of the trunk and flip it open. I go to settings to see if the owner's name and info has been input. Nothing. I tap the photos file, hoping to find a selfie. What I find makes my blood go cold.

The photo, the exact photo, that almost led to me and Skip's divorce mocks me from the screen. This is the photo that made me want to crawl in a hole and die; a close-up crotch shot. Tears stream down my cheeks, and I feel like I was kicked in the gut. Daisy barks and I hear a car turn into the oyster-shell driveway. I look out the window. Shit, it's Jake. I stuff everything back in the trunk, snap on the padlock, push it back into the closet, and shut the door.

Grabbing the pliers, I run to the basement door, taking the first two steps, before jumping down to the dirt floor. I fling them into the top of the toolbox and slide it back in place. Taking the steps two at a time, I sprint back upstairs and slide, stocking footed, into the living room. I pick up Davey and start dancing around just as Jake walks through the door. Davey's cheeks have gotten redder and he feels hot. He's definitely got a fever. He coughs and more mucus comes out.

"Are you havin' a dance party?" Jake asks, smiling.

"You bet," I say, out of breath. "No better way to burn calories and keep the kids happy."

"Skip told me to tell you he stopped for a beer. We had a hard day. Teak job gone wrong."

"Oh, that's fine." All I want to do is get out of here. I collect Davey's things and pack my bag.

Jake offers me a beer. "Do you wanna stay for a cold one?"

"No, no. Still have a lot to do tonight."

"Well, thanks for everything. I'll see you tomorrow."

Fat chance. There is no way in hell I'm stepping foot in this house again.

"Yeah, okay. See ya." I hightail it out of there.

By the time I get home, the shock is wearing off and I'm boiling mad. How could that back-stabbing bitch do that to us? And why? Yeah, Sydney and me haven't always been best buddies, but you wouldn't expect a few catty remarks would lead her to sabotage our marriage? How could she even think up something so horrible?

My mind turns to Cammie. Cutting nets is bad enough, but planting underwear to goad Shelby into hurting Cammie . . . I gag at the cruelty. I mean, Cammie could've died. I don't know who the poor guy was who fell from the balcony, but did Sydney somehow set that up too?

Holy Hell! My mind flashes to Mrs. Ennis and Sydney's burgundy CRV. I run to the toilet and puke. I don't think Sydney was lying about going back to Dollie's because she was cheating on Jake. I think she lied because she killed Eddie. I gag more, but my stomach is empty.

My anger is replaced with terror.

Sydney is crazy—like Charles Manson crazy. Even though I'm shivering, I'm wet with sweat. I splash cold water on my face and look in the mirror. My eyes look wild with fear. The raw spots on my skin shine fire engine red against my pale face. I shudder at a new thought—maybe my burns weren't an accident.

I run around the house and shut all the windows and lock the doors. Scooping Davey up, I take him into my bedroom and barricade the door. I crawl into the covers with him. I'm shaking. I know Sydney's in New York, but I feel the same way I felt after someone slashed my tires—violated. Dear God, could that have been Sydney too?

Oh my God! What am I going to do? I'm sobbing and gulping for breath. Upset at my tears, Davey starts crying too. I've got to get it together, for his sake. I pull him against my chest and pat his back until he calms. I force myself to breath slowly. When he stops crying, I switch on the TV and sit him beside me.

I grab my phone, intending to call 911, but what am I going to say? If I start ranting about someone killing Eddie and setting up me and Cammie, I'm the one likely to get locked up. Damn it! I have to get evidence—the phone, a piece of the net, maybe the bloody carpet—anything to prove Sydney's dangerous.

Wait, I have the photo! I go to my gallery. Dammit! You can't see anything but the boots and the letters and the edge of a baby blanket. It proves nothing, except I picked a lock on trunk and searched what doesn't belong to me. I almost delete the photo before I remember, in my hurry not to get caught red-handed, I just shoved everything back in the trunk.

I stop breathing. God help me. If Sydney's finds her trunk in a mess, she'll know it was me. My teeth chatter in fear. If she gave me chemical burns because I was a smart-ass to her, what will she do if she finds out I was searching through her private things?

My heart is hammering and I'm panting. I have to get back in that trunk! I have to put everything back in its place, and get photos of all the evidence! If I don't . . . If I don't . . . I look at Davey and tears run down my face. If I don't, I might not see him grow up. As much as I hate the thought of going back into her house, I have to.

I hear the front door open and I freeze in fear. Davey sneezes and I shush him.

"Deena, where are you?" Skip yells.

Relief floods my body. I move the stuff away from the bedroom door and fling it open. Clinging to Skip, I bury my head against his chest.

"Christ, Deena. What the hell happened? Did someone die?"

"No, no, no." I shake my head against his chest. "It's Sydney."

"What about her? Is she okay? Did something happen in New York?"

"She's going to kill me," I blurt out.

"Deena, I thought you two have been getting along great. Did you do something to piss her off?"

"I looked through her stuff. I'm not exaggerating, Skip, I mean she is going to really kill me—dead."

His mouth falls open and he groans. "Deena, for Christ's sake, why did you look through her things? What were you thinking?"

"That she's dangerous. She set up Cammie, and I think she caused my burns, and I'm pretty sure she killed Eddie."

He leads me to the couch. "Deena, honey, you gotta settle down. You're imagining things. Remember when you thought someone planted a bomb in your car after your tires were slashed? You're not thinking straight."

"She did that too," I wail.

"Planted a bomb in your car?"

I shake my head. "No, the tires. She slashed the tires."

He kneels down in front of me. "Deena, I'm really worried about you. You've been super edgy and your anxiety's been through the roof. Maybe we should get you in to see a doctor. You're acting crazy."

"I'm not crazy. Sydney is."

He grabs me by the shoulders and stares straight into my eyes. "Now stop! This is stupid. Sydney has proven herself as your friend. She's not going around the town hurting people. Eddie died of an overdose and your burn was a bad reaction to the sunscreen. Nothing more. I don't even know what the hell you're saying about Cammie. You sound nuts. Get yourself together."

I cry out of frustration. I knew no one would believe me. Without proof, everyone's going to think I'm crazy.

I clench my jaw. Skip's right. I've got to get myself together, because I'm the only one who can stop Sydney.

Davey cries from the bedroom. I stand up to get him.

"I'll go." Skip gently pushes me back onto the couch.

He walks back the hall and picks up Davey. From my spot on the couch, I can see Davey's cheeks have gotten redder and I can hear him wheezing.

"Jesus Christ, Deena," Skip barks. "Davey's burning up. How about we start worrying about real things?"

JAKE—June 21

This day is a fucking disaster. Deena woke me up with a panicked phone call at five. Davey couldn't breathe right so they took him to the ER. I called Maggie to see if she could watch Helly, but she ain't answering her phone. She didn't come home again last night. That's the third night in a row.

Not only am I out a babysitter, Skip's with Deena so I'll be a man short at work. The head honcho's driving in from Philly today and I got show-him-around duty. I can't drag a baby around with the boss, so I got no choice but to ask Tierney.

I'm trying to get a shoe on, but I got Helly in one arm and it ain't easy. She's squirmy and crying. I hop over to the stove to heat up a pan of water to warm her bottle. Daisy's under my feet whining to go out. On my way to open the door for her, I jam my other foot into a shoe and wriggle until my heel slips in. Two shoes on; that's progress.

I plunk Helly's bottle into the hot water and change her diaper on the couch. She's pissed 'cause she ain't been fed and kicks and screams. The diaper's crooked, but I ain't got time to fix it. I snap up her onesie and get her the bottle. Once the bottle's in her mouth, she's quiet.

While I'm feeding her, I wrangle Daisy into the house. I burp Helly and load up the diaper bag. Whew! I grab a yogurt outta the fridge, pull back the foil and squeeze the plastic container till the whole gob plops into my mouth.

I check the stove's off, and head out the door. After strapping Helly into her car seat, I'm on my way to the marina. When I hit the road, I let out a big sigh. I'll tell you one thing, after this morning, I got a helluva lot more appreciation for Sydney.

At ten minutes to eight I bang on Tierney's cabin door.

"Who's there?" I can tell she ain't too happy to be woke up.

"It's Jake. I need a big favor."

"Ok, coming."

She opens the door in teeny-tiny shorts and a see-through tank top with no bra. Her nipples poke out—more awake than she is.

"What do you need?" she yawns.

"A babysitter." I hand her Helly, as much to cover up her too-sexy nipples as to make sure she don't have time to say no.

"I uh, well, okay," she stutters.

"I hug her and plant a kiss on her cheek before she can change her mind. "You just saved my ass!" I hop off the boat to head to the office.

"Wait, Jake. Where's all her stuff?"

I grab the diaper bag from the catwalk and drop it onto her back deck. She takes a quick look into the bag. "I better watch her at your house, where she has everything she needs. Okay?"

I check my watch. It's eight. I gotta roll. "Yeah, yeah, fine." I wave as I walk away. "Car seat's in my truck. It's open. Just grab it. I'll be home by six."

MAGGIE—June 21

Ruby shoots out the door before I got it completely open. Poor dog. She ain't been out since six last night. I spent the night with Mitch again. A sleep over—not a sleep with. I ain't ready for sex.

I'm checkin' the house for piss or piles and hear a girl laughing. I look out. Some cute blonde bounces Helly on her hip. She sees me lookin' at her and gives me a crazy-ass wave that makes what little arm fat she got flap around.

She walks up on my porch. "Hi. You must be Maggie. It's soooo nice to meet you."

She must be the girl that helps Syd out, but where's Deena?

"Yeah, I'm Maggie." I kinda like people callin' me Maggie. "Who are you?"

"Oh sorry." She turns pink. "I'm just so excited to meet you I forgot my manners. I'm Tierney."

She got the same weird grey spots in her eyes that Swannee had, like dark freckles in the light blue. She steps up on the porch and gives me a hug like I'm her long-lost mother. What the fuck? Helly reaches for me and I take her from Miss Huggy Pants.

"Where's Deena?" I ask.

"Oh, I don't know. Jake showed up on my boat at the crack of dawn needing a babysitter. He was in such a rush he didn't tell me anything, just shoved Helly in my arms and ran."

Figures, the one day he needs help I ain't around.

Helly fusses.

"You want me to take her?" Tierney asks. "She's probably hungry." Tierney's gut gurgles. She puts her hand on her belly. "Guess I am too. After I feed her, I'm going to run into town and grab a sandwich. Jake's fridge is bare. Wanna join me?"

Why not? The day's shot anyways, too late to catch enough crabs to amount to anything.

"Sure. Let's eat at Millie's. I ain't seen her for a while and she's gaga over Helly. We'll make her day."

I get the dogs in the house and Tierney feeds Helly. The car seat's already in her car, so we take it. Helly's asleep before we's out the lane.

"This is great. I've been wanting to talk to you," Tierney says.

"Oh yeah. Why's that?"

"Well, Sydney's been filling me in on your job, and your and Jake's childhood. It seems so interesting."

Syd told me she wants to be a writer. Is she pokin' around for a juicy story? Get burnt once shame on them, get burnt twice you're a dumb-ass.

"Don't know 'bout that."

She whips her old tin can into Millie's lot so damn fast she almost takes out nosy Ned. When he sees me in the car he stops in his tracks. He circles like a shark around chum.

"Hey there young lady," he says to Tierney. "You oughta slow down. We don't put up with no speed racers 'round here."

"I'm so sorry." Her cheeks turn bright red. "I was so busy talking I almost missed the turn."

"Well, who might you be? And why you draggin' around with this old bag of hot air?" He points at me.

I roll my eyes. "Ned, you got so much hot air in you it's good your clodhoppers weigh twenty pounds or you'd float away."

He pats my back and laughs. "It's good to see you, Nails." He looks into Tierney's car. "Who's the kid?"

"It's Jake's baby, Helly, and this here's Tierney. She babysits for 'em."

"Why they need a babysitter? His wife don't work, does she?"

"She does," Tierney pipes up. "She's a writer, and actually she's in New York right now getting ready to publish her next book."

She just made his day. He'll tuck that juicy piece of info in his John Deere baseball hat for later.

"Hmph. Hadn't heard that. Good to know."

I grab Helly outta the car and push Tierney to the door before she blabs anymore. "We'll see ya, Ned."

We're barely through the door when Millie rushes over.

"Well, who do we have here?" Millie is happy as a pig in shit. "Is that the prettiest baby in the world?" She rubs Helly's cheek. "Hey Nails, it's about time you stop in to see me and who's this?" She turns towards Tierney and her mouth falls open like she seen a ghost. "My God, you're the girl version of a teenage Swannee."

"Yeah, she got his same eyes." I say.

Tierney turns even redder and sweat pops out on her lip. "Isn't that a funny coincidence? I guess I've found my doppelganger. Maybe when we get back home you can dig out a picture of him to show me?"

"Doppel what?" I say

"It means like a twin, right?" Millie says.

"Yes, pretty much, I mean, it's like . . . you look alike but you're not related. I mean, I guess you could have a doppelganger that's related, but well then, I guess that would just be a relative? Well, you know what I mean. I guess it's complicated. So yes, like a twin."

That was a helluva lotta words to say yes.

"Nails, if you can't find a picture, I know I can. She—what's your name?" Millie looks Tierney.

"Tierney."

"Tierney's got to see how identical they look."

"Yeah, I noticed the eyes right off, but now that you say it, she got his nose and his mouth too. I'll dig up a picture."

Millie shakes her head, still shocked. "Well, find yourselves a booth and I'll bring you a drink. Watcha want?"

"Water please," Tierney says.

"Sweet tea for me." I get Helly's seat settled in the booth. She plays with her toes and sucks on her fingers.

Tierney's face is back to its normal color. "It seems like Millie's tight with your family."

"She's like our second momma. Her and my momma were best friends pretty much since she moved here. She's a Pennsylvanian, like Syd, but she almost been around long enough to be a local."

"I'm jealous. Not only did you have siblings and a mom and dad, but a second mom too. I bet you and your brothers had a boatload of fun as kids."

I get a pang when I think of us as kids. We had fun, but I was scared a lotta the time. "Mostly fun. Catching fish, giggin' frogs, racing the bateaus—yeah, pretty fun."

"A childhood on the water. Is that what made you want to be a waterman—I mean woman?"

I started to work on the water to pay the fucking bills that my deadbeat husband let pile up. I ain't cut out to be a waitress or a bartender. I ain't lickin' the boots of no chicken necker for a lousy tip.

"Mostly I wanted to be my own boss. It ain't an easy job, especially in winter, but I don't got no one tellin' me what to do."

"I'd love to watch you work sometime. Your job is sooo interesting."

I already invited one newbie to crab with me, that's more than enough. "Yeah well, probably not. I like workin' alone. Ask Jake to show you the softshell pens. He likes showin' off."

"Sydney told me he loves the softshell business. Why did he join the Navy? Why didn't he just stay and be a waterman?"

More questions. She's nosin' 'round our family too damned much. "He had big ideas back then."

"Did he tell you stories about Navy life?"

"Okay ladies, what can I get you?" Millie asks, cuttin' off Tierney's questions.

"I'll take a bowl of the crab soup," I say.

"Yum!" Tierney says. "That sounds good. I'll have that too, but can I also get an order of your chicken salad? Sydney told me it's the best!"

Millie smiles. Ain't nothin' makes her happier than someone braggin' on her food. "Sydney eats like a horse! Hard to believe such a tiny thing can eat so much. She does love my chicken salad. I always add a little extra Old Bay for her. I'll do the same for you."

"Thanks!"

I take a slug of my tea. "You won't get a better crab soup nowhere. Millie and my momma came up with the recipe together."

"I can't wait to taste it. My mom and I make a mean Chicken Piccata. She got the recipe from her mom and we tweaked it to make it our own. Oh, you know what?" She claps her hands together. "I'm going to stop at the grocery store before we go home and grab the ingredients to cook it tonight. Jake's cupboard is bare and I'm sure he could use a home-cooked meal with Sydney gone this week. And then maybe he'll show me the crab pens, like you said."

She's pushy, asks a lotta questions, and sniffs around like a dog lookin' for a bone.

"I ain't sure Sydney would like that too much."

"Oh, I'm sure she wouldn't mind. We're really close. She's like my mentor. I want to be a writer too. In exchange for me watching Helly, she's teaching me the ins and outs."

Goddamn it! I knew it. "You writin' a book 'bout my family?"

She laughs. "Oh, I wish! I'm only going to start college in August. I'm not capable of writing a book."

"Then what's with all the questions?"

She turns beet red and her lips droop like flat tire. "I uh." She takes a gulp of water, "I guess I'm trying to soak in family life. It's different than what I'm used to, and I kind of like it"

Guess I was wrong. She's just a poor lonely kid.

Millie serves our soup and Tierney's chicken salad. Tierney digs in.

"Better than described!" she tells Millie.

Millie smiles from ear to ear. "I like this one." She pats Tierney's hand. "You all let me know if you need anything."

I eat a spoonful of soup. The taste brings back good memories; sitting at the table between Momma and Millie pickin' out the crab meat for the soup. I'd get one crab done to their three, but there wasn't no rush. Momma and Millie sipped their fun coffees—the Kahlua they added made 'em fun—and I'd have lemonade. We'd talk and laugh a Sunday afternoon away.

Tierney's voice brings me back to now. "I'm sorry if I was out of line. I wasn't trying to pry."

"Forget it. Just me bein' prickly."

She pats the corners of her mouth with a napkin. "No, I get it. I'm sure there were plenty of journalists and writers hounding you after what happened with your mom."

"What?" I snap. "How the hell do you know what happened to my mom?"

"Oh God. I keep putting my foot in my mouth. I'm sorry. Can we change the subject?" she asks like a timid little mouse.

"No. I want to know where you heard about it."

She sighs. "It was national news. I guess it's good that Sydney was the person to show up to write your story. At least she was willing to wait until you were ready for her to publish it. Other writers might not have cared what you wanted."

My mouth falls open. "You know about that too?"

"Yeah. I read all of Sydney's other books and figured it only made sense that she met you and Jake when she came to write your story." She hangs her head like she's ashamed. "I asked her to read it."

"And?"

"And, she said absolutely not. No one can read it before you and Jake give her the go-ahead."

Well at least that's proof Syd's true to her word.

I cross my arms. "Look, people 'round here don't know why Sydney came to Rock Narrows. Hell, most don't even know she's a writer. Course that'll change now that you blabbed to Ned."

She bites her lip. "Jeez. I never gave it a thought. I figured everyone knew."

"Believe me, in small towns it's best to keep shit to yourself."

She nods.

"Syd's got a hard enough time fittin' in 'cause she's from Pennsylvania. If people knew why she came here, it would make it worse. So, talk less, listen more. Okay?"

She nods again.

We eat the rest of our food without talkin'. Millie clears our plates and brings the check.

"Can I pay for yours?" Tierney asks. "Since I upset you."

"I ain't upset and I'll pay my own."

We split the bill. Millie can't let us leave without hugs all around.

"Now come back and see me soon," she says to all of us. "And if you can't find a picture of Swannee let me know. Tierney's got to see it."

We wave and get in Tierney's car. She don't start it.

She turns to face me and says, "The absolute last thing I would want to do is hurt Sydney, or really any of you. You've all been so kind to me. I know sometimes I can be a little much. It's hard for me to tell when I should rein it in. I'd still like to cook for Jake tonight, and for you if you'll come. Do you think that's okay?"

She's just an over-eager kid. I'm an asshole for thinkin' she was up to no good. I guess a lifetime of gettin' the worst makes me expect it outta everyone.

"I'm sure Jake'll be happy if he ain't gotta cook after work. Watchin' Helly by hisself is runnin' him ragged. It'll be nice."

She smiles, starts the car and heads to the grocery store. "Will you come?"

"No can do. Got a date."

"Ooh. With who?"

I look at her like are you fucking kiddin' me.

"Oh, right, right. This is the keep crap to yourself part . . ."

I just shake my head and smile.

JAKE—June 21

It's been a helluva day. When I hit my driveway, I put my truck in park, and crack open a beer from the six I picked up in town. I need a fucking minute of quiet before daddy duty.

I look over the crick and drink my beer. The sun's low in the sky. It'll set in another hour. All the watermen are in for the day and the crick's empty except for two sailboats anchored for the night. Shit. My beer's empty too.

I park in front of the house and head in. The table's set with real plates and something smells good. Daisy jumps up to be petted and Tierney comes out the hall from the bedroom. Her hair's messy like she just got out of bed.

She yawns. "Oh, your home."

"Yeah, sorry I'm late."

"No problem. I just got Helly down. She was cranky. I had to snuggle with her until she fell asleep."

I open another beer and put four in the fridge.

"Hard day?" she asks.

"Yeah. It started bad and got worse. Are you cookin'?"

"Yep." She smiles. "Chicken Piccata. Me and my mom's favorite recipe. Thought you might not feel like cooking."

"You're right about that. Thanks." I flop on the couch and prop my feet on the wood-cart thing Syd calls a coffee table.

Tierney's T-shirt shows her belly button every time she moves. She bends over and looks in the oven. Her ass peeks out from her jean shorts.

"Fifteen more minutes." She pours herself a tea and leans back against the counter. "I had Millie's crab soup and chicken salad today."

"Yeah? Whaddya think?"

"Ah-maz-ing! The Old Bay chicken salad was so yummy, and the soup was delish. It was cool to have whole claws floating in it."

"That was my mom's idea. Her and Millie came up with the recipe together."

"That's what your sister told me."

"My sister? She was at Millie's?"

"We went together."

I flip my legs off the cart and lean forward. "You and my sister Maggie went to lunch?" I ain't sure I heard her right.

"Yep." She fills up her tea, then opens the oven and peeks in. It smells good, Italian. "Want another?" She points at my beer.

I nod. She grabs me another beer and plops down beside me on the couch. I crack it open and put my feet up, sinkin' back into the couch.

"How did ya get Maggie to go to lunch?"

She answers, but I don't hear what she says. I can't concentrate on nothing but her long tan leg touchin' mine. I throw in a coupla "mm-hmms" and a few "okays" and nod my head a lot to make it look like I'm listening. The cushions give and I sink closer to her. She keeps talkin' and I keep thinking about having her legs wrapped around my back.

"You want to see it?" she asks.

See it? Holy shit! Is she askin' what I think she's askin'? My mouth goes dry and I swallow. "Sure."

She leans across my lap to grab something from the end table beside me. Her tits rub my chest and I get a rise in my pants.

"Here." She points at Swannee's senior picture. "Pretty incredible right?"

Her tits are pretty incredible. I lean in to her like I wanna look closer. I can smell her shampoo. If I turn my head just two inches more my lips will touch her neck.

The front door flies open. It's Sydney. I'm fucked. My dick goes limp

SYDNEY—June 21

The table's set, the smell of garlic is heavy in the air, and Jake is salivating over Tierney. She smirks at me, gloating over her success at playing house with my family.

"Oh, Sydney. You're home early! How was your trip?" She strikes up what I'm sure she thinks is a convincing tone of innocence.

Her composure is admirable, cluing me to her stealthiness. I mimic her calm demeanor. Now that I am certain what game we are playing, I don't want to tip my hand.

Jake, on the other hand, is transparently shaken. His slideshow of emotions is almost comical.

He jumps up guiltily. "Hey babe. I'm so glad you're home. Tierney was just showing me this picture." He snatches the photo out of her hand like it is incontrovertible proof that what I am seeing is totally harmless.

"Don't we look alike?" Tierney says.

I barely glance at the photo of Swannee, thwarting her attempt at distraction. "Indeed." I reply, my eyes trained on hers. "Smells like dinner is almost ready. Enough for three?"

"You bet! I was hoping Maggie would eat with us, but she had a date. I cooked me and my mom's favorite recipe. I hope you love it."

Apparently, it isn't enough for her to fixate on my baby and husband. She wants my sister-in-law, too.

"I arranged for Deena to stay with Helly. How exactly did this all come about?" I ask as if it's solely out of curiosity.

Jake mops his pitifully sweaty head. "Well, it was just one helluva day. Davey ended up in the ER, so Deena couldn't watch Helly. Maggie was nowhere to be found. And the head-honcho was at the marina today. I hadda go to work. Tierney bailed me out."

Tierney chimes in. "With you being gone all week, the fridge was empty so Maggie and I went out to lunch. We got talking about family recipes and that's when the idea hit me. After such a horrible day, I thought Jake could use a home-cooked meal."

She's smooth. I've got to give credit where credit is due.

"How thoughtful," I say, with nauseating sweetness. "That must be the southern belle coming out in you. Well let's taste this family recipe."

We enjoy a perfectly civil dinner followed by a nightcap for Jake and me, and a cup of tea for Tierney.

"This was sooo much fun!" she says, with what almost passes for sincerity. "Do you want me to watch Helly tomorrow?"

I need time to determine her punishment. "Oh no, dear. You've done enough, and I've missed her terribly. How about one or two days next week? I'll text you."

I walk Tierney to the door and hug her goodnight. Jake gives her a weak wave. The door clicks and I turn to face him. He looks like a little boy, knees knocking in his boots waiting for the belt.

"Nothing happened you know. I know it looked bad, but I swear, nothing happened."

Oh, sweet naïve Jake. I saw his erection. I saw the predatory gleam in her eye. Had I been twenty minutes longer I have no doubt I would've caught them in flagrante delicto.

"Jake." My voice is gentle as if I'm speaking to a traumatized child. "I saw your erection."

He crumples to the floor, devastated by his shame. "I'm so, so sorry. I swear to God, what you saw is all that happened. It was just a moment of weakness. I wasn't going to act on it."

Poor, poor weak Jake—led astray by a conniving bitch. In truth, Tierney's done me a favor. To be blunt, I have Jake by the balls. I will forgive him, but not too quickly. Let him grovel. Let him ponder a future without me and Helly, financially strapped by child support payments. When I do forgive him, I want him beholden to my magnanimity—for life.

"It did look very compromising." I force a tear down my cheek. "I need time to process. I think you should sleep on the couch tonight."

He doesn't resist. I graciously make up the couch with fresh sheets and a comforter, and kiss his forehead. "I love you Jake, but I'm hurt and I'm not sure I can trust you."

A broken man nods his head and climbs under the sheets. I have him exactly where I want him.

SYDNEY—June 22

My phone jolts me awake. This morning, Jake tended the pens, let the dog out, fed and changed Helly, and then laid her in bed with me so I could sleep in. A good start, but he has a lot more sucking up to do. Helly rolls onto her belly, and I answer the phone.

"Hello?" I yawn.

"Shit, did I wake you?" Deena whispers.

I look at the clock. It's almost ten. "Yeah, but no worries. I have to get up."

I texted her last night when I got home, so she knew she didn't have to sit with Helly today.

"How's Davey?" I ask.

"Much better. I'm so sorry I flaked on you."

"Couldn't be helped."

"I want to make it up to you. Why don't you let me stay with Helly today? Until you texted me, I was already planning to be there, and I think you deserve a me-day. I'm sure New York was exhausting."

TSP exposure as a behavior management technique has worked wonders. This version of Deena is quite pleasant. I put her on speaker and prop pillows on either side of Helly.

"That's sweet, but I'm good." I pad out to the kitchen to make coffee. "I'm kind of looking forward to a day at home. I might not even get dressed." I yawn some more.

"Are you sure? That new spa just opened in Bakerstown. I'd treat you to a facial or a massage. Really, you deserve it."

"No thanks, I'm not into spas. Once Davey's back to normal, you should go."

I pour my coffee, grab the newspaper, and head back to my bedroom. Not wanting to wake Helly, I carefully move the pillows and slide gently back into bed.

"Okay, well how about I sit with her tomorrow or Monday? I know how hard juggling work and motherhood is. You have been so kind to me, please let me give you a break. A day just for you."

I appreciate her gratitude, but her pushiness is getting tiresome.

I decide to throw her a bone. "Really, I don't need a me-day, but your company would be nice. You can come over tomorrow for brunch or we could meet at the pool."

"Um, well, yeah, okay. Yeah, it'll be good to see you too. Let's meet at the pool. Nine?"

"Ok, nine is good. See you then."

By the desperation in her voice, I think Deena's the one who needs a me-day.

*****

After a leisurely morning, I decide it's too nice to sit inside. Grabbing a rumpled T-shirt and a slightly-worn pair of jeans from the back of the chair, I get dressed. After I leash Daisy and sit Helly in the new umbrella stroller I bought in New York, I slide my phone in my back pocket and a poop bag in the front. There's something already in the pocket.

Hmm. I pull it out. Oh yeah, it's the one-year chip Shelby gave me. I hold the chip to my heart. Having witnessed a prior catfight between Cammie and Shelby, I knew it would be easy to provoke Shelby into giving Cammie what she deserved. It was a pleasant surprise to learn my well-executed plan had the bonus of a positive impact on Shelby's life. I'll stick that memento in my trunk after our walk.

149

Pushing the stroller through the oyster shells is like slogging through mud. It's a relief to get on the pavement. Helly gurgles and giggles, enjoying the warm sun on her face. The birds chirp in the pine trees. It's a wonderful summer day. It's a shame I have unpleasant matters to consider.

I have no illusions about men; Rob relieved me of those. Unfortunately for Rob, I didn't catch him *before* he disrespected me. I took care of his every need and he repaid me by sleeping with the neighbor's daughter. Obviously, that betrayal couldn't go unanswered. I wasn't sure of the outcome of loosening the balcony railing, but Rob survived his fall from grace with only a slight limp.

So, Jake is fortunate I stopped him before he could stray. After a few weeks of shaming, I'll let him off the hook. Tierney, on the other hand, is a threat. She has launched a hostile takeover—not just of Jake, but of Helly and Maggie too. What can I do to have her heading back to Norfolk with her tail between her legs?

After about a mile, I turn towards home, no closer to a plan. I usually do my best thinking while walking, but I'm at a loss for what to do with Tierney. I pick up the pace and try to clear my head. To quote Al-Anon, "you can't force solutions." The answer will come to me in its own time.

Septuagenarian Mrs. Clug, looking like a raisin as she sunbathes in her bikini, waves when we pass by. The Wheeler kids slam the screen door and run to their playset. The pleasant peace is spoiled when their mom comes out and starts the mower. Daisy strains to move faster and we run the last quarter mile.

Both Daisy and Helly are happy to settle in for a snooze after our outing. I pour myself a cup of freshly-made iced tea and retrieve the trunk key from its duct-taped position on the bottom of the silverware drawer.

Sitting cross-legged in front of the trunk, I slide the key into the lock and open it with reverence. The trunk is an altar to me, honoring my greatest achievements and commemorating my life. I'm dumbstruck. It's been ransacked.

I stare, appalled at the mess. I gently pull out each item to ascertain if anything has been stolen. The contents are intact. As I replace each piece and add Shelby's chip, my fury grows. After relocking the trunk, I pull down the attic stairs and struggle to carry it to its new location.

Only one person would have done this—Tierney. This changes everything. Now that she has violated my most private space, Norfolk is no longer an option. I need a more permanent solution.

MAGGIE—June 22

Liking sex is new to me. Before tonight, I only been with two men—one mostly by choice. Eddie was wham-bam-thank-you-ma'am. All I got was a wet ass. And Jed Donnelly, that above-the-law, so-called pillar of the community forced his privileged prick into me with as much meanness as he could. After he was done taking my virginity, he pulled his pants up and straightened his tie like nothing happened.

I was layin', legs spread, on his antique oak desk, ripped underwear hangin' from my ankle, and he said, "You're a smart girl. I'm sure you can see the wisdom of keeping our little escapade to yourself. I've got the power to make life tough for you and your family and I won't hesitate to do so. Besides, no one's going to believe the daughter of a white-trash drunk over the CEO of Donnelly Telecommunications." Then he threw me a hand towel from his ritzy bathroom. "Now clean yourself up and be out of here by the time I've finished showering. Oh, and as for you being my intern—you're not that smart."

He shut his bathroom door and left me to sop up the blood tricklin' down my legs. The handprints around my neck didn't show till a couple hours after Momma decided it was best to keep my mouth shut.

I stamp out the bad memories and spoon with Mitch.

He pulls me close and kisses my neck. "My God woman, you're amazing."

I ain't green enough to buy into his just-got-my-rocks-off sweet talk. I got close to no experience on how to make a man happy.

"It's only 'cause I'm your first piece since prison. I know I ain't nothin' special."

He straddles me and lays his hands on my cheeks. "Stop that! I don't ever want to hear you say that again." He looks at me so hard, like he wants to drill his words into my head. "Yes, the sex was incredible, but I am talking about you—Maggie Swann. You are amazing. I've never met anyone like you. I think I'm falling in love."

I dry heave and gotta run to the john. There's a collar of sweat 'round my neck.

He knocks on the bathroom door. "You okay?"

I puke and got the cold sweats.

He knocks again. "I'm coming in." He wets a washcloth with cold water and wipes my face. "Better?"

I nod. "I guess something ain't sittin' well."

"Like maybe my words? I think you're scared because you're feeling it too."

I get dizzy and slide down to the floor and rest my back on the toilet.

He slides down beside me and takes my hand. "We can take it slow Maggie. There's no rush. I just wanted to be honest about how I'm feeling."

I can't look in his eyes. "I ain't lookin' to get myself tangled up again."

"Maggie, we've all had bad break ups. I know yours and Eddie's was a doozy, but one bad relationship doesn't mean you're doomed to repeat it forever."

"I ain't doomed. I'm damaged. Damaged goods." Now I'm vomitin' words that been swallowed too long. "Yeah, me and Eddie's was a doozy all right. What I ain't shared with y'all in Al-Anon was he beat the livin' shit outta me for years, and I put up with it. And that ain't all I kept quiet. I was raped and I ain't done a thing 'bout it, just let Mr. Bigshot keep livin' his high and mighty life. So, you see, you don't want no parts of this. I ain't lucky in love."

He jumps up and paces 'round the bathroom. "That's not love! That's assault!"

Spit sprays outta his mouth while he's yellin'. After he splashes cold water on his face, he sits back down beside me so he can hold my hands.

"I'm so sorry that happened to you." He leans his forehead on mine. "But Maggie, never, ever, for one second think you're damaged. You are not what was done to you. You're a strong, resilient, incredible woman who had some really horrendous stuff happen. I can't imagine the pain and anger . . ."

He steams up again, pulls his hands away, and runs them through his hair. "Jesus, no wonder you're gun shy. I'm grateful you even let a drunk ex-con give you the time of day." He stands up and paces again. "I wish to hell those bastards would've been tossed in prison. Even in a building full of murderers and thieves, rapists and wife-beaters are considered the scum of the earth. The inmates would've taken a pound or two of flesh for you."

He sits on the toilet seat with his head in his hands. "I know in Al-Anon you said that burying Eddie gave you peace. What about the degenerate pig that raped you? You know it's not too late to hold him accountable. It might be too late to have him arrested, but you can let your community know what kind of monster is living beside them. In fact, they ought to know. I can't stand to think he'll go unpunished for what he did to you. Who is the scumbag? I'll take care of him myself!"

"You can't fix it, Mitch. Ain't you learned nothin' in Al-Anon?" I reach my arm up and pull him down to the floor beside me. "I talked enough. Other than my momma, rest her soul, you're the only person who knows."

"Your mother knew and didn't have him arrested?"

"You ain't a woman and you ain't come up in a barely-scrapin'-by family, so you got no room to judge."

"You're right. I'm sorry. Until you walk a mile . . ."

"Okay then. That's the last I'm talkin' 'bout it."

He nods and kisses my forehead. We sit side by side on the cold tile floor, holdin' hands.

We's quiet for at least ten minutes before he says, "My history has got to make you nervous. It's only fair that I do some sharing. You know I'm a recovering alcoholic, but I was nothing like Eddie. I was *never* violent. I drank to escape. I was one of those sad-sack, woe-is-me, blubbering drunks likely to collapse in a slobbering mess of tears."

"What did you want to escape?"

"Guilt. Shame. You know, the usual suspects." He gives me a half smile. "I had to get sober before I could start the hard work of making amends and learning to forgive myself."

"Forgive yourself for what ya did to land you in prison?"

"I wish that was all I had to be ashamed of. I was guilt-ridden way before that. I'm nauseous when I think back to things I should've done but didn't. But obviously what put me in jail is a biggie." He swallows loud like the words choke him. "I killed a mom of three."

I drop his hand like a hot iron. "Thought you ain't violent."

"No, no, no. It's nothing like that. I was drunk and fell asleep at the wheel." His lip quivers like he's holdin' in tears. "I crossed the median and hit her head on." He looks past me like he sees it all again. "But that isn't the worst of it. I was so smashed. I couldn't, I couldn't . . ." He pokes at the palm of his hand. "She didn't die instantly. She was trapped halfway out of the driver's window with the car laying upside down on top of her. She was moaning. The back of her head looked like she had been scalped. A bloody pulp." He lets out a sob. "I tried. I tried to call 911, but I was too drunk to dial the phone. By the time someone found us, she was gone."

He hangs his head between his knees. His shoulders move up and down. I don't say nothin'. What's to say? He cries till it turns to hiccups.

He lifts his head. His eyes are red and puffy. "I've got to live with what I've done, but I made up my mind in prison not to squander another life wallowing in guilt. My amends to Amy—that was her name—and her family will never be enough, but they're all

I can give. I've set up a trust fund for her three children, I make monthly donations to MADD, and I have vowed to stay sober. My life—since I still have it—needs to make a difference."

I touch his cheek. "You can't change the past, but *you* can change to make the future better."

He puts his hands together like he's prayin' and gives me a little bow. "Amen, my Al-Anon sister." He smiles. "Seriously though, I don't know what I'd be like without 12-step programs."

I answer with more stuff from Al-Anon, "You'd be the dickhead who keeps doin' the same shit every day expectin' different results!"

He laughs.

I feel like a wet towel that's been put through the wringer; but a cleanin' was overdue. I needed to squeeze some of that dirt outta me. I think Mitch feels the same.

He tucks my hair behind my ear. "Hungry?"

"Starved. Whatcha got?" I ask.

"Frozen pizza or sandwiches?"

"Sandwiches. I'm gonna take a shower while you fix 'em, okay?" I want a minute by myself to get back to normal.

"You bet." He gives me a quick kiss before he shuts the bathroom door behind him.

He got a fancy shower with three heads like a spa. I make the water just short of scaldin' and step into it. My ass turns bright red and itches from the heat. That's how I like it. Burns away my troubles.

Mitch is right about burying all the nasty shit that happened along with Eddie's ashes. It's dead and gone and I can move on. But what Jed Donelly did been gnawing at me all these years. Every time I see him wrote up in the newspaper for winnin' some award or making some big donation it's like rippin' off a scab.

I'm tired of bleeding. I ain't no dumb teenager no more; believing he's all-powerful. There's bigger names fallin' left and right for their bullshit: Bill Cosby, that gymnastics doctor, Harvey Weinstein. It'd feel damn good to out Jed. Show all the snooty society people what they been suckin' up to.

Shit, let's be real. I ain't gonna. I hated all the gossip after Swannee killed Momma. I sure as shit don't want people talkin' 'bout me again. But maybe Jed don't need to know that. I sure would like to watch him squirm.

SYDNEY—June 24

Deena and I rescheduled our pool day for tomorrow. After Saturday's discovery of my ransacked trunk, I needed a day to process and prepare to deal with Tierney. To her, the items in the trunk should just be random mementos, but I can't be too careful. Until I've formulated a plan, I'll keep her close and cement her trust. Sun Tzu's words have never been more relevant.

Tierney's coming at two to babysit Helly. I have a half-hour to kill. There's a light breeze and no humidity; a perfect summer day. I dress Helly in her mint green romper and sun hat and take her big fluffy quilt to lay in the yard. Maggie's loading her catch. Her biceps, as big as any man's, bulge under the weight of the basket as she throws it into the bed of her pick-up. It looks like she's caught three bushels.

"Hey there, stranger!" I yell to Maggie as I make my way towards her. Her yard is nicer for Helly. Ours is littered with holly leaves that could prick little fingers.

She looks up and offers a huge, welcoming smile. I soak in my achievement. I'm reaping the rewards of years of patient, careful cultivation. Our shaky start has given way to a rock-solid relationship; one that I will not allow Tierney to infringe upon.

"Hey yourself. Ain't she cute in her little hat?" She kisses Helly all over her face. "I'd hold her, but I got eel all over me." She holds up her arms to show me the salt splatters and eel slime covering her T-shirt and jeans.

"Good haul today?" I ask.

"Bushel of ones, bushel of twos, and half-bushel of papershells. Seen better, but ain't bad. Watcha up to?"

"Letting Helly breathe in some fresh air." I point to her yard. "Okay if I park her here?"

"Course. You know you don't gotta ask. Let me wash up my hands and I'll join you for an Arizona before I run the crabs out to JimBob. Grab us two from the cooler."

"Great. I feel like I haven't seen you in ages. Your new man is keeping you all to himself."

She turns and walks towards the house, but not before I see her cheeks flame red. I settle Helly on the quilt and she coos as the bay air skims her bare legs and feet. I lug two Adirondack chairs out into the yard under the Locust tree, grab the teas, and slide into the seat, reveling in the view. The sun shimmers on the water's ripples, flickering like butterfly wings. A blue heron sits on a piling, head bobbing every which way as he grooms his feathers. The earthy smell of marsh grounds you to the land.

"You out in La-La Land?" Maggie asks.

I startle at her voice. "Just taking in the view."

"Yeah. It's somethin'. Even when Momma forgot us, I know when she looked out over the crick, she knew she was home."

I smile at her sharing a memory. There was a time that Maggie wouldn't share more than a grunt.

"So, fill me in on Mitch. He's been keeping you out many a night and even a few days off work. He must be something special."

"You ain't changed much." She grumbles, but I see the hint of a smile at the corners of her mouth. "Still a nosy damn chicken necker."

I let silence do the work.

She mops her face with her shirt. "Yeah, he's special. I'm gonna take him trotlinin' soon. He was born and bred on the shore and ain't never held a dip net."

"Thought you hated teaching people to crab."

"Hate teachin' Pennsylvanians. He's from the shore." Tickled with herself, she throws her head back and laughs.

159

I roll my eyes at her. Although the anti-Pennsylvanian sentiment is strong in Rock Narrows, I know Maggie's only teasing.

"How's the sex?" I ask, enjoying the shock value of my question.

She gets flustered and flaps around in her chair like an angry goose. "What's wrong with you woman? Decent folk don't talk 'bout such stuff."

I laugh. By her total embarrassment I can tell they are indeed having sex. "Suit yourself." I shrug my shoulders. "So other than great sex," I say, ribbing her a little more. "What's so special about him?"

She swats me on the shoulder before answering. "He don't try to shut me up or control what I do. He likes me like I am. And I can tell him shit I ain't never told no one else."

I feel a green twinge at being usurped as her confidante. After a lifetime of Pavlovian conditioning to keep secrets, I alone was able to help her find her voice. Her defection seems thankless. But although she's on the right path, she does need continued encouragement. With the demands of a new baby and husband, and the added burden of a treacherous bitch nipping at my heels, I don't have a lot left to give. Passing the torch to Mitch may be a good thing.

"That's wonderful. You deserve someone like that. You are enough just as you are and should never change yourself for someone else. I'm glad he recognizes that. When do I get to meet him?"

She groans. "I'm gonna see if he wants to go trotlinin' on Wednesday. We could steam up the papershells we catch and have 'em for lunch."

I clap my hands in delight. "I'll see if Jake can join us."

"No way! One meddlin' family member at a time!"

"Fine." I agree quickly, before she changes her mind altogether. "I'm honored to be the first meddling family member to meet him!"

We both turn when we hear a car in the driveway.

Maggie juts her chin towards Tierney's car. "You got your girl helpin' you today? She ain't bad."

Poker face engaged, I make certain not a hint of disapproval or anger shows. "Yes, she mentioned you had lunch together. I didn't know you were a lady who lunches," I tease.

"Aaack. I was in a good mood is all. Kid seemed lonely."

Lonely my ass.

I paste a smile on my face. "She's a sweet girl."

"She wants Jake to show her the pens," Maggie informs me. "Well, she wanted me to take her trotlinin', but one newbie's enough, so the pens is the next best thing."

Of course, the softshell pens—Jake's courtship modus operandi—how poetic. The silhouette of a plan emerges.

"Oh, I'm glad you told me. He's so busy at work I wouldn't want to add to his load, but I'll be glad to show her the ropes. I'll start today."

Tierney hops out of her car. "Hey y'all."

She's wearing a yellow, purple, and orange striped mini-skirt, a powder-blue baby tee and lime-green flip flops.

"Ain't she all rainbows and unicorns?" Maggie whispers, blinded by garishness.

Tierney skips over to us, popping her gum. Add pig tails and knee socks and Humbert Humbert would be drooling.

"Wow! I get to visit with all three Swann women. It's my lucky day!"

"Well, it's a hi and goodbye for me." Maggie pitches her empty tea bottle into the recycling bin beside the dock. "Gotta get the crabs out the road before they die. Already spent too much time gabbin'."

She's walking towards the truck before she finishes her sentence. With a backward two-finger wave she jumps in and barrels down the driveway.

Tierney smells her armpits. "Do I stink?"

I mask my gritted teeth with an amused smile. "That's just her style. She doesn't mince words. She obviously likes you quite a bit. She never lunches and she did with you."

An eager puppy-dog grin lights up her face. "Yay! We had a really fun lunch. I hope we can do it again."

She's skilled. I can't detect even the slightest whiff of guilt over her snooping—or concern for what she found.

Time to launch my plan. "Maggie told me you wanted to learn to tend the pens."

"I do! Do you think Jake will teach me?"

I let her believe she has me snowed. "I'm sure he'd love to, but he's so swamped at work right now. How about I teach you instead?"

"I would love that!" she says with overblown exuberance.

Daisy lays protectively beside a peacefully sleeping Helly. "Let's start now, while Helly's asleep."

Because of Jake's patient teaching, my skills are proficient. I can easily identify a newly sloughed crab. I know the appropriate time to remove it from the water, and I'm able to properly prepare and position the crab to be sold to buyers.

When Jake tends the pens it's like watching a seasoned danseur perform a Pas de Deux—the crab his partner. His bare hands chasse dreamily through the waters, fingers delicately wooing the crabs, ending with the dramatic finale—a glorious lift of the softshell from the water. He'd razz me mercilessly for my flowery description, but the first time I saw it, that's how I felt.

I direct Tierney to stand beside me at the first pen. "So do you know anything about how this works?"

"Nope."

"Ok, we'll start at the beginning. The only crabs that get put in the pen are ripe peelers. That means they are ready to slough their too-small shells."

She interrupts. "Ok. How do you know they're a ripe peeler?"

I put on my glove and pull out a crab to show her. "You see this red ring around his backfin?"

"Yes."

"That shows he's a peeler. If it's red, he's ripe and can go in the pen. If it's pink, he's a green peeler and needs a couple more days before it's safe to put him in."

I motion Tierney to follow me to the top of the dock, and pull up the line that's attached to the first pier. "This is a slough box. Jake's dad built this one. You see it has a screen bottom to let the water in. The wood sides make it float and the slatted wood top keeps the herons from eating the crabs. It's tied to the pier to keep it from floating away. That's where we put green peelers to ripen."

"Why isn't it safe to put him in until he's ripe? Will he die?"

"He won't, but every softshell will. Once a crab molts, it's defenseless. Its claws are too soft to protect itself. A green peeler is still hard and still eating. He'll rip a softshell to shreds and eat it."

She shudders. "Cannibalistic."

"Survival of the fittest."

"Okay, so what happens next?"

I scan the pen to find my next visual aid. "Look closely at this crab. See how the back part of his shell has just started to lift?"

"I do. Is he molting?"

"He is. Right now, he's called a crackshell. He literally just cracked his shell from his body. When he pulls away from it a little more, he'll be called a buster. Once he's completely out of his shell, I'll give him about a half-hour or so to firm up and then I'll lift him out."

"Why do you want him to get firm?"

At least she's asking intelligent questions. "If he's too soft he won't travel well. We need him tough enough to transport, but soft enough so he's not leathery. That's why the pens need to be checked every two or three hours."

"Got it. Now how do you know which ones are softshells?"

"First you find the sloughs, the empty shells." I point into the water of the pen. "See, here's one. Now I know I have one soft crab. Look around the empty shell. Softshells are usually bigger and darker than the peelers. Can you spot him?"

"Is that him?" She points to the correct crab.

"Yep. Do you want to lift him out?"

"I don't know about that. I'd rather watch you do it first."

I understand her hesitancy. Sticking your hands into a pen full of crabs seems unwise. My first attempt was disastrous. Nearly every crab latched onto my glove. I got so discombobulated I flung the glove off of my hand and had crabs scurrying all over the deck.

"Okay. There's another one." I point out another softshell. "I'll show you how to do it." I pull the half-full tray out of the refrigerator we have on the dock to keep the crabs alive, and sit it on the work station across from the pens. I slip on my second glove and calmly glide my hands through the water. I gently scoop up the softshell from underneath and hold him above the pen to let the excess water drain. "Did you notice how slowly I moved my hand through the water?"

Tierney nods.

"That's critical. You need to stay cool, calm, and collected or you'll rile up the other crabs. Now watch how I position him on the tray. Fold each claw into his body to protect them."

She nods again.

"Are you ready to try it?"

"I guess so." She sounds uncertain.

I hand her the gloves and she slides them on backwards.

"Tierney, you have to turn them around. The knit side is on the top of your hand and the latex protects your palm."

She picks at the tiny slashes in the latex. "What are all these little holes from?"

"From the crabs. Every once in a while, they take a pinch at you."

"I was afraid you'd say that."

She swallows hard, girding herself for what's to come. Easing her hands into the water, she gradually slides them towards the softshell. Not a single crab moves. Mimicking my lift, she sweeps the crab up with one fluid motion. She has the same tranquil energy as Jake.

She folds the softshell on the tray and asks, "How did I do?"

"You're a crab whisperer, just like Jake."

She beams. "That was amazing. I feel like I was born to do this. When it's time, can I check them again?"

Satisfaction suffuses my body. "Absolutely."

The groundwork has been laid.

DEENA—June 25

I am a nervous wreck and have been since I opened Sydney's trunk. I can't sleep. I have no appetite. I jump at the slightest thing. My plan has got to work.

My hands are shaking so much, it's a struggle to strap Davey in his car seat. I check the time. 9:10. Perfect.

Me and Sydney agreed to meet at the pool at nine, so she should be there now. I still have her house key, so I will slip into her house, get photos of the evidence, and fix the trunk.

At 9:20, I pull into her driveway and park in front of her house. Nails's bateau isn't in the slip, so I don't have to worry about her. I roll down all the windows, and leave Davey in his seat. When I hit the first step of the porch, a jumble of news stories about kids dying in cars invades my brain and I run back to get him out. With Davey on my hip, I climb the front porch steps, key in hand. Just as I slide it in the lock, Sydney opens the door.

I jump and knock the key out of the lock. It lands on the porch with a ping. Sydney looks at it.

"What are you doing here? We're supposed to be meeting at the pool at nine."

Having not yet thought of a good answer, I blurt, "It's past nine."

"Yeah. I'm running late. Didn't you get my text?"

I feel my back pocket. In my nervousness for what I was about to do, I forgot to bring my phone. "Damn, I forgot it."

"What's with the key?" She picks it up and tucks it into her back pocket. "Were you sneaking in?"

She's smiling, but I can't tell if she's teasing or threatening.

"I, uh. Where's your car?"

She points to the far side of the house. "Around the side."

How stupid. I didn't even bother to check the side.

"So," she says, eyebrows raised. "What's with the key?"

"Oh, I, uh, I think I left Davey's lovey here when I babysat. I thought you were already gone, so I was just going to pop in and get it."

She swishes the corner of the little blue blanket Davey's holding. "I thought this was his lovey."

Think, Deena, think.

"Yeah, this is his favorite lovey, but we have a spare. That's the one I thought I left."

"Got it. Come on in. We can look for it."

I hope with every fiber of my being she bought it. If not, I may be dead man walking. I follow her into the house.

"You check the main room and the mudroom and I'll look in the bedrooms. *Please,* be quiet. Helly was awake most of the night. I just got her to sleep. That's actually why I texted you to tell you I'd meet you at the pool when she wakes up."

We both scan the house for the non-existent lovey.

"No luck, sorry."

I shrug. "Oh well. At least we have his favorite. See you at the pool."

My chest tightens, my hands are sweaty, and I'm gulping for air as I drive out their lane. I fight back tears. Without the house key, how am I going to get in to fix the trunk? My face and neck are burning up and I feel like I can't catch my breath. If I don't do it soon, Sydney will figure out I was snooping. And if she figures it out . . .

My body starts shaking uncontrollably and I get tunnel-vision. Luckily, I'm at the marina. I park and rest my head on the steering wheel trying to calm myself. I flinch at a rap on the window. It's Skip.

"Take it easy, Deena. It's just me."

He opens the car door. "What's wrong? You're shaking and white as a ghost."

I fight to get my anxiety under control. Skip's been watching me like a hawk since I blurted out my suspicions about Sydney. If he gets any more worried about me, I'm afraid he'll have me committed. "I'm okay."

He bends down to my eye-level. "Deena, what happened?"

"A car pulled out in front of me and I almost hit it. Shook me up. Really, I just need a minute and I'll be fine."

Despite his reassuring squeeze of my shoulder, I see the doubt in his eyes. "All right. Chillin' at the pool is just what you need." He unhooks Davey from his car seat, hands him to me, and grabs the beach bag. "You want the baby pool too?"

"Yep." I force a breezy smile onto my face. "He loves splashing in it."

At the pool gate, Jeremiah waves me through. Skip spreads my towel on the lounge. "Are you sure you're okay with being *here*? You look jumpy."

It's my first time at the pool since Banana Boat Burn, but that's not what has me rattled.

"I guess I'm a little edgy, being my first time back since . . ." I let my words trail off and adjust the floppy sunhat I'm wearing to protect my healing skin.

"That makes sense. Plus, the near-accident didn't help." He seems relieved that I have "real" reasons for my tension. He unrolls the baby pool. "Let me go get an air pump. You'll blow your lungs out inflating this thing. Be right back."

I rub a test-patch of zinc sunblock on my hand and take slow, deep breaths to calm my nerves. Five minutes later, as I'm slathering it on Davey and me, Tierney sashays in, looking amazing in her yellow string bikini. It's clear Jeremiah thinks so too, because he peeks around the corner to watch her make her way across the pool. I cover my muffin top and dimply legs with Davey's towel and vow to sign up for Zumba.

"Hey Deena! Can I sit here?" Tierney asks.

167

"Sure."

She spreads out her towel, applies her sunscreen, and pulls out *Images of America—Rock Narrows.*

"Where'd you get that?" I ask.

"In Bakerstown, at the B-town Creamery. They have all kinds of local souvenirs." She flips the book open to a dog-eared page and points at a photo of a waterman tonging for oysters. "Look. It's Gilbert Swann, Jake's grandfather." She flips to another page. "And here's Sarah Beall. That's Helen's mother, Jake's grandmother."

"How and why do you know that?"

She shrugs. "Genealogy's kind of my thing."

The book is a nice distraction from my racing thoughts. "Did you see any Clarkes or Marshalls in there? Those are my family names."

She's searching the index when Skip returns with the pump.

"Hey, Tierney," Skip says, averting his eyes from her swimsuit-model body.

"Hi Skip," she says, not looking up from her book.

As Skip pumps up Davey's pool, his walkie-talkie squawks.

Jake's voice booms from the radio. "Skip, where you at?"

"The pool. What's up?"

"I'm on my way."

Jake strides into the pool like a man on a mission. He smiles when he sees me and Tierney.

"Ladies." He pats Davey on the head. "How's the kiddo?"

"Good," I say. "I'm sorry I left you hanging."

"No worries." He juts his chin towards Tierney. "She bailed me out."

I turn towards Tierney. "Well then, thanks to you."

"You bet! It was fun. I had lunch with Maggie and got to cook my mom's Chicken Piccata for Jake."

Skip shoots me an oh-shit look, and tries to change the subject before we find out something we don't want to know.

"Whaddya need?" he asks Jake.

"The 42' Ocean ain't blocked right. Get it fixed and make damn sure no one touches it before it's good. We don't want a repeat of what happened to Kendall."

"Will do," Skip says to Jake. He leans down, kisses me and whispers, "You'll be fine. See you tonight."

Jake turns to leave. "You ladies have a good pool day."

"Do you have a sec?" Tierney asks Jake.

"Yeah, what's up?"

"I'm dying to show you what I found." She flips her long legs off the lounge, sits sideways, and pats the spot beside her. "Look at these photos."

Jake sits beside her. Their shoulders touch and he leans over to look at the book.

Tierney points to the same photo she showed me. "Here's your grandfather. What's hand-tonging?"

"That's how you catch oysters. See this?" When he points to the tonging rake, his fingers brush her hand. "There's a rake head on each side and when they squeeze it together, on the bottom of the bay, it rakes up the oysters."

Out of the corner of my eye, I see Sydney and Helly coming through the gate. The ease I was just starting to feel is replaced with dread.

Helly looks adorable in her blue and white striped bathing suit. Sydney's wearing a Kimono style cover-up and has oversized sunglasses propped on top of her head. When she spots Jake leaning over Tierney, she stops in her tracks.

Her jaw tightens and she shoots daggers with her eyes. If looks could kill, Tierney would be dead. My stomach flips and my mouth dries up when I think of Sydney levelling that stare on me.

Sydney gives her head one hard shake and her face changes. She relaxes her jaw and puts on a warm, friendly smile. Jake and Tierney haven't seen her yet. As Sydney pushes Helly's stroller closer to us, her smiles broadens but her eyes scare the hell out of me. Her pupils are so big her eyes look black, and the white part is weird too—kind of shiny. I think she notices me staring because she slides her sunglasses down to cover her eyes.

"Hi guys," she says casually.

Jake jumps at her voice and whips his hand off the book. He stands and gives her a hug. "Did Helly finally get some sleep?"

"She did." She rolls the umbrella stroller to the other side of Tierney and spreads her towel on the lounge chair.

"You want me to put sunscreen on her?" Jake asks, taking Helly out of her seat for a snuggle. "I know you hate that zinc stuff."

"No, I'm good. I'm sure you have plenty of other things to do." She's acting so calm it reminds me of that movie—*Stepford Wives.*

"Okay. Text me before you leave so I can come say goodbye." He hands off Helly and waves to me and Tierney. "See y'all."

I'm on pins and needles. I've got no idea what's going to happen next. I know Sydney was not happy with what she saw when she walked in.

"So," Sydney says to Tierney, as she's putting sunscreen on Helly. "What were you and Jake looking at?"

I root around in my beach bag like I'm searching for something.

Tierney swings her legs to the other side of the chair and leans towards Sydney. "Look at this." Her excitement seems genuine. "This is Jake's grandfather. His grandmother's in here too."

"Interesting," Sydney stretches to look at the book. "You're digging up all kinds of things about my family."

"I am!"

I heard the sarcasm—and subtle warning—in Sydney's response, but I don't think Tierney did.

Helly waves her arms up and down and grunts. "Can I take her in the pool?" Tierney asks Sydney.

"Sure."

After sliding swimmies onto Helly's arms, Tierney wades into the pool. I can't tell for sure because of the sunglasses, but I think Sydney's watching me as she pulls her Banana Boat sunscreen out of her bag. I've never seen her use that brand.

Rubbing it on her body and face she asks, "How's your healing coming?"

It feels like a threat. Fear zings through my body and my heart pounds.

"Oh, you know what else I found?" Tierney yells from the pool.

"What?" Sydney's hands tighten into fists.

For one selfish, shameful second I hope Sydney keeps her focus on Tierney instead of me.

"Sarah Beall's father also served in the Navy, just like Jake."

"Mmm," Sydney says. Her nostrils flare.

Tierney's clueless. The more she talks, the more she pisses Sydney off.

Feeling guilty for my horrible thought, I try to cover for her. "She's really into ancestry stuff. You know tracing family trees and finding out family histories."

Sydney presses against her temple and shakes her head, as she lets out a long sigh. Reaching for her water bottle, she takes a few sips, stretches, then turns to face me.

"Deena, speaking of finding things . . ." She slides her glasses up onto her head, clasps her hands in her lap, and gives me an unblinking stare.

This is it. She found the trunk. My throat tightens and sweat coats my palms. The pressure pushing on my chest makes it hard to breathe. I swallow, clench my teeth, and use every bit of focus not to squirm.

My voice quivers when I answer. "Yes?"

"Did you find Davey's lovey?"

MAGGIE—June 26

I'm showin' Mitch how to trotline today. Most times, I don't bother to brush my hair before work, but I might spiff up a little. When Mitch's headlights shine across the yard, I get a flutter in my gut. I'd like to chalk it up to too many beers last night, but I'd just be lyin' to myself. I head outside.

He flicks off the lights and gets outta the car. "Damn! I can't see a thing. Are you there?"

"Hold up. I'll come get ya." I run up to him and use my flashlight to show him the way. Can't have him trip over shit.

He reaches for my hand. "It's kind of creepy out here by the water when it's dark. You guys ought to get those motion-sensitive lights."

"And wake the neighbors with a light flickin' on and off every time me or Ruby moves? They'd fucking love that."

"Hadn't thought of that."

At the top of the lighted wharf, I flip off the flashlight and grab my gear.

Mitch grabs the cooler and follows me down the dock. "What time does it get light?"

"5:30."

Ruby hops into the bateau. I get in next and reach my hands up to take the cooler. Mitch jumps in with a thud and rocks the boat so much Ruby yelps.

"Sorry." He turns tomato red.

I shrug like it ain't no big deal, but hold in my laugh. I throw the lines off and putter out to my lay. Away from the dock, it's pitch black. I made this trip so many times, I could do it with my eyes closed, but every so often I switch on my spotlight and scan the water for floatin' logs.

"I don't know if I like being on the water at night." Mitch says. "It feels kind of claustrophobic. Like the dark is pressing in on me." He's quiet for a minute. The only sound is a few crickets chirping. "It's like when they closed the cell door for the very first time."

"Here." I hand him the spotlight. "Shine it on the water ahead of us and look for shit stickin' up outta the water. If you're busy, the dark won't bother you."

I steer to the right past the duck blind and turn the bateau around to head back towards home. The black sky turns to gray and you can start to make out the shapes of trees on the shoreline.

"This is my lay." I throw my float into the water and lift my line on the ringer arm.

He shines the light on my line so he can watch what I'm doing. I inch the bateau forward real slow, letting the line feed out into the crick. Twenty minutes later, I drop the end float.

"Now we wait," I say.

"Oh my God, look." Mitch points to the horizon. "The clouds are glowing."

The white clouds shine and the risin' sun makes the sky and water look pink.

Mitch stands and reaches for me. I rest my back against his chest and we watch the sky turn to purple then blue.

"I'm going to get sappy, so don't make fun of me," Mitch says.

"I might."

"Being here with you and seeing that sunrise feels like all the darkness I've been carrying cracked away and opened into the brightness of a shiny, new life."

That ain't the way I woulda said it, but I know what he means. It feels like hope.

*****

I stink, my hair's stuck to my head from sweat, and I'm up to my elbows in rotten eel.

Mitch puts his hands on my cheeks and gives me a whopper kiss. "That was terrific. And so are you."

It was a great. After a kick-ass sunrise, the sun was warm but not burnin'. The water was smooth as glass, reflectin' the sky and shore like a mirror, and the crabs was bitin'. Mitch only missed half a dozen or so till he got the hang of it.

"Well, it ain't over yet," I tell him. "There's still work to be done. We got eel to chop and a line to bait. Then we gotta run the crabs out the road. The bateau needs scrubbin' and the coolers need a good cleaning."

"Aye Aye, Captain." He gives me a dumb-ass salute. He's cornier than Sydney and that ain't easy. "What do you need me to do?"

"You chop the eel and I'll bait the line."

He whistles *Pop-Eye the Sailor Man* while he works. I must got it bad. If it was anyone else, I'd throw the damn cleaver at their head to get 'em to shut up.

"You know," he says. "I never realized how much is involved in catching crabs. No wonder they're so expensive."

"I do it old school. The way my old man taught me. Not everyone trotlines; especially not with a dip net. If they're gonna trotline they use auto-dippers. They don't even gotta look at the line. They just run it and the net scoops up the crabs."

"Seems like it'd be easier."

"Easier yeah, but boring as hell. Pop used to say there's skill to workin' the water. Where's the skill in lettin' a machine do all the work?"

"Yeah, I see what you're saying. Your way takes a lot of finesse."

"And it gives the crabs a sporting chance. Keeps ya from strippin' the bay. Hell, auto-dippers ain't the worst of it. Out in the

bay, lotsa watermen don't even bother to run a line. They pot 'em."
My blood starts to boil. "And don't get me started on the greedy
bastards in Virginia. They pot and then dredge crabs all through the
winter. Sponge crabs and all. How they expect 'em to restock?"

"What's a sponge crab?" he asks.

"Are you sure you're from the Eastern Shore?" I tease him. "A
sponge crab is a female that got a sack of eggs attached to her. The
sacks can have over a million eggs, and the blockheads keep 'em
anyway."

"You're a regular Norma Rae for the crabbing industry." He
laughs and I feel stupid.

"Well, it's how I make my livin' you know. If there ain't
crabs, I don't get paid."

"That was a compliment."

"Hmph. Didn't sound like one."

"I mean it. I love your passion and your respect for the water."
He walks over to me and puts his salty hands on either side of the
line barrel and kisses me. "In fact, Maggie Swann, I love you."

SYDNEY—June 26

I catch Mitch kissing Maggie. She looks stunned.

"Hey lovebirds!" I yell, as I walk across the lawn.

Maggie glares at me. "Ain't you got somewhere to be?"

"Yep, right here for lunch."

Her thorniness has no impact on my good mood. Jake told me this morning that he has to work another boat show July nineteenth weekend. His absence will give me the perfect opportunity to deal with Tierney.

I only wish it was sooner. Tierney is using every ploy—like a book about his grandparents—to get close to Jake. She's good, but I'm better. This is one tug-of-war she won't win.

"Hi, I'm Mitch," Maggie's beau introduces himself. "I'd shake your hand, but . . ." He lifts his hands and shows me his slimy, eely palms.

I laugh. "I'll pass on the hand shake. It's nice to meet you."

He's tall and trim with unusual green eyes, which look adoringly at Maggie.

"I hear I did worse than you when you first learned to dip. I missed four or five," Mitch says.

"More like six," Maggie chimes in.

"I was too afraid to miss under pain of death," I answer dramatically.

"Really?" Mitch teases. "I didn't even get yelled at."

"Aah. It must be true love."

Maggie rolls her eyes at both of us and tosses the last of her line into the barrel. "Enough yakkin'. Finish choppin' those eels. We gotta get the crabs out to JimBob."

"Tierney's in the house with Helly. I can run them out for you while you clean up the boat," I volunteer.

I actually increased the number of days I'm having her babysit. Better to keep her out of Jake's sight. Unfortunately, I think he's too vulnerable to her charms.

"Yeah, all right," Maggie says. "Leave two dozen papershells. I'll steam 'em up when I'm done with the bateau. And pick up some corn at Ned's on your way home."

"Will do. I need to grab my purse and let Tierney know, then I'll be on my way."

I hear Tierney on the phone as I'm opening the door. She has it on speaker. I stop and listen. There's clattering and lots of people laughing in the background.

A woman's voice says, "Well honey I've got to pour some shots. You know these sailor boys have no patience. I'm glad you met Maggie. Maybe you can get me a copy of the picture of Jake's brother. I'd love to see it. I miss you. Love you, baby girl."

"Love you too, Mom. Bye."

I close the door loudly and Tierney startles.

"Hey. It's just me. I caught the tail end of your conversation. Was that your mom?" I ask innocently.

Worry flits across her face, as if she's concerned about what I might have overheard. "Yep. She's at work so she couldn't talk long."

"Where does she work? Sounds noisy."

"It is. It's an Irish pub near the docks. Actually, I'm named after it—Tierney's Ale House. Mom's been a bartender there since before I was born."

Name your daughter after a bar, interesting choice.

"I heard her say she'd like a picture of Swannee. Does she mean the one you showed me the night I got home?"

"Yeah, I was telling her how much we look alike."

I barely glanced at the photo that night; I was focused on other things. But thinking back to Swannee in the courtroom at his change of venue hearing, I don't see much resemblance. Maybe a little around the eyes.

"We can scan it and you can email her a copy. While we're at it, let's send her some photos of you holding Helly, and tending the pens."

"She'd love that!"

And I would, too. Photographic evidence will bolster my version of the events.

"Super. We'll do that tomorrow." I need a little time to prepare. "I have to run Maggie's crabs out and pick up some produce. You good here with Helly?"

"She's sound asleep, so no problem."

"Good. I won't be too long."

Actually, while I have Maggie *and* Mitch as witnesses, why not add some more blocks to my plan's foundation?

"You know what, Tierney, why don't you tend the pens by yourself today? I'll ask Maggie to do a quick double check when you're done to make sure you didn't miss any."

She claps her hands together with excitement. "Yeah! I'm ready!"

"Great. Bring the baby monitor and walk out with me, and I'll give Maggie the heads up."

Maggie and Mitch are sitting in the Adirondack chairs under the tree. Her face, normally taut, is open and relaxed. He's holding her hand. Something he says makes her blush and giggle—neither of which I'm accustomed to seeing Maggie do. They're so engrossed in each other they don't see us coming.

"Hey guys," I say to get their attention. They both look at us. "Mitch, this is Tierney my"—I choose my next word purposefully; subdue the enemy without fighting—"protégé."

Tierney's delight shows I chose wisely.

"And babysitter," she adds with an ear-to-ear grin.

"Pleasure," Mitch says.

No, the pleasure is mine. A tingle of sweet anticipation warms me, as more of my plan falls into place.

"Tierney's going to tend the pens while I run out," I say to Maggie. "Would you double check and make sure she does it right? It'll be her first time doing it alone."

"You bet. Grab some tomatoes too. Tierney, you wanna join us? We got plenty."

I didn't think her grin could get any wider, but it does. "Is it okay with you?" she asks me.

Lunching with her is much better than letting her tease Jake with her perky little ass. Besides, I cannot let even a whiff of animosity show.

I force my smile to match the exuberance of Tierney's. "Glad to have you join us."

For the little time you have left.

MAGGIE—June 27

It's 3 a.m. and my brain won't quit. Since Mitch said he loves me, my heads been spinnin'. I already cleaned out the refrigerator, scrubbed the tub, and mopped the kitchen floor. Nothin's workin'. I slide into my work boots, leash up Ruby, and grab a flashlight. I gotta walk.

Once I hit the road, all I hear is bullfrogs croaking. They're so loud they drown out the crickets. Ruby pulls me into the grass to take a piss. It's already wet with heavy dew.

I hear a rustle in the woods and shine the light. Two eyes shine back at me. It's a deer. She's frozen in place, too scared to move a muscle. Kinda like me. I sure as shit don't wanna go back to my old ways, but I ain't sure I'm ready to jump ahead. I still got a lot of bullshit weighing me down.

I drag Ruby outta the grass and keep walkin'. We get to the first houses past the woods. Mrs. Brewster's dog hears us and barks. The light flips on upstairs and I see her head poke out the window.

"It's me, Nails," I yell up to her so she ain't worried someone's lurkin' around. "Sorry, I couldn't sleep."

"Yeah, well I could," she yells back and snaps the blind down.

I keep going. I pass the house with the swing set and above-ground pool. The yard's overgrown and full up with toys, balls, and bikes. Then I come up to Willy Klug's house. He's eighty-six and he got married a month ago, for the first time in his life. It just goes to show it's never too late.

Goddammit, that means for me, too. I do love Mitch. And it ain't too late for me to be happy.

More barkin' and more bedroom lights flip on. I see the new Mrs. Klug peeking out her window. I wave. I better turn back before I wake the whole goddamn neighborhood.

Ruby trots ahead like it's normal to take a walk in the middle of the night. She don't have a care in the world. Dogs don't lug their hurts around like people do.

If I'm gonna be with Mitch, I wanna be like Ruby. No baggage. No garbage stinkin' me up inside. That means I got one more piece of rot to deal with. No more pussy footin' around. I'm gonna do it tomorrow. Jed Donnelly, it's time to pay the piper.

He probably ain't gave me a second thought in seventeen years. But that's gonna change. I'm gonna march into his office and tell 'em he'll have the starrin' role in the next #MeToo post. That oughta have him shittin' bricks.

SYDNEY—June 27

Jake went to work and it's minutes before Tierney will arrive. I hurry out to the wharf and the pens to take one last look. Yes, everything is properly staged. After all, the photos will be evidence. They need to document the correct story.

Daisy's bark warns me of her arrival. I dash back to my front porch. When she turns the corner, I wave enthusiastically, sincerely glad to see her. Helly's in her playpen on the porch. I lift her out and give her belly a raspberry. She giggles.

Tierney pops out of her car. "Morning." She points at Helly. "Her outfit's adorable. I love the little honeybees."

"I wanted her to look cute for the photos. I thought we'd take them outside while the light's so pretty."

"She can't look un-cute. How about I hold her on the rocker?"

"No, too shaded. Let's do a few shots at the end of the wharf with the water behind you."

Today, the dock has a gangplank-esque quality, as Tierney walks down it. Her steps seem interminably slow. She reaches the end, less than six inches from the water. She turns and reaches her arms out for Helly. I hand her my daughter and direct the photo shoot.

"Lean against the piling. okay, now sit sideways with Helly in your lap. Hang one leg over the edge. Perfect." Using her phone, I snap several photos of each pose. "They're great." I scroll through the options, deleting a few. "Now let's get you tending the pens. I'll put Helly back in her playpen."

We repeat the process, but this time at the softshell pens.

"Slide your hand in the water." I snap the photo from a few angles, making sure each shot will corroborate my story. "Now hold up a buster. Let me get one as you arrange him on the tray. Do you want a video of you lifting him out?"

"Yeah, that'd be awesome!"

I shoot a video with Tierney explaining what she's doing.

She takes off her gloves and lays them on the worktop. "I can't wait to text my friends."

"And don't forget your mom," I remind her. "I scanned the photo of Swannee last night. I'll text it to you now."

Her phone pings. "Got it. Let's take a selfie at the end of the dock. I want a pic of us together."

As we walk out the dock, she grabs my hand and gives it a squeeze. "Thanks for everything. You're making my summer really great."

I squeeze back. "You're welcome."

She snaps a few selfies with the water behind us, then swipes through the shots. "Check 'em out. Aack, you look crazy in this one."

She's right. My eyes are huge and bugging out. I laugh. "That one's got to go."

She giggles. "Yeah, if that got out it'd be bad PR." She deletes it.

"Send them to your mom," I encourage, wanting to ensure they're sent. "She'll love them."

She taps her phone a few times. "Done."

Foundation complete.

MAGGIE—June 28

Seventeen years ago, I walked through the door of Donnelly Telecommunications wide-eyed and innocent, with big ideas of bettering myself. I limped out bloody and shamed. Today's gonna be a helluva lot different.

Jed's office is on the top floor. Of course, he ain't gonna have no one above him. I got Swannee's old guttin' knife strapped under my shirt. Ain't takin' any chances. That flabby, white piece of shit won't ever hurt me again.

His secretary ain't at her desk, so I don't gotta deal with that. I fling open his door and barge right in. He got his feet propped up and he's leaned back in his fancy leather chair. His mouth drops open.

"Albert, I've got to call you back. I have some urgent business to attend to," he says to the guy on the phone before he hangs up. "Who the hell are you?" He damn near snarls at me.

I put my hand on the knife and walk around his desk so we's face to face. "Look me in the eye, you piece of shit. Do you remember my blue eyes? Do you remember them beggin' you to stop before you ripped my skirt off?"

He pushes his chair back to get further from me. "I, I, I . . . Young woman, I have no idea what you're talking about."

I got him nervous.

"When I was a young, innocent girl I came here to apply for an internship and you threw me on this here antique desk. You ripped my panties and skirt right off me and laughed at my tears,

You squeezed my throat till I couldn't breathe and shoved your worthless dick inside of me, rippin' me to shreds as you went."

Behind me, I hear the door open. It's the same sound I heard when I was trapped under Jed, but this time I ain't desperate to be saved. Now I got the power. Let whoever it is hear what I got to say.

I poke my finger hard into his chest. "You raped me and now the world's gonna know it." I spit in his face then turn to see who opened the door.

It's Mitch. Why the fuck is he here?

His face is green and he looks like he's gonna hurl. "Maggie, what the hell? Oh my God, Oh my God. Is this who raped you? Oh, Jesus Christ, Maggie. I didn't know."

"You know this deranged woman?" Jed asks Mitch, tryin' hard to make his voice sound offended. "I have absolutely no idea what she's talking about. She stormed into my office and is accusing me of reprehensible behavior. I won't tolerate it. I'm calling security."

Mitch is on him faster than a scalded dog. I hear the crack when his punch lands square on Jed's nose. Blood spurts all over, makin' puddles on the desk. Jed's white shirt looks like boardwalk spin art with only red paint.

Mitch grabs Jed by his necktie and lifts him half off the seat. "Stop your goddamn lying, Dad."

Dad? No. Did I hear that right? This is Mitch's old man? Holy fuck.

Mitch twists his tie tighter and tighter, cutting off his air. "I saw you; you perverted bastard. I saw how you hurt her. It's burned into my mind."

It was Mitch who opened that door and didn't help me.

A sharp pain doubles me over. I can't breathe. It's like I got the wind knocked outta me. My head spins and I gotta hold onto the side of the desk. Mitch saw his old man rapin' me and didn't do a goddamn thing to stop it. Sour acid burns my throat. My ears ring and my head throbs.

"Maggie, please, please. You've got to forgive me," Mitch begs.

When he calls my name, I turn and look at him. Everything's in slow motion. I mighta shook my head no, or I mighta just thought it. I dunno. It's like I'm here watchin' but ain't a part of it.

Tears run down Mitch's cheek, but he don't loosen his grip on Jed's tie. His old man's eyes bulge and his lips look blue. Jed kicks and flails, but Mitch got him pinned in the chair and ain't easing up. Ain't gonna be too much longer before the old man is dead. I think about steppin' in, but my body don't move, like when you can't run in a nightmare.

"You worthless scum." Mitch's words sound like a growl. He lifts Jed outta the chair, throws him on the floor, and sits on top of him.

Jed takes a big gasp of air before Mitch tightens the tie again. With his free hand, Mitch lands a punch beside Jed's eye. The force whips his head to the side and the blood from his nose splatters all over Mitch's face.

Mitch's face is tight. "You already ruined half my life. I tried to escape the flashbacks of seeing what you did with booze and pills. And now, after I finally got my shit together and am starting life over, you're going to destroy it again."

I hear pain in Mitch's voice and Jed's grunts. I swirl my finger in the blood on the desk. It's sticky, like when it was dryin' on my naked, bruised legs. But now it ain't mine. I wipe it on my shirt. An ugly scream, like cats fighting, snaps me back to full speed.

"I'm calling the police!" Jed's secretary yells from the doorway.

Mitch don't even look up. He pops his old man again. Jed squirms under him, scared shitless. Payback's a bitch.

I walk over to the secretary and say, "Best to let his boy take care of him. If you call the cops, I'm gonna have to tell 'em the reason Mitch is beatin' the hell outta his daddy is 'cause Jed raped me."

Her jaw falls damn near to her knees. She turns around and shuts the door behind her. Mitch stands up and gives Jed two hard kicks to the ribs, surely breakin' a few. Jed coughs and moans.

Mitch comes 'round the desk and tries to hug me. "Maggie, please. At least let me explain."

I push past him. Jed's layin' in his own piss and blood. His neck and eyes is already purple. For half a second, I feel sorry for him, and then seventeen years of rage take over. I slam my foot down on his crotch and grind his dick into the floor. He squeals like a stuck pig and pukes from the pain. With any luck, I broke his dick permanent and his rapin' days is over.

I go into his bathroom and pick up one of his monogrammed hand towels. Leaning over his snot and blood-smeared face I drop the towel on his chest. "Clean yourself up, you disgusting pig." I turn my back on Jed and walk towards the door.

Mitch grabs my arm. "Maggie, don't let him ruin what we have. Don't let him take more from us."

I slap his hand away. "Let go." I walk outta the office, past the skittish secretary bitin' her nails to the quick, down five flights of stairs, and out the front door.

SYDNEY—June 28

It's almost noon and I just woke up. Between make-up sex and tending the pens, I got zero sleep. Though I'm still miffed with Jake, I allowed him back into my bed because everything needs to appear back to normal before he goes to the boat show.

I settle into the rocker with my first cup of coffee. Laughs echo across the water. A group of four stand-up paddleboarders glide by my dock. Daisy, always interested in new friends, trots down to the end of our pier and barks a greeting. A guy with a man-bun and flowered boardshorts paddles over to pet her. She wags her tail so fast her whole back-end shakes.

"You made her day," I call down to him.

He smiles and paddles away, catching up to his group.

An eagle soars overhead, gliding through the cloudless blue sky. He lands in the treetops of the small island across the creek from our house. A heron sits motionless on the top of a piling waiting for prey. It's like living in a David Attenborough program.

I hear Maggie's truck in the lane. She truly is the first friend I've ever had. Feeling sentimental, I stroll over to meet her, still in my pjs and slippers.

"Morning," I say as she steps out of her truck.

When she steps out of her truck, her knees buckle and she almost falls. She's sheet-white and shaking.

"What happened?" I ask.

She just stands there unmoving, arms limp by her side, like she's shell-shocked. I wrap my arms around her. Her skin's cold, but slick with sweat. For a least a minute, the only movement is her body trembling. What starts as a slight rise of her shoulders, morphs into heaving sobs.

She pulls away from me and doubles over, barely able to catch her breath, and then she screams. Again and again at the top of her lungs.

Sounds carry across the water and the paddleboarders turn back towards our docks to see if help is needed. I wave them away.

She kicks her bucket full of bait and the salted eel spills over the grass. Daisy rushes to eat them. She grabs the Adirondack chair and throws it on its side. The arm cracks. Picking up a stack of bushel baskets, she hurls them into the yard. She stands tall, throws her head back, and stares into the sky. As she shakes her fists in the air like she's cursing God, one long, plaintive wail is dredged from the depths of her bowels. Daisy howls along with her.

She collapses on the ground. When she uses her shirttails to wipe her face, I notice blood on her shirt and hands. The hair rises on my neck. I'm afraid of the answer, but I have to ask.

"Did Mitch hurt you?"

She stands up slowly, like an arthritic woman, and shakes her head dolefully. "Not the way you think."

"Talk to me, Maggie. I'm here for you."

She caresses my cheek and gives me a weak smile. "You always been. Even when I didn't like you." She plods wearily to the porch steps and sits on the top one, slumping against the rail. Patting the space beside her, she invites me to sit.

Ruby scratches at the door but Maggie's too depleted to get up, so I let her out. She wedges herself between us, licking Maggie's face. Dogs can always sense their owner's distress. Maggie buries her face in Ruby's neck. Voice muffled by fur, she begins her story.

DEENA—June 29

Four more days have passed since I tried to get back into Sydney's trunk. Four more days for her to have discovered I snooped. I know I'm running out of time.

All I want to do is hunker down in my house, but I've pushed myself to keep my normal routine so as not to tip Sydney off. When I get to the pool, I see Tierney, looking lean and lovely, stretched out on a lounge chair. Helly's between her legs and they're playing peek-a-boo. She waves me over to an empty lounge beside her.

I drop my load and tubby body on the lounge and spread a towel out for Davey. I look around.

"Where's Sydney?" I ask.

"She'll be here in a few hours."

I imagine her at home opening the trunk and making her plans to get back at me. My anxiety flares.

"Is she working?" I ask.

"No, errands in Bakerstown."

I've got to grab the chance while I have it. My brain kicks into high gear. "Crap, I forgot to take my meds this morning. I'm going to have to run home and take them." I pick up Davey. "Will you watch my stuff?"

"Sure, I can watch him too if you want." She smiles at Davey.

Breaking and entering will be a lot easier without a child.

"You're a peach. I should be back in less than a half hour."

I stroll out of the pool, but as soon as I'm out of Tierney's vision, I sprint to the car. I need every minute. After stopping at

Bayside Foods to pick up a mixed bouquet of fresh flowers—for my cover story if I'm caught—I race the mile to Sydney's house. Dear God, I pray I can pull this off.

Nails's truck is in the driveway, but the bateau is gone. I park at the side of the house, grab the flowers, and walk up on the front porch to try the door. It's locked.

I hurry around the back and try the mudroom door—locked. I lift a few rocks and knick-knacks on the back porch looking for a hidden key. No luck, but there's a screen in the kitchen window. I reach up to test if I can open it from outside. It slides open an inch. I need something to stand on to lift it any higher.

A cooler is propped upside down to drain and dry. I slide it under the window and climb onto it. The screen slides open easily. Now, if I can haul my too-big butt up and in, I'll be in business.

I push up with my arms and try to swing my leg onto the sill. The cooler tips and I'm hanging. I drop back to the ground. Just as I reset the cooler, Ruby trots around the corner and barks. Shit. That means Nails is back. I hop up, pull down the screen, and put the cooler back where it was. I pick up the flowers and walk around to the front of the house.

"Hey." I'm trying to play it cool.

Nails walks across her yard to meet me. "Syd ain't around. You need somethin'?"

"Well, I wanted to surprise her with these." I hold up the flowers. "She's been so good to me. I thought it would be a nice thank-you."

"You want somethin' to put 'em in?" she asks, walking back to the wharf.

I follow her. Here goes nothing. "Well, I know Sydney has a vase in her cupboard. Can you let me in and I'll fix them for her?"

"Nah, but I got this." She adds water to an empty bucket.

Dammit! I'm not getting into her house today. I'm tempted to spill my guts and tell Nails everything I found. If I thought there was any chance she'd believe me, I would. Maybe I can at least get her thinking.

I reach for the bucket. "Yeah, okay. This will work."

Tearing open the cellophane, I arrange the flowers. Nails wheels a bushel of crabs up to her truck and throws them in the bed.

"You done for the day?" I ask.

"Yeah. Gotta clean up around here before I run out to JimBob's."

I'm not great at being sly, but if I want Nails to figure out what Sydney's up to, I've got to give it a go. "Speaking of JimBob, I saw one of his sister's old friends the other day."

"Where? At the crack house?" She unrolls the hose and pulls it down the dock to her boat.

"Want me to turn it on?" I yell.

She shakes her head no and hops on the bateau.

I walk down the dock in front of her boat. "No. Not at the crack house. She was working at the bistro in Bakerstown. It was Shelby. Do you remember her?"

Nails stops for a second. "Yeah, I just . . . Yeah, I remember her." She soaps up the bottom and sides of the boat.

"You wouldn't recognize her. She looks great, and is doing great. She was glad to run into us because she wanted to thank Sydney."

Nails scrubs the salt off every surface. "Uh-huh. Go turn the water on, will ya?"

Trying to keep my courage up, I take a big breath on my way up the dock. I turn the valve and the hose fills up with water. Okay, this is the big moment. Silently, I practice what I'm going to say while I walk back to her boat.

"Well, you know Sydney; always helping. I guess she heard money was tight for Shelby, so she took food for her and her dog to her trailer."

"Oh. Didn't Shelby thank her then?"

"I don't know. Apparently, a lot went down right after Sydney's visit. Shelby found a pair of Cammie's underwear in the trailer. That's why she beat the hell out of Cammie and ended up in jail."

Nails lets the hose hang over the side of the bateau and leans on the handle of the scrub brush. "Cammie's? JJ's the last person Cammie would screw."

"Yeah, I know." I slap confusion on my face. "That's the part that was weird, but Shelby found the underwear right after Sydney left, so . . ." I pause to let that sink in, then bring up Jake in hopes that Nails makes the connection. "I mean none of us are fans of Cammie after what she did to Jake, but she didn't deserve a beating."

Nails scrubs more. I can tell I got her thinking. "Why'd Shelby think they was Cammie's panties? Coulda been anyone's, right?"

"Except the panties Shelby found were monogrammed with a C."

"Sounds like Cammie, thinking her pussy's too special for regular panties." Nails rinses off the head of the scrub brush and hands it up to me. Then she rinses the boat. "You can put that brush up by the crab pens and turn the water off, okay?"

I do as she asks. She hops out of the boat and winds up the hose.

"You know," she says. "Even if Cammie was screwin' JJ, I don't see her leavin' her panties. She's slutty, but she ain't stupid."

I keep quiet and let her chew on that.

We both turn when we hear a car in the lane.

Nails frowns. "Christ, what's goin' on around here. It's like Grand Central Station today." She starts chopping eel.

The car pulls up close to the dock and Bev Simms steps out. "Hey there. How y'all doin' today?"

"Fine, and you?" I say.

Nails nods and keeps chopping.

"Hey Nails, I was wondering if you know where Whitey is. I haven't seen him for over a month."

Nails wipes her nose on her shoulder. "He told me you kicked him out."

She shrugs. "I did, but you know how it is. He always turns back up after a couple weeks, and I always take him back."

Something is picking at my brain.

193

Nails slides the cut bait into a bucket. "I do know how it is and maybe you shouldn't take his sorry ass back. Let him hit bottom."

Bev shakes her head. "I know, I know, but what can I say, I love him."

Whatever's worrying my mind is just under the surface, but I can't grab it.

"Well, last time I saw him he was drunk as a monkey. Syd had to drive him out the road to Hooper's Point."

Oh my God.

Sour acid comes up and I feel the blood drain from my face. I shiver from fear. I remember why the anchor necklace seemed familiar. It was always around Whitey's neck.

Now it's in Sydney's box of trophies and Whitey's missing.

MAGGIE—June 30

I putter out and float by the duck blind to give the crabs time to latch on. Air's already like molasses and the sun's only just comin' up. The clouds glow pink with patches of blue between 'em. I hear locusts, but not much else. It's quiet and I can think.

A lotta shit went down on Friday. Syd thinks I gotta "process" it. That's her favorite fucking word. But she's wrong. I'm done with Jed. Grindin' his prick under my boot was damn satisfying. I don't gotta waste no more time on him.

Now Mitch, I dunno. When I was trapped under Jed and heard the door open, I damn near burst with relief. For the first time in my life, my prayer was answered. But the help didn't come. That tore me up almost as much as the rape. When the door clicked shut, I stopped fighting. I had no more hope of stopping that son-of-a-bitch from rapin' me than stopping Pop from beatin' on Mom and us kids. So, I gave in. My lot in life was to be a punchin' bag.

But I ain't that no more. I found my spine and I ain't sure I can love a man without one.

A wake rocks the bateau when a speedboater zooms past me. Christ, I don't know how long I been drifting. I look around. The crick's full up with chicken neckers pretending to be watermen. One's fixin' to lay his line over mine. I run my bateau alongside his boat.

"You blind? Don't you see my line?" I point at my floats.

"Oh, I uh, didn't notice them." He stutters and gets all red in the face.

Course he didn't. I'm sure he didn't even look. Damn weekend boaters think they own the crick.

"Well go on." I shoo him away like a mosquito. "Go find your own goddamn lay. I got work to do."

He hightails it outta there like a scared rabbit and I smile. Swannee woulda got a kick outta that. His favorite thing was tormentin' chicken neckers.

After I hook the trotline and lay it over the ringer arm, I run the line, nettin' one crab after another without even thinking. Now crabbin' comes easy, but it ain't always been that way.

Damn if I could get the hang of steering the bateau and dippin' at the same time. The old man had no patience. If you missed a crab, you'd get a swat on the ass or a backhand across the face dependin' on how many whiskeys he slugged back. No kid of his was gonna suck at crabbin', so he made me keep going out.

To try and spare me the smacks, Swannee and Jake would take me out to practice. I always got the tiller stick confused. I'd push it front when I wanted to go right. Course it was opposite. Then I'd be so upset that I'd miss the crabs. I finally caught on. Then Pop just found something else to swat me for.

That's the thing. Even though Swannee and Jake couldn't protect me, or Momma, or even themselves from gettin' beat, at least they tried. Mitch didn't even try.

JAKE—July 1

I'm still dozing when Syd plops Helly in the bed beside me. I don't start work till noon today 'cause tonight we're having a shindig for the slip holders. I'll be cleanin' up till midnight.

Syd gives me a quick kiss. "I'm heading out."

I look at the clock. It's only eight. "Where you going so early?"

"I've got a million things to do to plan for the party. Take Helly to Maggie's when you leave. She's watching her today."

"I gotta leave at 11:30. Maggie won't be in by then."

She rolls her eyes at me. "Oh, for Pete's sake. You should know I don't leave things to chance. I already arranged it with Maggie. She worked yesterday so she could take care of Helly today. Tierney will come by and tend the pens. So, everything's set."

"Can Tierney do it alone? Don't she still need help?"

"Maggie will make sure she's doing it right. Seriously Jake, just worry about your event. You know I've got everything handled."

She blows me a kiss and heads out the door. It's good to see her in charge again. Motherhood rattled her and she's just now getting her footing.

After a half an hour of peek-a-boo my brain needs coffee and a grown up to talk to. I text Maggie, *Got coffee?* She texts back, *I'll make some. Come over.*

I dress Helly in a onesie, throw on a pair of jeans and a T-shirt, splash some water on my face, and head over.

"Trade." She hands me the coffee and takes Helly.

Maggie sits on one end of the couch with Helly on her lap, and I sit on the other end with Ruby on mine. Ruby don't want the baby being the only one to get attention.

"What's up stranger?" she asks. "We ain't said more than hi and goodbye in weeks."

"I know. Work keeps me hoppin'. That's why I didn't wanna be the boss. And I guess Syd told you I got another damn boat show comin' up."

"No. She didn't tell me nothin'. When you goin'?"

Damn, I wish Syd had already told her. I don't wanna be the one to break the news. "July nineteenth weekend."

Maggie's mouth drops open. "You won't be home for it?"

"No."

She looks at me like she can't believe it.

"I know Maggie. I ain't happy. Hard enough to deal with it together. But I can't get out of it. I tried."

Our tradition is to drink ourselves silly on July twentieth, the day Swannee killed Mom. I feel horrible that I ain't gonna be here. I tried to get the big boss to cover for me, but he's gonna be in Aruba. And now Maggie's hangdog eyes make me feel even worse.

I scrounge around in her fridge and pick out a leftover porkchop. Mom loved eating a cold porkchop between two slices of buttered white bread. "Can I have this?"

"Sure, but I'm outta bread."

"It's okay this way." I chomp into it.

"Syd said Tierney'll come by later and check the pens."

I rub my face. "Yeah. That's what she said."

Maggie stares at me. "What's that look for? Don't you like the kid?"

Maggie always could sniff out when something was up with me.

"She's not really a kid, you know. She's eighteen."

Maggie shifts a sleeping Helly to her other arm. "That's a kid in my book."

I finish my chop and wash my hands. "You want something to drink?"

She scrunches up her face and glares at me. "Don't try to change the subject. What's up with Tierney?"

I shrug my shoulders. "Nothing."

Maggie puffs up her chest and squares her shoulders like she's ready to box my ears. "Jake, don't even tell me you's been thinkin' with your dick again."

My face gets hot. I hate admitting I'm such an asshole.

"Jake! What the fuck!" Maggie yells and startles Helly. She rocks her and whispers, "Spit it out!"

"The night Syd came back from New York, she kinda caught me."

She grits her teeth. "Caught you what, Jake Swann? Caught you what?"

I hang my head, ashamed. Helly whimpers.

She rocks Helly and whisper yells, "Tell me you didn't fuck her."

"I didn't, but I woulda tried," I admit. "If Syd hadn't come in when she did."

"So, Sydney figured out what you was gonna do?"

"Yeah. It was pretty obvious."

Forgetting to whisper, she yells, "Jesus Christ, Jake! You're a moron! You'd throw away your perfect life for a blonde piece of ass."

I shake my head with shame. "I know. I know. And I almost did, but I won't. It woke me the fuck up. I ain't gonna mess with what I got. I think Syd forgives me. At least she let me back in our bed."

"You're damn lucky. I'm surprised she's givin' you a second chance."

"I know. That's why I don't get what's up with Tierney. Syd's teaching her to write and now she's teaching her to tend the pens. I don't get why she'd take her under her wing."

Maggie rolls her eyes, "Pfff. To keep her away from you, you dumbass."

I shake my head and sigh. "Yeah, I'm sure that's it. Don't be mad. I promise I'll get my shit together."

"You better. Blood's thick, but if you fuck up with Syd, I ain't sure which side I'll take."

Maggie lays Helly on a fluffy comforter on the floor and grabs herself a tea. She gives my shoulder a sisterly punch, letting me know we're all good, and plops back on the couch.

"Besides Jake, you know Syd. Always tryin' to fix shit. She ain't happy unless she's got a project. Tierney must be her new one."

I smile. Me and Maggie joke about Syd's help. Don't get me wrong, she's done a lot for us. A helluva lot. But sometimes she goes a little overboard.

"True," I agree. "Since Deena's healed up, she probably needed someone new to help."

Maggie guzzles her tea. "Hey, speakin' of Deena. Do you think Cammie'd ever fuck JJ?"

"Get real. Cammie's a slut, but even she ain't low enough to screw the guy that killed her husband. What's that got to do with Deena?"

She shakes her head and waves her hand. "Oh, nothing. Never mind."

SYDNEY—July 1

Food is ordered, supplies are bought. I'm ready for our July 4th picnic. Onto the next task on my to-do list—take down Jed Donnelly.

Maggie thinks since she confronted Jed, she'll be able to leave the past in the past. But I know she needs to see him held accountable. Fortunately, I have a plan.

Mitch has agreed to meet me at the Burger Barn in Jonesboro, about thirty minutes north of Rock Narrows, away from prying eyes. Burger Barn is just that—a country barn retrofitted to be a burger joint. The tables are covered in red-checked cloths and have wooden bench seats. Drinks come in mason jars and the condiments are kept in a stainless-steel milking pail. And a life size resin cow greets you at the ice cream bar. I arrive ten minutes early and choose a table in the corner.

My server wears overalls and a straw hat and greets me with, "Howdy! What can I get to wet your whistle?"

Let's hope the food rivals the gimmick.

"Unsweetened ice tea, and I'm waiting for a friend, so bring two menus please."

"Yes ma'am," she replies with her interpretation of a country-bumpkin accent.

Mitch plods through the door right on time. I wave him over. He slides onto the bench across from me. His hair's disheveled and his shirt buttons are in the wrong holes. He looks like he's been on a bender. Maggie told me he's a recovering alcoholic.

I'm direct. "Are you drinking again?"

"No," he croaks. "But I sure as hell want to."

Our perky hillbilly returns with my tea and menus. "Howdy there, partner! Can I get you some old-fashioned lemonade or maybe a root beer float?"

"Water." He doesn't look at her.

She pouts at his underwhelming response and mopes away.

"You're a mess."

"You're damn right I am. So much shit is rolling around in my brain, I don't even know which way is up." He puts his elbows on the table and lays his head in his hands.

The server, who I've dubbed Daisy Mae, brings his water. "Are you ready to order?" she asks, with substantially less animation.

"I'll have a classic burger with fries."

"Same," Mitch growls without lifting his head.

He takes a sip of water. "I'm so disgusted with myself." He shakes his head and stares at his lap.

"Then fix it."

He raises his head and looks at me with blood shot eyes. "How?"

"Make your father pay for his crimes. You didn't save Maggie then, but you can support her now. She needs to see your father held accountable for what he did to her."

"The shit will hit the fan when she outs him."

"She's not going to. After the publicity she endured surrounding her mom's murder, she's not willing to become fodder for the gossip mill again. She said confronting him was enough."

"Shouldn't you take her at her word?"

"Don't be obtuse," I snap. "Do you really think she's okay watching him continue to live his charmed life and being recognized for his positive impact on the community? Plus, do you think she's the only one? You know damn well there are other victims." I let that sink in for a minute before continuing. "Seventeen years ago, you skulked in a doorway and watched your father devastate a young girl's life. You shoved what you witnessed out of your mind and took every advantage he offered you, education, money, connections—"

"STOP!" He slams his fist on the table. The other patrons stare. He takes a sip of water to compose himself. "You don't know what it was like. I replayed that scene every day. I had nightmares—"

"Nightmares?" White hot anger boils up inside of me. "Poor little Mitch had nightmares? Maggie *lived* the nightmare. Don't you think she has flashbacks? Don't you think she smells his fetid breath and feels him tearing her apart? Am I supposed to feel sorry for you?"

"No. I don't deserve sympathy." His voice cracks. "I know that. You're right. I did take what he offered, every damn bit of it. I tried to drink and drug away my guilt, but I just made more bad choices. That's how I ended up in jail."

"And your dad—the man that ripped away Maggie's innocence and ruined your life—lives unrepentant. What are you going to do about it?"

"Tell me how to fix it. How do I make amends? I love Maggie. I'll do anything to get her to forgive me."

Our server arrives with our burgers and delivers them with speed. After Mitch's outburst I suspect she's wary of our table.

Mitch shoves his plate to the side and takes my hands in his. "I have been haunted by what I saw and have prayed every day for a chance to make amends. Maggie won't take my calls. Please help me. What can I do?"

I squeeze his hand, hard. "Find someone willing to talk. Find the other victims. Stop being that spineless boy and become the man you were meant to be."

His head sinks into his shoulders, exhausted before he even begins, but his eyes crackle with resolve. "I will."

MAGGIE—July 4

Jake got it wrong. Really wrong. I just spent four hours listening to Tierney jabber while me, her, and Syd got everything ready for our cookout. Tierney ain't lookin' to get in Jake's pants. Far from it. She's lookin' for what she never had—a daddy and a family to go with him.

Tierney couldn't get enough stories 'bout our childhood. I only told her the good stuff. No point in dredging up the bad. Sydney was into it too. I bet that's why Syd took Tierney under her wing, reminds her of herself—a lonely kid.

The first batch of crabs is steamed and everyone starts rollin' in. Deena brings a giant bowl of cucumber salad. Millie brings fried chicken. Syd cut up fresh peaches and strawberries, and bought the coleslaw and a Smith Island cake. I got plenty of crabs and two dozen ears of corn. There's so much food it covers one whole table.

Deena and Sydney drag some chairs around the two giant blankets they spread out on the yard for the kids. Tierney's on the blanket playing patty-cake with Davey, and Millie bounces Helly on her knee. I go to play horseshoes with Skip, Jake, and Harry. Even though I'm mad at him, Jake and me team up, and Skip and Harry are partners. My first throw the shoe clinks against the peg and bounces off. My second throw's a ringer. We beat 'em in no time.

I hand Jake my horseshoes. "I gotta get another pot of crabs on. Get yourself a new partner."

He holds the shoes in the air. "Takers?"

"Me!" Tierney jumps up from the blanket. "Will you teach me?"

Jake kinda squirms. "Yeah, okay."

Me and Deena both look at Sydney. She's cool as a cucumber.

"I bet you'll do great," Sydney says.

After I get another pot of crabs cookin', I grab a beer and sit down with the women.

"I've been teaching Tierney how to tend the pens," Sydney says to Millie and Deena.

Millie laughs. "I hope she picks it up quicker than you. I remember you telling me how you flung crabs all around the deck the first time you tried it."

Sydney smiles. "It's true. I was awful, but Tierney's a natural, like Jake. She's actually already good enough to do it on her own. I might even ask her to stay with me when Jake has to go the boat show on the nineteenth. Trying to take care of an infant and tend the pens alone is exhausting."

"Infants in general are exhausting," Deena says.

Must be stressful too; lately every time I see Deena, she's wound tight, and her knee ain't stopped boucin' since she sat down.

Metal hits metal and Tierney cheers. "I got a ringer! I got a ringer!" She runs over and gives Jake a hug. "You're a great teacher."

Jake turns red and Syd's eyes turn black.

"Finish up," Sydney yells to the players. "It's time to eat."

Sydney puts vinegar and Old Bay on the table and makes sure everything's set. I tong the hot crabs onto a big tray. Deena comes over to help me.

"Nails, I'll hold the tray. You fill it up." The tray jiggles in her jittery hands. She leans in closer to me and whispers, "Why does Sydney put up with that?"

"With what?" I know what she means, but I ain't gonna add fuel to the fire.

"That girl's sniffing around Jake like a bitch in heat."

I shrug. "I don't think it's like that, Deena. But even if it is, I know better than to mix in someone's marriage. I sure as shit didn't want no one in mine."

"Ready?" Syd yells to me.

"Yep." I carry the tray of crabs over and dump it in the center of the table.

The Old Bay is strong and my mouth waters. Deena brings the corn and Syd makes sure everybody got a beer. We all dig in. The food's so good there's more eatin' than talkin'.

Around three we take a break. The men and Tierney play horseshoes again, and the rest of us move our chairs under the locust tree. The sun's beat down on us all day and we need some shade. Sydney feeds Helly, Millie and Deena get a piece of cake, and I grab myself another beer.

Deena shares her piece with Davey. "This is so good. Where'd you get it?" she asks Sydney.

"Mrs. Ginder, of course."

"Hers is the best," Millie says.

Helly fusses on Syd's lap. Syd pats her bottom and groans. "She's wet. Again." She goes in the house to change her.

"Mrs. Ginder lives by Mrs. Ennis, right?" Deena asks me and Millie.

"Yeah," Millie says.

Deena squeezes her eyebrows together. "You know, I was surprised I haven't heard more about it, but did you know Mrs. Ennis swears she saw a woman coming out of Eddie's house the night he died?"

Millie puts her hand on her heart. "Really? I haven't heard a thing. Who told you that?"

"Miss Mary. She overheard the Sheriff's phone call about it. The police were even considering whether or not his death was accidental."

Millie's eyes bug out and she leans towards Deena. "What does it mean?"

Great, now this crazy rumor'll be all over town.

"It means he's dead." I say, pissed they're bringin' this shit up again. "Find somethin' else to gossip about."

I walk away before I get mean. Syd's back and settles Helly in the playpen. I walk over to them.

She pats Helly's back. "I think she'll take a nap. Damn, I forgot her pacifier in the nursery."

"I'll get it."

"Great, thanks. It's probably on the changing table."

I take my time, to let myself cool off. I could use a tea. I grab an Arizona out of Syd's fridge—she always keeps a few for me—and lean back against the counter. Sydney bought new tea towels when she got the fridge. One hangs on the stove handle, folded in thirds, and even back to front.

I remember my bathroom towels, and again I flash to Eddie's kitchen. I know Eddie ain't the one who folded that tea towel and hung it on the stove, and now I hear Mrs. Ennis seen a woman in his house the night he kicked it.

"Goddamn it!" I say out loud. I grab the tea towel and throw it on the counter. That's why I hate gossip. It makes your mind spin in ways it shouldn't spin.

DEENA—July 4

Dammit! Nails storms off before I can bring up Whitey. I need to plant the seed and pray she makes the connection. I can't be the only one who knows how dangerous Sydney is.

When I try to talk about it with Skip, he looks at me with pity. I know he thinks I'm losing it. If I'm not careful, I think he'll have me committed. That's why I won't share my suspicions with Nails outright. I need her to reach the same conclusion on her own.

After settling Helly in the playpen, Sydney rejoins our circle.

"What pissed Maggie off?" She stares at me as she says it.

Crossing my arms, I tuck my fists into my armpit, so no one sees me shaking. I force a chuckle. "Oh, just me putting my foot in my mouth again."

"Don't mess with my family," Syd says with a cheesy mobster accent.

Millie laughs. I don't. Sydney delivered the message like a joke, but I know it's anything but. My stomach rolls with nausea and I feel lightheaded. If I'm going to come out of this alive, I need to return her mementos to their original place and get proof of what she's done. Today. Before she figures out I'm onto her, and I become another trophy in her trunk.

I pop two Benadryl to settle my nerves. Tierney joins Millie, Sydney, and me under the locust tree, and Nails is back outside, playing horseshoes with the men. It's clear the cookout is winding down. If I don't get to the trunk soon, I won't have a chance.

I take Davey down to the shoreline to dip his toes in the water. The boats coming by make gentle waves. He giggles each time one rolls over his toes. Ruby barks at Sydney, begging her to throw a stick into the water. My heart hammers in my chest as Sydney walks over to me and Davey.

She tucks a stray curl behind her ear and rolls her eyes. "This dog."

She wings the stick into the waves. Ruby bounds after it. Davey giggles more.

"His laugh is adorable," she says.

I paste on a big smile and swallow the stomach acid rising in my throat. "It is. Always makes me smile."

She looks me up and down. Fear chills my insides.

"Deena, you're really making progress on dropping the baby-weight, aren't you?"

Yeah. That's what living in terror will do for you.

I hope my smile is convincing. "Sure am! Glad you noticed."

I shiver thinking about what else this sociopath has noticed. *I* have got to stop her. There's no one coming to rescue me. I suck in a deep breath and dive in.

"Sydney, would you mind staying with Davey for a few minutes?" I rub my belly. "The crabs have my stomach torn up; I need to hit the bathroom."

Her smile looks evil as she takes Davey's hand. "My pleasure."

The hairs on my neck raise. Is it safe to leave Davey with her? I almost change my mind, but I'm pretty sure she won't do anything to hurt him in front of everybody, and I know this is my only hope to save myself.

"Thanks, back in a few."

"No hurry. I'll take care of him."

I wince at her choice of words. That's what I'm afraid of.

I suck in courage, and walk into her house, peeking in each room to make sure no one else is there. Sliding my handmade picks out of my pocket, I hurry to her room, praying I'm able to open the lock fast—I've been practicing every day. I close the bedroom door so if anyone comes in the house they won't see me, and slide open the closet door.

I freeze in fear. The trunk is gone.

I have to find it. I look under her bed—nothing. I fly through the house, searching every closet, opening cupboard doors, looking under couches, and the shelves of the basement. No trunk. God protect me, Sydney knows! She knows—and she's got Davey.

I sprint out of the house terrified of what she might have done. She's on the shoreline and he's giggling when the water hits his toes. I try to control my breathing. Sydney turns. Her eyes shine black. She sees my shaking and a scary smile curls the corners of her lips. Slowly, she lifts Davey, taunting me. My gut clenches and I stifle a scream.

Her arms wrap tight around him. Too tight. He squirms. Tears flood my eyes and slide down my cheeks. She walks towards me. Cold sweat coats my healed skin; skin that I'm sure she burned off me.

"Are you okay?" I hear the cutting sarcasm in her voice.

My chest is tight and I'm struggling to breathe. I can't get any words out.

"Let me get you some water." She runs into her house, with Davey still on her hip.

Panting, I follow. I can't let Davey alone with her. She meets me on the porch with a glass of water. I start to take a sip, but stop. It's probably poisoned. I let the glass fall out of my hand. It shatters and the water splashes on our feet and the porch. I'm gasping for breath now.

"Skip," Sydney yells. "Come quick."

She runs back in the house and gets a paper bag. "Here." She hands it to me. "I think you're hyperventilating. Breathe into this."

"What happened?" Skip asks, when he sees me breathing into the bag.

"She's having a panic attack."

He lays his hand on my back. "What the hell, Deena? What are you panicking about?"

"We . . . need . . . to . . .go," I force out between breaths.

"Take her home, Skip," Sydney says. "I'll keep Davey and bring him later."

"NO!" I yell.

"Okay, okay." She pats my back and I flinch at her touch. "I'll gather his things and strap him in the seat. Don't worry. I've had panic attacks before. It'll pass. Just keep breathing slow and easy."

Skip walks me to the car, but I won't get in until Davey is strapped in his seat.

"Sorry," Skip mumbles.

"Not a big deal," Sydney says. "Call me if you need anything."

Only when I'm at home, locked in my bedroom, under the covers, with Davey on my lap, can I catch my breath.

Later that night, after Skip's been asleep for hours, I rip a piece of paper from the tablet on my desk and write, *If I am hurt or killed, it was Sydney.* I fold the paper and slip it in our fire box in the closet, between the pages of my will.

SYDNEY—July 5

As I scroll through headlines trying to find a new story, my mind keeps returning to Deena's behavior yesterday. Skip told Jake he's going to insist she see a doctor. He thinks her anxiety has worsened dramatically since her chemical burn. I think it's something else.

I saw absolute fear in her face when she flew out of my house, and Maggie mentioned Deena heard the police are looking into Eddie's death. I think Deena's getting suspicious. And I think she may have been the one to ransack my trunk.

I'm so disappointed. I thought the sunscreen incident had finally rid her of her incivility. We were getting along so well. I sigh out my frustration and—again—add Deena to my to-be-dealt-with list.

In light of this new development, I might have let Tierney off the hook—at least until I'm certain if it was she or Deena who broke my trust—but Tierney is shameless. She is relentlessly insinuating herself into our lives. I've worked too hard, carefully cultivating each relationship, to create my perfect life. No snot-nosed brat is going to push her way in. Whether or not she searched my trunk, her time is limited.

I turn off my computer and saunter outside. Tierney is stretched out on a blanket reading a story to Helly. I grab a lawn chair and join them.

"What are you reading?"

"Ten Little Fingers. Ten Little Toes. She loves the part where I wiggle her pinky toe."

I tuck a frizzy curl behind my ear. "You're really good with her."

"I just love her so much. She's going to have the best life growing up here on the water. Catching crabs, tending the pens, having a mom, a dad, and an aunt spoiling her."

Her covetousness is apparent. Time to set the wheels in motion.

I smile. "I have a big favor to ask, but since you seem to love it here maybe you won't mind too much."

She sits up and crosses her legs. "I'm sure I won't mind at all. What's the favor?"

"Would you stay with me the weekend of the 19th, while Jake is at the boat show? Between tending the pens and Helly's care, I get no sleep if I have to do it all myself."

She claps her hands together. "Are you kidding me? I'd love it! Yay! Sleepover!"

More like game over.

DEENA—July 7

They found Whitey's body. Bev went looking for him. When she found all his stuff on his friend's boat, she called the cops. The news said they recovered his body from the bottom of the bay, right beside the dock. His rubber boots filled with water, anchoring him in place.

Once I realized the anchor necklace belonged to Whitey, I knew he'd be found dead. And I know Sydney did it, but the cops ruled it accidental—just like Eddie—and I can't do a damn thing about it.

I'm terrified to leave the house and had to call in sick every day this week. Every time I hear a car on the road I freeze until it passes. I check the locks every ten minutes, and have chairs propped under the doorknobs. I've only dozed a few hours a night, and as for eating and drinking, unless it's in a sealed bottle or box, I won't. I'm depressed, exhausted, and I feel like I'm losing my mind.

Skip and the doctor he insisted I go to think so too. I'm taking the Xanax like a good patient, but I don't think it's working. The fear is relentless.

Davey cries to go out to play. I don't want to take him out, I really don't, but he's been shut up inside with me for three days. I reason with myself. My yard should be safe—unless Sydney buried a mine. I shake my head to clear it. That's ridiculous. Where would she get a mine? A copperhead snake would be more likely.

I make Davey wait in the doorway, while I sweep the yard with a broom to scare anything out of the grass. A cricket hops and I fall backwards. Davey laughs. My chest feels tight, like it did at the picnic. I try to do what the doctor said and breathe slow and deep.

"Momma, pway," Davey yells from the house.

"Okay honey, just wait a minute."

I finish my check of the yard. I use the handle end of the broom and dig it around the sand in Davey's turtle sandbox. It looks clear.

I carry Davey down the porch stairs. He toddles over and climbs into his sandbox. Using his chubby hands, he buries his toes, then wiggles them until they pop up through the sand.

"Wittle piggy," he says every time they pop up.

I move my lawn chair beside him and keep the broom across my lap. Lifting my face to the sun, I try to calm down. My breathing slows and my chest feels less tight. Davey's laugh soothes my nerves.

My phone vibrates to notify me I got a message. It's probably Skip checking on me. He'll be glad to know I'm outside. I slide the phone from my back pocket. It's not from Skip. It's from Sydney.

My body tingles with fear and my throat feels like it's closing. I swipe to open the message. *Your search is over.*

I snatch Davey out of the sandbox and run into the house. He lets out a wail, mad and scared that I grabbed him so fast. I lock the back door and slide a chair back under it. My phone vibrates again as I'm checking all the locks. Davey squirms under my arm, but I hold him tight. Only when me and Davey are locked in my bedroom do I open the second message.

It's a photo. My fingers shake when I tap to open it. The circle on my phone spins round and round, trying to download it. I realize I've stopped breathing and take in a gulp of air.

Davey yells, "Pway, pway, pway."

I crack the bedroom door, peeking into the living room.

"Pway, pway, pway." Davey is on his belly, kicking his feet.

I tiptoe out, grab the tub of blocks, and zip back into the bedroom. After relocking the door, I dump the whole container on the floor. Davey wipes his tears and stacks blocks.

My phone vibrates again with a third message from Sydney. *Found it in a gift shop in Bakerstown. I'll give it to you next time I see you.* I tap the photo file on my phone again. This time it opens. It's a picture of a little brown puppy head with a silky blue blanket body, an exact copy of Davey's lovey.

A shiver runs down my spine. To anyone else I'm sure this would look like a sweet gesture, but to me it feels like a threat.

JAKE—July 8

I throw my lunch in my truck and am getting ready to hop in and head to work when Bev's seen-better-days Hyundai pulls into the lane. Poor woman. I bet she's still in shock that Whitey's dead. I know I was when I seen it on yesterday's local news.

I lean against my car door and wait. She parks beside me and eases her body out like everything hurts. Her hair's skinned back in a ponytail and her eyes are red and damn near puffed shut.

"Hey Bev." I walk over and give her a hug.

She holds on like I'm a life preserver. "Oh Jake, it's all my fault. I shouldna kicked him out. I'm so sorry."

Her body bucks with her sobs and I keep huggin' her till she's cried out. Sydney hears the commotion and comes out with a cup of coffee and a box of tissues.

I guide Bev up to our porch and settle her in a rocker.

She blows her nose and takes the coffee from Sydney. "Thanks."

I kneel down in front of her. "Bev, it ain't your fault. Whitey was pushin' it, drinkin' all the time. It was bound to happen. Ain't nothing you did wrong."

"The last words I said to him were 'don't come back.' How can I live with that?"

Her tears start up again.

I pat her knee. Sydney sits the coffee on the table and moves in front of me to wrap her arms around Bev. "It's okay. He knows you loved him."

"I was gonna take him back. I always did."

Syd pats her back. "Shh, shh. He knew that, Bev. He told me the night you kicked him out that you just needed some time to cool off."

Bev blinks her eyes. "He did?"

Sydney nods and hands her another tissue. "He did. On the way to Hooper's Point, he couldn't stop talking about you. Bev, he loved you so much. He was sorry he kept pushing you; the alcohol just had a hold of him. But he knew you still loved him too."

Bev nods. "I do. I did."

Syd hands Bev the coffee and she takes a big swallow. She sniffs. "Sorry for all the tears. I came here for a favor. I hate to ask you, Jake. I really do. But I don't got enough money to bury him."

I give her shoulder a squeeze. "Don't worry 'bout that. I got it covered."

She hangs her head and stares at her feet. "I'll pay you back. It might take me a while, but I will."

"You ain't paying me back. He's family."

Sydney takes Bev's hand. "Absolutely. And, if you'd like, I'll go with you to help make all the arrangements."

I mouth, "Thank you," to Syd. I joke about Syd's constant helping, but I really am lucky to have such a caring, generous wife.

Bev wipes her eyes. "Would you? I really didn't wanna do it alone. Thank you."

Syd smiles at her. "Of course, that's what family's for. Does tomorrow morning work for you?"

Bev nods. "Yep."

"Okay, I'll pick you up at eight," Sydney says.

Bev sets the half-empty mug on the table and stands. "I'll get out of your way. I know you gotta get to work."

"Come by any time," I say.

She shoots us a sad smile. "Thank you both so much. I don't know what I'd do without you. I'll see you tomorrow, Sydney."

Once Bev's car is out the driveway, I say to Syd, "Did Whitey really say all that stuff when you ran him out the road?"

She sighs and shakes her head. "No. He was beyond drunk. He passed out and drooled all over my window. I really struggled to get him into the boat. I just wanted to make Bev feel better."

I kiss her. "Thank you."

"For what?"

"For being so good to my family."

"Always."

She stands on her tiptoes and kisses me and I wrap my beautiful, kind wife in my arms.

MAGGIE—July 9

I'm packing my cooler and see movement down by the wharf. Last time someone was creepin' around in the dark it was Whitey, poor dead bastard.

I look out the front window. It's Mitch. Shit. I grab my stuff and me and Ruby walk down to the dock.

Mitch holds out an egg sandwich and a bottle of Arizona tea. "Peace offering. Can we talk?"

Night is changing to purple.

"I gotta lay my line before sun up." I motion to the bateau. "Ride along if you want."

Mitch follows me down the dock. Me and Ruby jump in the boat, but Mitch damn near falls in. He ain't got sea legs, that's for sure. He sits on the bench seat and I cast off the lines.

About half way out I take the egg sandwich and say, "Okay, talk."

"Maggie, the Mitch that walked away was a weak, scared, privileged little boy, shaking in the shadow of his all-powerful father. I'm not that boy anymore. And I'm not the damaged, ashamed drunk that killed Amy. I've grown into a strong man. One who will never again cower to a thug. I'm a stand-up guy who accepts responsibility for his mistakes and makes amends. And I'm a man who is healthy enough to love—myself and others—specifically you. Will you give me a chance to prove that to you?"

I lay my trotline up on the ringer arm and let it feed out. I'm glad it's still too dark to see his face. Makes it easier to say what I got to say.

"Mitch, seventeen years ago, when that door clicked behind you, it tore me up more than what your old man was doin' to me. I couldn't fucking believe that anyone could walk away without helping. I lost all hope and I lost all trust in people."

I pull the line off the ringer and the weight sinks it to the bottom. Mitch sits on the bench with his face in his hands. I feel kinda bad for him, but I gotta tell it like it is.

I crumple the sandwich wrapper and shove it in my pocket. "I been makin' headway. I sure as hell ain't as closed off as I used to be, and I found some people that I know I can trust. But, I ain't sure you're one of them. You let me down big time. I know you say you changed and I know *you* believe it, but *I* gotta believe it or I can't see you."

He nods, face still in his hands. I run the bateau back into the wharf to give the crabs time to latch on. Once I'm tied up, I jump out and offer Mitch my hand to help him up to the dock. He grabs it and holds on longer than he needs to.

He looks me dead in the eye. "I will prove it to you, Maggie Swann, because I love you."

*****

A few hours later, I run back in to let Ruby piss. Tierney's waitin' on the dock to throw me a line.

"Morning!"

She's too damn chipper.

I tie off the bateau. "Why are you here?"

"Sydney is helping Bev with Whitey's funeral arrangements today, so I'm tending the pens for her. I'm really sorry about your cousin."

"Yeah. It sucks." I hop off the boat and walk towards the house to get another tea. It's only nine, and I'm already sweatin' my ass off.

Tierney follows me up. "Are you going back out?"

"Yeah. Soon as I grab more tea."

"Can I go with you?" She holds crossed fingers beside her face.

Don't know why I got a soft spot for this kid.

"Yeah, all right. Go grab yourself a drink and a hat. But, make it snappy. Don't need the crabs eatin' up all the bait."

She hauls ass into Syd and Jake's house. By the time I grab more tea and round up Ruby, Tierney's already sittin' on my bateau.

"I'm so excited. Thanks for letting me crab with you."

"Yeah, well for now you're just gonna watch. I got a feelin' there's some fat, black ones on the line and I can't afford to have ya miss 'em."

My hunch was right. The line hangs low, heavy with crabs. I put the dip net in my right hand and steer with the left. Four baits in a row got number ones on 'em. After the fourth dip, I flick the net and toss the crabs into the basket. Every time you throw one in, all the crabs get riled up and scrabble around tryin' to climb over each other to escape.

Tierney scoots to the far side of the bench. "Can they get out?"

"Nah, that's why I stack a bottomless bushel basket inside the one I'm fillin', so it's too high for them to climb out."

She's still jumpy. "Are you sure?"

"Yeah, I'm sure. They'll scratch around a little and then settle down."

She keeps her arms in tight, anyhow. "How can you tell when a crab's on the line?"

I can't look at her; this is a great run and I gotta keep my eyes on the line. I'm usin' bull lip for bait. Thought I'd give it a try. Snooks swears by it. It's cheaper than eel and he said it holds up just as good. So far, he's right.

"The line stays deeper. You gotta dip before the crab's at the surface or he'll drop off. Stand behind me and watch."

Three baits pass, floatin' high. The fourth one's sunk lower. I point my chin at the line. "See, line's heavy and hangs low. We got one comin' up. The sixth bait got a sook. I net her, and toss her into a plastic tub.

"Why did you do that?" Tierney asks.

"It's a sook—a female. I ain't gonna keep her. First off you don't get much for 'em, and if we catch up all the breeders how they ever gonna repopulate? If you ask me, it's a dumb-ass waterman who keeps a sook."

"Well, if you're not going to keep her, why did you put her in that tub?"

"When the tub's full up I'll run 'em up the crick and dump 'em away from my lay. If I toss her overboard now, she'll end up back on my line. Sooks'll strip a line of bait in no time."

She squeezes her eyebrows together. "How can you tell it's a sook?"

This is why I hate teachin' people. Too many fucking questions.

"Sooks got red tips to her claws. Jimmies, males, got blue tips. And I saw her belly. Sooks got aprons shaped like a bell and jimmies got aprons shaped like a dick."

Tierney looks in the basket at the jimmies and in the tub at the sook. "Ok, yeah. I see what you mean. How did you learn all of this? It seems like so much."

"Been doin' it since I can remember. Pop had us out here pretty much since we could walk. There's a picture of me on the bateau in diapers."

She smiles. "Yeah, I saw it. So cute."

I'm pretty sure that photo is in the end table beside my bed. "When did you see it?"

Her cheeks turn red and she looks like a puppy who got caught pissin' in the house. "I, um . . ." She rubs her eyebrow. "I must've seen it at Sydney's. She has a bunch of photos from when you, Jake, and Swannee were little."

Maybe Syd made a copy of it, but then why does Tierney look so guilty? I get a funny feelin' in my gut. What if all her questions ain't so innocent? What's this kid up to?

JAKE—July 9

I cut outta work a little early. Syd's CRV ain't in the driveway when I get home. I guess she ain't back from helping Bev. Tierney's on the porch in shorts so short it makes me uncomfortable. Her tits jiggle when she jogs over to my truck.

"I was really sorry to hear about your cousin."

I shake my head. "Yeah. Thanks. You just never know how much time you got left." I open the passenger side and slide out a case of Natural Light.

"Should I grab the food?"

I got take-out from Millie's. "Yeah, thanks."

A slice of tan belly shows when Tierney reaches for the bag. She runs up on the porch and opens the front door for me.

I set the case on the counter and unload the cans into the fridge. "Everything go all right today with the pens?"

Her smile lights up her face. "Not a hitch. Maggie took me out trotlining. That was so fun! I really had a blast. I can't wait for the weekend of the nineteenth!"

I take the food from her and shove it on the top shelf. "Oh? Why's that?"

"Sleepover with Sydney and Helly! While you're at the boat show."

"Oh. First I heard of it."

"Yeah, I'm going to tend the pens through the night and help Sydney with Helly during the day. Sydney said it's just too much to do alone."

I don't know what the fuck to make of that.

"Well, glad you can help her out."

"Me too!" She twirls a strand of blonde hair around her finger. "So, I just finished checking the pens before you pulled in. Do you want me to stay to do it again or do you think Sydney will be back in time?"

There's no way in hell I want to be alone in my house with Tierney for two hours.

"Nope. All good. If she don't get home in time, I'll do it." I slide two fifties outta my pocket and hand them to her.

She waves them away. "Oh, no. I didn't expect to get paid."

I shove 'em towards her. "Take 'em. You're soon to be a broke college kid."

She tilts her head and smiles. "True. Okay. Thanks."

I try not to watch her slide 'em into the back pocket of her tight shorts. "Thanks, Jake. I'll see ya!"

Once she's out the driveway, I splash cold water on my face and crack open a beer. Me and Daisy kick back on the front porch until I hear Maggie's bateau putter in. I head over to help. She swings three baskets of crabs on the dock, and I wheel the cart down to them.

"Hey."

"Hey."

She wipes her forehead with her arm. "Some shit about Whitey."

We haven't seen each other since we heard the news.

"Yeah. Syd's with Bev today. Picking out a coffin and shit."

"Yeah. That's what Tierney said. How's Bev taking it?"

I shake my head. "Not good. Blames herself 'cause she kicked him out."

She wipes her sweaty forehead with her arm. "How the hell did he drown? He's a good swimmer."

"Fell off the dock and split his head open on the cleat. Knocked him out cold. Guess he never had a chance."

"Shit." She jumps up on the dock.

I push the cart to the back of her truck. "So I hear you took Tierney crabbin'."

She crawls up in the bed and I hand her the full baskets of crabs. She slides 'em to the back, jumps down, and slams the tailgate shut. "Yeah. She leave already?"

"Yeah. When I got home. I'm keepin' my distance like I promised."

She hops off the back of her pick-up. "Good thing. Hey, while I'm thinkin' of it, do you know if Sydney made copies of my photos. You know the one's when we were kids?

I shrug. "Probably. I know Syd wants to make a photo album of all our old photos for Helly. Why?"

She rubs her face. "No reason. Forget it. Not important." She whistles for Ruby. "You wanna ride out the road with me? We can stop at Dollie's for a cold one."

"Nah, I picked up take-out for when Sydney gets back."

Maggie opens the passenger door and Ruby hops in the truck. "Sounds good. Make sure you keep your ass outta the doghouse." She wags her finger at me. "Don't do nothin' stupid."

I salute her. She flips me the bird.

MAGGIE—July 10

I overslept and am barely back in the house from layin' the line when little Robby Kendall wings the Keene County News onto the porch. I check the clock—six. He's early. He took on the route after his old man's leg got crushed under a dry-docked boat that no-good drunk, Buster Miggins, didn't block right. Robby runs the route in the morning and bags groceries after school. Hard worker, that kid.

I make coffee, let Ruby out to piss, and grab the paper. Ruby scratches to be let back in before I got the paper spread out on the table. She wants food. I feed her, pour myself a cup of coffee, and sit down to see what gossip's fillin' the pages.

Another kid overdosed. Why the hell can't they just booze it up? At least you pass out before you bite it. Marni Matheson graduated from University of Maryland. First of her family to go to college. Snooks got picked up on a DUI. I flip the page.

Holy fuck! I jump and knock the mug off the table. The crash scares Ruby and she yelps. I grab my chest. I can't fucking breathe. Page five knocked the wind right outta me. Christ, I don't know if I should laugh, cry, or cuss.

The top half of the page got a picture of Jed Donnelly lookin' sleazy and the bottom is filled with a letter from Mitch.

Dear Keene County residents,
My father, Jed Donnelly, is a serial rapist and I have finally realized that if I remain silent, I am complicit. I can no longer live

with the shame of my inaction, and I can no longer let his brutality go unpunished.

Seventeen years ago, I witnessed him savagely raping a young woman. He showed her no mercy, laughing at her cries of pain and terror. I am utterly humiliated to admit—because of my fear of his power—I walked away without trying to intervene. I know that no amount of repentance will absolve me of that crime.

To my horror, in the past few weeks I have also discovered three other victims of his barbarism. All four of these women rightly fear the repercussions if they talk. After all, as everyone in Keene County knows, my father is a powerful man. None of these women want to subject themselves to the scrutiny inherent with reporting his crime. I can't blame them; they have been violated enough.

So, it falls to us, me and you, to make him pay. We have a responsibility to hold him accountable. We must demand his immediate removal as CEO of Donnelly Telecommunications and boycott the company if it does not act. We must strip him of all power and status in our community. Because of the statute of limitations, we cannot jail him, but we can shun him. We can revoke his country club and chamber of commerce memberships. We can ban him from dinner parties, charity galas, and cigar-club gatherings. We can turn our backs when we see him on the street. We can encourage and support any additional victims who would like to come forward, and we can send healing prayers to the women who suffer in silence.

Jed Donnelly is not untouchable. The real power lies with all of us. Don't let this monster walk amongst us unscathed. Help me mete out his punishment.

Sincerely, ~Mitch Donnelly

Wow. Just fucking wow.

I don't got a clue what to do with that. I would love to be a fly on the wall when Jed gets a look at this. That miserable prick won't be able to show his face nowhere. He deserves to get called out, but knowing he hurt more girls makes me wanna puke. I ain't surprised, just sad.

And then there's Mitch. What am I gonna do about him? Payin' to get his letter published took a lot of guts. He filleted himself open to the whole damn county. A man with no backbone don't do somethin' like that.

Sydney beats on my door, still in her pajamas. She plasters the paper on the window and yells, "Justice!"

I open the door and pull her in the house. Don't need nosy neighbors connecting any dots.

"Shush up. You're gonna wake the dead with your squawks."

She bounces around like the Energizer bunny. "Did you read this? Aren't you thrilled? Can you imagine what the fallout is going to be? He's done."

"He hurt more girls. What's to be thrilled about?" Her excitement seems too much. I pick up the pieces of the broken mug. Ruby's lappin' up the coffee.

"What happened?"

"Dropped a mug."

She gets a wet rag from the sink and scrubs the coffee off the edge of the rug. "You're right, of course it's horrible there were more women, but today it stops. In my book that's a win."

"Better not be a book 'bout this." I'm half-sarcastic, half-serious.

She rolls her eyes. "You know what I mean."

After rinsing out the rag, she throws it in the sink. I pour us both a cup of coffee.

She plops down in the seat across from me. "So, are you going to make up with Mitch? I mean this was a huge gesture. There's not much more he could do to make it up to you."

"I hope he ain't done it to get back with me. I hope he done it 'cause it was the right thing to do."

"Can't it be both?"

I shrug. The sun's just starting to come up. I can't wait to get out on the crick.

"Are you going to call him?" Syd pushes.

"Drink up. I gotta get to work."

She means well, but I don't need her meddlin' today. I slug back my coffee and pack my lunch for the day.

She crosses her arms. "Maggie, we need to talk about this."

"*You* need to talk about this. I don't."

SYDNEY—July 10

Though I'm extremely pleased my meeting with Mitch resulted in Jed Donnelly paying for his brutality, I thought Maggie would be more appreciative of Mitch's grand gesture. I do hope she'll forgive him. With a little more of my expert guidance, I think he could be a good match for her.

Excited to hear how the rest of the Rock Narrows community is taking the bombshell revelation about Jed, I head to Millie's Place. The diner crackles with chatter. Every booth is occupied. I take the one empty stool and slide Helly's carrier behind the counter, tucking her out of Millie's way. Millie's wearing her signature rooster apron, a bright yellow sweatshirt, and her mom jeans. She's harried. Sweat beads around her hairline and she's running in circles.

"Oh honey, I'll get to ya as soon as I can. It's been a tornado since the paper came out."

I wave her away. "No worries. I have time."

Like everyone else, I came to hear the scuttlebutt.

"He always did think his shit don't stink. Never did like him." Mick said to Snooks.

"Goes to show what money'll do for you," Snooks grumbles. "Hell, I might get jail time for havin' one too many beers and this cock-sucker's been hurtin' girls and's still walkin' free."

"I cancelled my cable first thing this morning," Doris preens. "I had to wait over thirty minutes to get through because they were getting so many calls."

"I cancelled cable, internet, and my phone service, and wrote a letter to the board of Donnelly," Rhonda says, one-upping Doris.

My chest swells with pride at what I've accomplished. I can't take the trauma from Maggie, but I can make her victimizer bear the consequences of his heinous crimes.

Millie pours me a cup of coffee. "Hi sugar. You want the usual?"

"Please. Quite the commotion around here."

"Ain't been nothing this big since Swannee shot Helen. Dear Lord, to find out the biggest employer in this county is a rapist is just, just . . . jaw-dropping."

Ned mumbles under his breath on the stool beside me. "I guess ain't no one gonna talk about the elephant in the room. Seems mighty suspicious that Jed's son is outing him now. Now that he's 'rehabilitated' hisself and is a good age to take over as president of Donnelly. Damn convenient none of the women wanna speak up. All comes down to Mitch's word. Something smells rotten to me."

"Ned, I swear if you met Jesus himself, you'd doubt his motives," Millie says, clearly annoyed at his comments. She turns her back on him and goes to place my order with Harry.

"What do you think, girlie? You ain't dumb."

Swallowing my irritation at being called girlie, I answer loudly enough that anyone with doubts is certain to hear. "I am quite certain that if Mitch was trying to finagle his way into Jed's position, he would not have disclosed his culpability. Yes, Mitch's letter outs Jed's monstrous behavior and leaves the company no choice but to remove him. But it also reveals Mitch's failings. Certainly, no board would replace a rapist father with a son who turned a blind eye."

I see nods of agreement throughout the restaurant. Ned grumbles a little more and goes back to eating his breakfast.

Millie brings my food and takes a minute to give Helly a little attention. "Hey there dumpling. You're just the sweetest little baby on earth."

Helly smiles up at Millie and giggles.

Doris peers over the counter at Helly. "She is a cutie. Millie, let me pay you. I'm showing the Garrett house and can't be late."

"No doubt to more out-of-staters," Ned grouses.

"Why Ned Wheeler, you're especially charming this morning," Doris retorts. She turns her back on Ned. "Sydney, are you and Jake going to bring this adorable little baby girl to the fish fry on the twentieth?"

"Nope. Jake will be at a boat show so I'll have my hands full with Helly and tending the pens."

"My goodness. He shouldn't leave you alone. That's too much for a new mom to handle."

Thank you, Doris, for giving me the perfect opportunity to broadcast my weekend plans.

"You're right about that, Doris. I lose enough sleep with Helly, but I won't be alone. Tierney's helping me out. She'll stay at the house and tend the pens overnight."

Doris hands Millie her credit card and waits for the receipt. "Is that the cute little blonde who's spending her summer here?"

"Yep."

"I saw her and Jake at the pool when I was collecting donations from the marina for the Ladies Auxiliary Benefit Auction." Doris signs the receipt and pockets her copy. "Tierney's teensy-weensy bikini had all the dock boys walking in circles."

It takes a lot of effort and concentration to replace my tightened jaw with a natural smile. "She is a looker. And such a sweet girl. I'm lucky to have her help."

"Well, I'm off," Doris says, with a dramatic wave.

My buoyant mood has been ruined by her comments. I take a deep breath and clear my head. Soon enough I'll be done with that mosquito of a girl.

JAKE—July 10

I'm holed up in my office to clear my head. Mitch—the guy Syd told me Maggie's dating—is Jed Donnelly's son. Jed Donnelly is a rapist. And I'm queasy. I think I know one of his victims.

Back when I was in the Navy, Maggie wrote to me. She was all excited to interview for an internship with Donnelly. When I was home on leave, I asked her how it went. Her and Mom got all squirrelly. Mom said it ain't no place for a young girl to work, and that was the end of that.

I didn't think nothin' of it at the time, but when Sydney saw the letter in that gossip-rag of a newspaper and tore over to Maggie's, that memory popped up. I hope to hell that ain't been what's goin' on with Maggie, but my gut tells me it is.

Poor Maggie. She finally let somebody in and now this. If Jed did . . . hurt Maggie and she found out Mitch is Jed's son—what a sucker punch. Hell, she coulda been the one Mitch saw and walked away from.

I'm sweaty and my head thumps. I scrounge up some Tylenol from the first aid kit and mop off my hands and face with the alcohol wipes. Someone bangs on the office door.

"Give me a damn minute!"

Skip yells, "Jake, come quick."

I fling open the door. Skip's breathing heavy.

"A dock plank came loose. When Tierney stepped on it, she lost her balance and fell off the catwalk. Thank God Tony saw her fall. She hit her head on the side of the boat and it knocked her out.

Tony fished her outta the drink, but she ain't breathing. I called 911 and Tony's doing CPR."

I grab the AED and we run. I hear sirens. Tony's got her laid out on the back of her boat. By the time I hit the top of the dock, she vomits water and gasps for breath. Tony sinks down beside her, exhausted. I jump onto the boat and sit behind her, straddlin' her body with my legs. I lean her back against me. She coughs and gags up bay water. A three-inch split on the back of her head is bleeding all over my shirt.

"Give me your shirt." I yell to Skip. He whips it off and throws it down to me. I press it against her gash. "Go meet the ambulance. Show 'em where they need to come."

Skip runs out the parking lot to flag 'em down.

Tierney's coughs change to cries. Don't know whether it's from pain or fear.

Tony tries to calm her down, "You're all right. Everything's fine. Paramedics will be here in a minute and get ya all patched up, good as new."

She nods her head and wipes her snotty nose on her arm.

Smitty and June, the paramedics on duty, roll the stretcher down the dock to Tierney's boat. Me and Tony start to lift her, but Smitty yells, "Wait."

He jumps onto the boat and checks her out. He listens to her heart, looks at her eyes, and puts a clip on her finger to check her breathing. After he puts one of those hard collars around her neck, June hands him a folding stretcher. Smitty helps Tierney onto it and straps her in. Me, Tony, Skip, and Smitty lift her outta the boat and lay her on the gurney. June and Smitty wheel her up the dock and across the parking lot to the ambulance. Me, Skip, and Tony follow.

I bark out directions. "Skip, call home office and report the accident. Tony, gather all the men and check every plank on every dock. Fix anything with the slightest give. I'll follow the ambulance to the hospital."

Before they slide her in the back, I ask Tierney "Should I call your mom?"

"Yes, please." She sniffles and hands me her phone. "She's under my ICE contacts listed as Mom."

June pushes the gurney into the ambulance.

"What's her name?" I yell.

I hear her answer just before the doors slam shut. "Julia. Julia Burke."

The realization hits me like a ton of bricks. I drop the phone and stare shell-shocked at the flashing lights of the ambulance.

DEENA—July 10

The Xanax must be helping. I'm still scared, but I feel much more in control. I finally got a full night's sleep and ate a decent breakfast.

To protect myself, I've started taking basic precautions. Instead of screened windows, we're using air conditioning. Having learned how easy it is to pick a lock, I installed bolt latches on all of our doors. Skip raised his eyebrows at that, but let it slide. I bought motion-activated outdoor lights and I've tucked Skip's deer-gutting knife between my fitted sheet and the mattress. I also have a bottle of mace and a switchblade in my purse. I still jump when a car passes our house, but I feel better prepared for attack.

I refuse to let Sydney interfere with my life anymore, so I'm going to work today. I load up Davey's backpack with a change of clothes, a few snacks, and his lovey.

Before taking him out to the car, I check for bombs. I made a makeshift inspection tool out of a hand mirror, tied to a broomstick. After checking under the car, I look at the exhaust pipe and gas tank to make sure nothing is stuck in either spot, and I check under the hood of the car. Once I'm confident the car is safe, I put Davey in his seat and we're off.

Half a mile from home, my phone rings. It's Skip.

"Hey, babe. I'm on my way to work," I tell him, proud of my bravery.

"Good, that's good Deena. Hey, I need you to ask the sitter to keep Davey till you get off. I'm not gonna make it outta here until late."

"Why, what's up?"

"There was an accident. Tierney tripped on a loose board on the dock. She fell overboard and hit her head on the way down. Knocked her out cold. She damn near drowned like Whitey."

My gut flips and adrenaline pumps through my body. I do a U-turn and head back to my house. My heart's beating out of my chest and my eyes dart in all directions, searching for threats. A loose board on Tierney's dock has Sydney written all over it. From the way Sydney glared at Tierney at the pool, I should've known she'd be a target, too.

"Deena, Deena, can you hear me?" Skip asks.

"Yeah. Sorry. Is she okay? Is Tierney going to be okay?"

"She was talking when they wheeled her to the ambulance, so I think so. Jake's following the ambulance to the hospital. When I know more, I'll text you. So, will that work? With the sitter?"

"I'll take care of it, Skip."

No way in hell am I going to work and dropping Davey off with a sitter. We'd be sitting ducks.

Once I'm home, I rush inside, bolt all the doors, and close the blinds. Spreading a blanket in front of the couch, I dump a tub full of blocks out for Davey to play with. After setting my phone and mace on the end table, I unlock Skip's gun cabinet, pull out his shotgun, and load three shells. I sit down on the couch, facing my front door, holding the gun across my lap.

An hour or so later, Davey insists on being snuggled and I realize how messed up this is. What am I going to do? Live the rest of my life behind locked doors with a gun in my lap, waiting to be killed? Or pack my family up and leave town for good?

Dammit, no! I want my life back.

As terrified as I am, I've got to deal with the situation. I can't just sit back and wait for her to attack. I've got to stop her from hurting me or anyone else. I have to prove what Sydney has done and have her arrested.

I unload the gun and lock it back in the cabinet. I take a big breath and steel myself for what's to come. No matter what, I have to get into the trunk. There's no other way.

I'm not very smart or brave, but I can do this. I have to.

MAGGIE—July 10

It's good to be out on the crick. It's dead calm and dead quiet. Makes space to think. I know Syd means well, but sometimes her chatter gets on my last nerve.

I can't deny Mitch manned-up. It takes balls to do what he did. If I don't forgive him, who am I punishing? Who wins?

The sun is high in the sky and beats down on me. I dip a rag in the water and wrap it around my neck to cool off. My tea's hot, but I swig it down anyways. I only catch one crab on this run. When I'm puttering back to the start of the line, I think about the past, and I think about what I want.

All my life, I settled for whatever shit came my way. Didn't think I deserved better. Now I know different. I changed, I found my backbone, and I made my life good.

I'm my own boss. I live on the water. I'm tight with my brother. I got a best friend and a niece. But I don't got a man, and I want that. And goddammit, I deserve it.

Yeah, Mitch fucked up, but ain't we all. If I give him a second chance, it don't make me a doormat. Besides, it's past time I make myself happy. I take the bull by the horns and text Mitch to meet me when I'm done work.

I feel a little giddy, like a girl waitin' for her date to pick her up for prom. I crack open my last cold tea. It's probably the heat.

I run the line a few more times and only dip six crabs. It's like pullin' teeth. I decide to try another spot. After reelin' in the line, I check my phone. No messages.

I cruise over to where Pop used to lay. He liked it further out the crick towards the bay. It ain't my favorite spot 'cause there's too many other watermen out there, but hell, this day's been a bust. Might as well give it a try. I drop the weight and lay the line over the ringer arm to feed out.

Snooks runs up alongside me. "Hey Nails, dead as shit today, ain't it?"

"Yeah, I only got a half bushel so far and most of them is twos."

He wipes the sweat off his face with his arm. "You got any extra water? I'm spittin' dust."

"Got an Arizona. Want it?"

"Yeah."

I toss it over to Snooks. He cracks it open and swallows half in one gulp.

"Thanks." He lets out a long burp. "I got a bushel of twos and a bushel of trash. I'm gonna call it. Wanna join me at Dollie's for a cold one?"

I check my phone again—nothin'.

"Nah, I'm gonna stick it out and fill this bushel. JimBob's countin' on the crabs. He got some big orders to fill. Be sure to get yourself a ride home. I don't wanna see your ass in jail. One more DUI and that's where you're headed."

"Yeah, ain't that some shit. They might send my ass to jail for havin' one too many and that prick, Jed Donnelly's walkin' around free. Don't make no goddamn sense if you ask me."

Christ, I can't even get away from Jed on the crick. This fucking town is too small.

I shake my head. "Yeah, that's some shit."

I steer my bateau to the start of my line. Snooks takes the hint.

"Well, all right. A cold beer is callin' me." He heads in for the day.

Still no messages. Maybe my phone's dead. I check my battery—sixty percent.

After two more slow hours of only catchin' four or five crabs per run, I finally fill the basket and pull up my line. Before I head to shore, I check my phone again—nothin'.

What the fuck? Mitch been after me every day to talk, and now that I said yes, he don't text me back. What a dick.

Maybe he's gonna just show up like I told him to. He damn well better show up. Man, I hope he shows up.

SYDNEY—July 10

I'm keyed up after our morning outing to Millie's Place, and Helly is cranky. I spread a fluffy quilt onto the floor and surround it with throw pillows. Daisy immediately curls up on half of it. I settle Helly beside her and switch on the TV. The noise distracts Helly and she stops fussing.

Cashing in on the adrenaline buzz, I mentally review my plan for Tierney. All i's are dotted and all t's crossed. Everyone who attended our 4th of July party and now—thanks to Doris—everyone at Millie's knows Tierney will help me tend the pens while Jake's away.

If all continues as expected, Maggie will be spending nights with Mitch by the nineteenth. If not, I have a backup plan; a sleeping pill to crush into her Natural Light.

Although probably overkill, since the neighbors sleep like the dead, I will "forget" to bring in my sheets from the clothesline, conveniently blocking the view of the dock. The photo Tierney emailed to her mom captured her lifting a softshell from the water, and a clamp light hanging precariously over the pens. I'll choose between Friday and Saturday night based on cloud cover dimming the moonlight. I've left nothing to chance.

A breaking news alert blares across the TV screen. The headline scrolling across the bottom reads, *Hostage situation at Donnelly Telecommunications.* Daytime TV is replaced with the news station, and the local anchor begins his report.

"The situation is unfolding as I report to you. State and local police, as well as hostage negotiators, are on the scene at Donnelly Telecommunications. What we know so far—all but three employees safely escaped when Jed Donnelly began waving a gun and making threats throughout the office building.

"According to Jed's private secretary, he called a meeting with the COO, the CFO, and his son. She heard yelling and threats. Mr. Donnelly came out into the top floor's lobby area and shot into the ceiling, screaming 'Get out, all of you. There's no company without me,' before barricading himself in his office with the hostages.

"This bizarre behavior comes on the heels of Mitch Donnelly's shocking accusations published in the Keene County News this morning . . ."

I scoop up Helly, holding her on my hip, as I hop around trying to get my shoes on. Grabbing my phone, I call Maggie. She doesn't answer. I fling open my front door and look out. Maggie's truck is in the driveway and her workboat is in the slip. Daisy moseys out into the yard and pees on the dianthus. I shoo her back into the house, closing the door behind her, and sprint, as best I can carrying a baby on my hip, over to Maggie's house.

I bang on her locked front door and yell, "Maggie, Maggie, you've got to answer the door."

She doesn't come. I peer in the front door windows while calling her again. Her phone lights up from its spot on the farm table. I drag Helly around to the back door to check if it's unlocked. It is.

I barge in yelling, "Maggie, where are you?"

No answer, but I hear the shower running and rap on the bathroom door. "Maggie, it's me. I'm coming in."

She pokes he head out from behind the shower curtain. "What the hell is wrong with you? I'm takin' a damn shower."

I'm panting from running. "It's Mitch! His dad's got him at gunpoint."

Maggie shuts off the shower and grabs a towel. "He what?"

"Yeah, Jed's holding him and two other people hostage at the Donnelly building."

"Oh my God!"

She wraps a towel around herself, runs into the living room, and switches on the TV. The news anchor repeats what I just watched, adding no new information.

"I gotta go." She races back to her bedroom.

I follow her. "Go where? There's nothing you can do."

"I can be there when he comes out." She struggles to slide her jeans over her wet legs and hips.

"I'll go with you."

"No!" She fastens her bra and pulls on a T-shirt. "Are you fucking crazy? You ain't takin' that sweet baby to a hostage scene." She pulls her wet hair into a ponytail. "I'll call you when I know somethin'." Brushing past me, she yells over her shoulder, "Let Ruby out for me."

A moment later she guns the truck and kicks up a plume of oyster dust behind her.

JAKE—July 10

Stunned, I'm frozen in the parking lot staring at the taillights of the ambulance. All the pieces fall together in a giant mess of truth. Julia Burke, a bartender at Tierney's Ale House, is a girl I dated on and off when I was in port in Norfolk. Tierney said her dad ain't been around and she's got Swannee's eyes. She's my daughter.

I puke on my shoes. I got so much disgust for myself I'm heavin' it up. I lusted after my own flesh and blood. Jesus Christ, I'm a goddamn pervert.

I pick up the phone and climb in my truck. This is some shit. The daughter I didn't know I had got a busted head, and damn near drowned. Now I gotta call her mom. The last time I saw Julia, she caught me sneakin' outta her bed before dawn, not even man enough to tell her I was shippin' out for a six-month stint in the Mediterranean Sea.

I decide to wait and call her till I get an update from the docs. I pull out of the marina parking lot and head to Bakerstown. About two blocks from the hospital, Oak Street is blocked by fire police. I turn onto Chestnut. Damn! It's blocked too. So, I turn on Water Street to try to get to the back side of the hospital. It's blocked too.

I roll down my window and yell to the cop, "Hey man, I gotta get to the hospital. How the hell am I supposed to get in there?"

"Watcha need at the hospital?" he asks.

"They just took my daughter by ambulance. I gotta be with her." It feels wrong sayin' she's my daughter.

"Ok. I'll let you through. Go straight to the back lot and park in emergency. We got us a situation at the Donnelly building and don't want extra people mucking around."

Holy shit! I completely forgot about Mitch's letter in this morning's paper with all that went down. I nod to the cop and do twenty-five mph down Water Street to the ER. The Donnelly building is across the road, a few blocks down on the corner. I see a million flashing cop cars and a row of TV vans parked behind yellow caution tape. I'm too far away to get a good look at what the hell's happening.

I walk into the ER waiting room. Every TV has Jed Donnelly's face on 'em. He got Mitch and two other guys holed up in his office threatening to shoot 'em. I pull my phone out to call Maggie, but stop. How's it gonna help to tell her? Ain't nothin' she can do but worry. I hope to hell she's still out on the crick and ain't heard what's going down.

I go to the ER desk. "I'm here for Tierney Burke. They just brought her in by ambulance."

The sharp-nosed receptionist asks, "Are you family?"

I swallow hard. "I'm her dad."

"She's in Bay 4. They took her for a CAT scan, but she should be done soon. I'll take you back now."

She leads me to Tierney's bed and pulls the curtain aside. I sit in an uncomfortable chair and wait. I'm glad she ain't here. It gives me more time to figure out what the hell I'm supposed to say.

MAGGIE—July 10

Oak, Chestnut, and Water streets are all blocked, so I park a half-mile away and hoof it. I don't get too close before I'm stopped by yellow caution tape and a pain-in-the-ass cop tellin' me to stay back. I ain't never seen nothin' like it. Cruisers are everywhere. Behind the car doors, dozens of cops are pointin' guns at the windows of Jed's office.

Some guy in a suit got a megaphone and yells something I'm too far away to hear. TV cameras and reporters with mics are set up all along the row of tape. And people are comin' outta the woodwork to rubberneck. It's a goddamn circus.

I walk along the outside of the tape, trying to get close enough to see what the fuck is happenin'. I got a better angle from the yard of the Nationwide Insurance building. Now the guy with the megaphone is on a cell phone. He paces and talks, but I still can't hear what he says. He looks pissed and slides his phone into his pants pocket. A guy in jeans and a flannel shirt, with a big-ass gun strapped to his hip, brings him water. Megaphone guy drinks the whole bottle down in one gulp. They talk for a minute and then I guess his phone rings 'cause he pulls it outta his pocket and starts talkin' again.

A guy bumps into me tryin' to get closer. "Sorry. Never thought I'd see the day something like this would happen around here."

I turn my back on him and walk a few feet away. The wind musta changed 'cause now I catch a few of megaphone guy's words.

"Mr. Donnelly . . . if you . . . send . . . out."

My gut's clenched so tight I'm barely breathin'. Megaphone guy motions a cop over. Whatever he tells him makes the cop run back and yell something to all the other cops. More guns are drawn. Half point at the window and half at the front door. Megaphone guy gives a thumbs up. Christ, I hope that don't mean shoot.

The automatic doors slide open and two guys in suits come out with their hands up. Their faces are so white they look like clowns. Two cops run up to the door and grab the men, and drag 'em to the ambulance. They ain't Mitch.

The men sit on the back of the ambulance and the crew wraps silver blankets around 'em while the cops talk to 'em. They look scared shitless.

Megaphone guy yells something else into the cell phone. He rubs his hands over his face like he ain't happy with what he's hearing on the other end. He holds his hand up in the air and makes some kinda motion with fingers. Six cops sneak up the fire escape on the side of the building.

The TV crews see it too and they to push each other outta the way to get a shot. The guy in the flannel shirt and a few other police tell them, and everybody else, to move back. I step back without turning around.

The men on the fire escape get to the fourth floor. The whole fucking place goes quiet. Not one cop moves, not one person talks. We all hold our breath to see what's gonna happen.

A gun shot. From inside. I drop to my knees. The cops on the fire escape move fast. I'm so fucking scared, I'm shaking. What if Jed shot Mitch?

Just when the cops reach the top floor there's a loud crack. Jed's office window shatters and a screaming man falls out the fifth-floor window. His tie floats up like the line of a parachute that ain't never gonna open. Jed Donnelly lands on the roof of his fancy red sports car and bounces off onto the street.

JAKE—July 10

When the orderly wheels Tierney back into the ER bay, my throat gets a lump and I feel like I gotta puke. What the hell should I say?

"Did you call my mom?" Tierney asks in a lost-little-girl voice.

"Not yet. I wanted to wait for your test results, so I don't panic her."

Tierney sucks in her bottom lip and nods.

An intern pushes the curtain aside and brings in a tray of tools and a needle. "Her results will be up shortly. I'm going to go ahead and stitch her wound."

Tierney reaches out her hand. It's shaking. I take hold of it with both of mine and get a jolt—the same kind of buzz I felt the first time I held Helly. I blink my eyes to stop the tears.

The intern picks up the needle. "This is to numb the area. It'll feel like a bee sting."

"I hate bees," she says, and squeezes my hand. Her face crunches up when the needle goes in.

Not letting go of her hand, I scoot my chair so I'm right beside her head. When he starts to stitch, I lean close and whisper, "I know I'm your dad and I'm so happy."

Her eyes get wide and then she covers them with her free hand. Her shoulders shake and I can tell she's crying.

I rest my hand on her shoulder. "You okay?"

When she nods, the intern tells her to hold still so she smiles instead. "I was so afraid you wouldn't want to be my dad."

The intern stops and looks at both of us, like he ain't quite sure what he got in the middle of.

My smile runs ear to ear. "I'm her dad."

He shoots me a weird look. "Okay dad, let's stop talking until I finish these stitches."

I look at Tierney. Tears roll down her cheeks and over her smiling lips.

"Okay," she says to the intern and squeezes my hand.

He finishes the last stitch. "The ER doctor will be in with the test results soon."

"Thank you," I say.

Once he's outta the bay the words tumble from Tierney's mouth. "I've waited my whole life to meet you. I can't believe you finally know. I didn't know how to tell you. You have the perfect family with Sydney and Helly and I was so afraid you'd think I was messing everything up."

I lift her chin and look her in the eye. "Are you kiddin'? I'm over the moon. Tierney, I didn't know. Your mother never told me. I'm so sorry I wasn't there for you."

"Oh, I know, Dad. Can I call you Dad? It sounds funny coming out of my mouth. Maybe I should just call you Jake."

I shake my head. "Not a chance. No daughter of mine will be callin' me Jake."

She laughs and it sounds different now that I know she's my girl. In fact, everything's different now that I know.

She scooches up in the hospital bed and I tuck a pillow under her.

"So anyway, Dad—ooh, I like how that sounds."

I wink at her. "Me too. So anyway . . . what were you going to tell me?"

"Yeah, right. So, when I turned sixteen, Mom told me about you, but she made me promise not to try and meet you before I turned eighteen. She wanted me to think it through. She wanted to make sure I'd be okay if you weren't nice, or you didn't want me

251

around. She and I decided my graduation gift would be the chance to get to know you and decide if I wanted to tell you the truth or not. That's why she rented me the boat at the marina."

I get a pang in my heart and ain't sure I want to ask the question, but I do anyway. "Are you glad I figured it out?"

She sits up quick. "Of course!" Her face turns green and she looks woozy.

"Take it easy, there. Your head took a really hard hit."

"Yeah, I'm a little dizzy." She lays back on the pillow. "Ja—I mean Dad, I wanted to tell you the first day I met you, but then I got scared. And then when I met Sydney and Helly and Maggie . . ." She twists the edge of the sheet.

I tuck a stray hair behind her ear. "Then what?"

She sighs. "There's nothing I want more than to be a part of your family."

"You *are* family."

She smiles and tears fill up her eyes.

The ER doctor comes in with her clipboard. "Hello." She holds her hand out for me to shake it. "I'm Dr. Montrose."

"I'm Jake, this is my daughter Tierney." It's starting to roll off my tongue.

"Well, your daughter was very lucky. Her CAT scan came back clear. No swelling, no bleeds, no skull fractures. She does, however, have a minor concussion. Because of that, and the fact that she took in some water, I'd like to keep her overnight for observation. We're going to move her up to room 208. You may stay the night with her if you like."

"Okay. Sounds good," I say.

The staff gets Tierney ready to move.

I pull out her phone and hand it to her. "Why don't you call your mom? She'll be less freaked out if she hears your voice. I'm gonna go call Syd and let her know I'm stayin' with you. I ain't gonna tell her our news over the phone, though. Better to do that in person."

Tierney nods and I lean down and kiss her forehead. She calls her mom as they wheel her up to her room.

MAGGIE—July 10

People kick into high gear. EMS swarm around Jed. Cops charge through the front doors. All the TV cameras start filming. I sit on the ground. My gut rolls like waves in a nor'easter. I pull out clumps of grass scared shitless for what comes next.

They load Jed into an ambulance and scream out the road. He must be alive. I hope to hell his son is.

There's a fuss by the front doors. I stand and move closer. Someone's comin' out. It's a cop. He yells to a paramedic to bring a gurney. My knees buckle. I sink to the ground and put my head in the grass and pray. *Dammit God. Don't be so cruel. I finally know what I want. Don't take it from me now. Please God. Give me some happiness.*

I hear yellin' and look up. The doors open again. Two cops is holdin' Mitch up. They help him onto the gurney. I can't take it.

I duck under the tape and run towards him yellin', "Mitch! Mitch!"

A cop tries to stop me but I push him away to get to the stretcher.

"Oh my God, Maggie." Mitch opens his arms and I damn near jump on top of the gurney. I'm ugly crying and I don't care.

The paramedic pulls my shoulder and says, "Ma'am, let us take care of him. He needs to go to the hospital."

I ain't even looked to see where he's hurt. I pull back and look him over. He got trickles of blood all over his face, hands, and arms. Jagged little pieces of glass are stuck all over him.

Mitch takes my hands. "It's okay, Maggie. I'm not shot. It's just from the fight and the glass. I'll be fine."

"I'm going with you." I don't even ask the crew; I just crawl in the ambulance.

They roll Mitch in and we take the two-block ride to the ER. They take Mitch through the back and make me go in the front to wait till they get him cleaned up. I turn the corner and almost run smack into Jake.

"What are you doin' here?" we say at the same time, shocked as hell to see each other.

I point to the TV. The reporter says, "Jed Donnelly is in critical condition after a fall from the fifth floor of the Donnelly Building. Moments ago, his son, Mitch, was taken to the emergency room in stable condition and is expected to make a full recovery."

"Holy Shit!" Jake says.

"Right?"

"Did Jed . . . Was it you?" Jake's voice quivers.

"Yes, but it's over. One-hundred-fucking-percent over. Ain't nothin' I gotta waste one more minute on. Got it?"

Jake pulls me tight in a bear hug. "You got a spine made of steel. I'm damn lucky you're my sister."

I push him away and cough to keep tears from starting. "So, you know why I'm here. Why are you?"

"Tierney fell off the dock and busted her head open. It knocked her out and she damn near drowned."

"Christ, we don't need another drowning. She gonna be all right?"

"Yeah, but they're keeping her overnight. But that ain't the big news."

"There's more?" I blow out a sigh and rub my face. "This day is fucking unbelievable."

"Yeah, well you ain't gonna believe this. I'm still in shock." He rakes his fingers through his hair. "Tierney's my daughter."

I punch his shoulder. "Get the hell out! That is some big news!"

That explains the picture and all the questions. My gut was right after all. Tierney was lookin' for a daddy—her daddy. I shoulda guessed it. She's damn near a twin to Swannee. I ain't never met anyone else with those eyes. Shoulda known she's related.

"Well, Dad, fill me in."

"I dated her mom back when I was in port at Norfolk."

"Dated or banged?"

"Mostly banged. Neither one of us was out to get serious. We was just having a good time."

"Did you know she was pregnant?"

His face turns black. "Hell no! What kinda man do you think I am? Julia, Tierney's mom, was getting clingy though, and I wasn't lookin' for that."

"So, you stopped seein' her?"

"Not officially. I shipped out on a six-month Med. cruise and once I was back in Norfolk I went to other bars. I ain't seen her for eighteen years."

"So, you ghosted her? That was a dick move."

He hangs his head. "Yeah, but I didn't know she was pregnant. I woulda married her."

He looks like a beat dog. Guess I was a little hard on him.

I pat him on the shoulder. "I know you woulda. Tierney's a good kid. We got ourselves another new Swann. That's damn exciting! Did you tell Syd?"

"Not yet. I wanna tell her in person. I was just getting ready to call to tell her I'll be here late. I'm gonna stay with Tierney till her mom gets here."

Once Jake tells Sydney, I guess she'll be relieved. A grossed-out shiver goes up my back, when I think about Jake havin' the hots for Tierney. I push that picture so far down it ain't never gonna see the light of day again.

"Good plan, Jake. That ain't something you should spring on Sydney over the phone. What room's Tierney in?"

"208. Why?"

"Cause I ain't gonna stand around this waiting room with my thumb up my ass. They won't let me back with Mitch yet, so I'll go welcome my new niece into the family."

He holds his hands up like he surrenders.

I laugh. "Make your call. And tell Syd I'm okay and I'm staying at Mitch's tonight. I'll catch up with her tomorrow."

"Okay. I'll meet you in my daughter's room."

His grin takes over his whole face.

SYDNEY—July 10

My eyes have been glued to the TV and I've been pacing with the phone in my hand for hours. No amount of herbal tea is calming me down. I feel the vibration and answer it before it finishes one ring.

"What's happening with Mitch?" I yell into the phone.

"He's in the emergency room, and he's stable." It's Jake, not Maggie.

"How do you know that? Where are you? What the hell is going on?"

He sighs. "It's a long story."

"Is Maggie okay? Is she with you?"

"Sydney, if you stop askin' questions, I can fill you in."

"Fine. Speak." I clamp my mouth shut, extremely irritated that he cut me off short.

"I am at the hospital. Maggie's here too. Mitch is getting patched up in the ER, but like I said, he's stable and he's gonna be fine. Maggie'll take him home and stay with him. She said she'll talk to you tomorrow."

"Thank God!"

While I'm relieved, I'm miffed that Maggie forbid *me* to be with her, but called Jake.

"When did Maggie call you to come be with her? Were you at the Donnelly building when it all went down?

"Maggie never called me. I'm at the hospital because of Tierney."

Tierney? I've passed irritated and am heading for infuriated. "What does Tierney have to do with anything?"

"She had an accident at the marina this morning. A board was loose on her catwalk. When she stepped on it, it flipped her off the dock. She smashed her head on the side of the boat and was knocked out. She woulda drown if Tony hadn't seen it happen and pulled her out."

"Oh my God! You're going to be sued." As soon as the words are out of my mouth, I realize my mistake.

"Probably, but I ain't worried about that right now." Jake snaps, clearly annoyed with my insensitivity.

I take a breath and work to smooth ruffled feathers. "Well, of course not. Forgive me. I didn't mean to be callous. I just naturally put the welfare of my family first. I'm like a lioness protecting her pride. How is Tierney?"

"She'll be okay. But they're gonna keep her overnight. I'm gonna stay with her till her mom gets here."

Like hell. I'm not going to allow Jake to be sucked in by her vulnerability.

"I'm on my way, Jake. I'm sure you have a boatload of paperwork to get started on regarding the accident. I'll be glad to stay with Tierney until her mother shows and let you get to work."

I start packing Helly's diaper nag.

"No. I'm staying. Besides there's no need to drag Helly to a hospital. You stay where you are and I'll be home in five or six hours."

Jake never says no. "No, really Jake. I want to. You know I've grown close to Tierney. Helly will be fine. Plus, I can check on Maggie."

"Sydney, this ain't a negotiation."

His voice is unyielding and his adamance stops me in my tracks. I have no option but to relent. Pushing could raise doubts in the future.

I sigh loudly. "All right. If you're sure—"

"I am."

"Okay. Well, give her my best and keep me posted."

GREEN PEELER

He hangs up and I'm furious. Tierney's claws are obviously embedded in Jake. Her removal can't come too soon.

MAGGIE—July 10

Mitch's face looks like a pin cushion. He got little red dots and lines all over it. Only a few cuts was deep enough to need steri-strips. He signs the discharge papers and they wheel him out to my truck.

After I saw Tierney, I walked the four blocks to get it and park it in the hospital lot. The cops still got the street right around the Donnelly building blocked off, but all the other roads is open.

The orderly helps Mitch into the passenger side and slams the door.

"Stay with me tonight," Mitch says.

I pull out of the lot and head to his house. "Nah, I was gonna drop you off." He looks surprised, and I roll my eyes. "Of course I'm gonna stay, dumbass."

He laughs and then he gets all serious. "About my letter—"

I hold up my hand to shut him up. "Stop there. Apology accepted. Subject closed. I ain't visiting there no more."

"But Maggie, shouldn't we talk about it?"

"If you need to talk about it, take it to your sponsor. I'm done. I dealt with it and I'm movin' on."

He nods. "Okay, fair enough. Then let's talk about your big news, a new niece."

"Yeah, ain't that some shit?"

I pull the truck into his driveway. He's outta the truck before I can go around to help him. He can tell I'm pissed he didn't wait.

"I got some cuts and scratches. My legs aren't broken."

"How can I take care of you if you don't let me?"

"I don't need taken care of. I need you."

He puts his arm around me and I feel like butter on a hot biscuit. We go in his house and he sits up at the kitchen island. I open the fridge to see what I can find. We's both starved. He got ham, Swiss, mustard, and bread. Sandwiches it is.

"What do you think of your new niece?"

I grab two plates from the cupboard and open a few drawers to look for a knife.

"Third drawer on the left," he says.

"She's a good kid." I lay a slice a bread on each plate and spread 'em with mustard. "I'm kinda pissed at her momma for keepin' her from us. Woulda been nice if my momma and Swannee coulda met her."

"Do you know why her mother didn't tell Jake?"

I pile ham on the bread and cover it with two cheese slices. "Jake kinda disappeared. He got shipped out and left without tellin' her. And when he got back, he never looked her up. Guess she figured he didn't want nothin' to do with her."

"Still. Jake never was given an opportunity to make it right. Feels a little selfish to me."

I lean across the island and kiss him for stickin' up for my brother. "Yeah. Jake woulda manned up." I shrug. "Oh well, what's done is done. At least we got her now."

"What did Sydney think about Helly not being an only child?"

"She don't know yet. Jake wants to tell her in person. I ain't sure how's she gonna take it." I slice our sandwiches in half, grab two napkins, and sit down beside him. "Some shit went down that Sydney ain't too happy with, but then she kinda took Tierney under her wing, so it's hard to say. Lately Sydney seems off."

I didn't know I was thinkin' that till I said it. But it's true. Lotsa little things been buggin' me about Sydney lately.

JAKE—July 10

Julia flies in the room, straight to Tierney's bedside. "Oh my God, are you okay?" She puts her hands on each cheek and kisses Tierney's whole face. "I was so worried. You poor thing. Does it hurt?"

Tierney laughs. "Mom, stop. I'm okay. I'm on pain pills so it doesn't hurt. My hair will cover it. You won't even see a scar."

"You're coming home with me. I want you double checked by a specialist. We have to make sure nothing is in your lungs. Oh, my dear girl, what would I do without you?" Julia nuzzles her face into the crook of Tierney's neck.

Julia's blonde hair is shoulder length. Now that it's shorter, it got waves. Her body's still smokin' hot—trim waist, tight ass—and that's just the back. I clear my throat. She is so focused on Tierney, she ain't noticed me.

She turns, keeping her hands on Tierney's shoulders. Anger flashes in her blue eyes before she gets control. "Jake. It's been a long time."

I don't know why the hell she's mad at me. She's the one who kept me from my own daughter all these years. "Yeah."

She gets up, walks over to me, and pulls herself up to be as tall as she can. "How could you let this happen?"

I feel like slappin' her. "How could you not tell me I got a kid?"

"You're the one who left." She spits the words out.

"Cause the Navy sent me to the Med. If you told me you was havin' a kid I woulda stepped up."

"Would you?"

"Well, I sure as shit didn't get the chance to prove it to you, now did I?"

"Mom, Ja . . . Dad. Stop!" Tierney interrupts our fight.

Julia throws her hands up and puts her nose in the air. "Fine, fine. No argument. I will be suing the marina, and that's that."

"No, you won't!" Tierney yells.

Tierney grabs her head. Me and Julia both run to her side.

"Stop fighting. It makes my head hurt."

I take a deep breath to calm down. "The marina will be paying for all medical treatments including all follow-ups or physical therapies. We'll also be offering her a pain and suffering settlement."

I talked to the owner earlier and he told me to do what I needed to make a lawsuit go away. And now that I know she's my daughter, I'll fight to get her the best deal possible.

"Mom, this is ridiculous. It was an accident. I don't need pain and suffering."

I answer before Julia got time to open her mouth. "Yes, you do. It's only fair and it will help with college expenses. And so will I, personally. I don't got a ton of savings, but I'll do what I can."

Julia's ramrod back softens when she sees I'm all in. "Well, I'm still taking you home while you're recovering," she says to Tierney.

"Mom, I can't. I promised Sydney I'd tend the pens while Ja . . ." She smiles 'cause she almost called me Jake again. "While Dad is at the boat show. I can't let her down."

"That ain't till the nineteenth. We can get Maggie to help," I say.

"No. I promised and I want to. I'm not ready to go home. Especially not now that you know I'm family."

I grab her hand and give it a squeeze. My heart just filled right up.

263

"Okay," Julia says. "We'll compromise. I'll take you home and have you checked out. As long as the doctors say it's okay, I'll bring you back on the eighteenth. Fair?"

Tierney beams. "Yes, fair."

"Then I'm gonna go on home," I tell her. "I'll see you on the eighteenth, before I head out to the show. Call me and let me know what the doctors say, okay?" I bend down and kiss her forehead.

"Give Helly a kiss for me and tell her I'll see her soon," Tierney says.

I nod and wave.

Julia says, "I'll walk you out."

She stays quiet till we're at the elevators. "Look, Jake. I've gone over my decision more than a million times, and am no closer to knowing if I was right or wrong. The last time I saw you, I didn't know I was pregnant. Once I knew, you were gone. You had made it very clear you weren't looking for a relationship, and I certainly didn't want you to marry me out of duty. I just couldn't see the point in telling you. It would've complicated things. Maybe I was wrong."

I'm boiling mad that she stole my chance to be Tierney's dad, but what's done is done. I gotta find a way to live with it. It ain't fair to Tierney for her dad to hate her mom. Just puts her in the middle of things.

"You were wrong, Julia—dead wrong. And I ain't gonna lie, I'm mad as hell. You took her childhood from me. It's gonna take me some time to get over it. But what I ain't gonna do is drag Tierney into the fight. I'm gonna be in her life, and you're gonna be in her life, so we gotta figure outta way to make that work."

She holds out her hand and I shake it.

SYDNEY—July 10

The sky is clear and the pale light of the quarter moon creates dancing shadows in the water. A few random crickets chirp, but otherwise it's quiet. Feeling antsy and annoyed at being shut out of everything that's happening, I decide to take advantage of Jake and Maggie being away.

I step off of my porch and into the night. The summer air envelops me like an old friend. I look around. Nebulous shapes litter the dark yards. A chair could be a bush, or vice versa. If I keep my porch light off and use the back door, I'm sure I'll never be noticed exiting my house.

I slink over to Maggie's house and let Ruby out. I scan the yards again from her porch. This vantage has the clearest view. I can begin to distinguish shapes about three feet from her lighted dock. Stealthily, I creep across the driveway to Rhonda's rancher. I tiptoe under her bedroom window and survey the yard and dock. Even if she would wake up, if my sheets are on the line, she can't see the pens.

I have one more angle to check. I scoot across Maggie's yard, through my backyard, to Lolly and Bob Johnson's house. Their bedroom window faces the side of my house, so unless they'd be on their porch, they couldn't possibly see the wharf. I sneak up on their porch. The pilings that support the roof over the upper part of the dock obscure their view of the pens. As long as I stand in line with the piling, they won't be able to see me.

I hurry back to the pens and check the sight line so I know where I'll need to stand. It'll work. I take a piece of duct tape and mark the spot, smoothing it repeatedly to make sure it sticks. I tuck a stool within easy reach of the mark. Of course, I'll recheck before *the* night.

I glance at my phone—11:30. Time to tend the pens. I glide my hands deftly through the water, skimming just above the crabs. Ruby meanders in and out of my legs, hoping I'll drop a softshell.

An image of Tierney laughing with Jake flashes into my head. I tense and a crab pinches the glove. I breathe. There's no need for anxiety. It will be over soon. The crab releases and I continue scanning the pen. Tierney has foolishly underestimated me—a grave mistake. There is nothing I won't do to protect what's mine.

I hear oyster shells being pulverized under Jake's tires. Ruby barks once in greeting. Once parked, he's slow to get out of the car. I finish with the pens and walk towards him. When he opens the car door, Ruby runs to him. Stepping out, he pets her head. He looks tired, but content, like he's enjoyed a day well spent.

I meet him half way and he wraps me in a hug.

He smells my hair and kisses my neck. "I missed you."

I hold back a sarcastic retort. "I missed you too."

He takes hold of my hand and pulls me towards the dock. "It's beautiful tonight."

We walk to the end of the wharf and sit, dangling our legs over the edge. A fish jumps and the ripples are illuminated by the moonlight.

He leans his head against mine. "I have something to tell you."

My gut clenches and my jaw tightens.

Jake notices. "It's good news."

I force myself to visibly relax. "Okay, what is it?"

"Tierney is my daughter."

My hand tightens over the edge of the dock and a splinter pierces my palm.

MAGGIE—July 11

The phone rings and wakes me and Mitch up at three. It's the hospital. Jed took a turn for the worse. He probably ain't gonna make it to sunrise. Mitch slides his jeans on and sits on the side of the bed with his head in his hands.

"Christ," he says. "I might have killed my father."

I crawl across the bed to sit beside him. "What choice did you have? He was gonna shoot you."

He shakes his head. "You should've seen his eyes. He was crazed, like a rabid dog. I swear to God, he was frothing at the mouth."

I seen that look before, in Eddie's eyes, but I don't say nothin'.

"When he pointed the gun at me, I knew he wanted to kill me." He rubs the bruises on his neck and shoulder. "I dove for him, but I couldn't get the pistol." Mitch stares across the room like he sees it all again. "He was a lot stronger than I expected, like a bull seeing red. I had him pushed down on his desk, but he kneed me in the balls. I let up for a split second and he shot. I swear to God, I felt the bullet whizz past my ear and then all I could hear was a painful buzzing, like if you were standing beside a band saw."

He stands up, paces round the room, and throws on his dirty shirt. When he sees the blood stains, he strips it off, sits down on the floor in front of me, and lays his head in my lap.

He chokes on the words. "I knew then it was him or me. Maggie, he wasn't going to stop. I was wrestling him for the gun.

When I got him in front of the window, I pushed him as hard as I could. I damn near went through it with him." His shoulders buck up and down.

I pat his head. He stands up and rubs his face, makin' one of his cuts bleed again.

He grabs my hand. "I know I have no right to ask this of you. And if you say no, I completely understand, but will you come to the hospital with me?"

The last fucking thing I wanna do is hold a bedside vigil for that cock-sucker, but I ain't gonna make Mitch go alone. "I'll go, but I ain't going in his room."

I throw on my clothes. My T-shirt's still damp from my nervous sweat, and it don't smell pretty. Mitch puts on a clean shirt, grabs his wallet, and we're out the door. It takes us less than ten minutes to get to the hospital.

Mitch punches the elevator button, but when it don't come that second, he gets antsy and we take the stairs. The ICU's on the third floor. Jed's room is easy to find 'cause two cops stand outside of it. From the hall, I can see Jed got tubes stickin' out everywhere. It don't make me sad, but Mitch's suffering does.

He's looks at me like he's being torn in half. Like he ain't sure he oughta leave me and go in.

"Go. No matter what, he's still your old man. I'm okay. I'm gonna go visit Tierney. Text me when you need me."

He hugs me hard. "I love you, Maggie Swann."

The cops check Mitch's ID and then lets him in to say goodbye. I head down to 208.

I scoot by the nurse's station and into her room before they catch me. Visiting hours are way past over. Tierney's hair looks like a halo around her face. I can't believe I got an eighteen-year-old niece. A blonde woman's asleep in a recliner by Tierney's bed. Must be her mom. She opens her eyes and jumps up. I guess it's kinda freaky finding a stranger starin' at you and your kid.

"I'm Maggie. Jake's sister."

"Oh. Hi." She wipes the sleep outta her eyes. "I'm Julia."

Two years in Al-Anon taught me to say what I mean, mean what I say, but don't say it mean. "Look, I ain't happy that I only found out I got a niece when she's damn near grown. And it ain't right that you didn't give Jake a chance to see his kid grow up. My momma and pop didn't even know they had a grandkid and that ain't fair. What's done is done, but now that I know she's family, I'm in her life for the long haul. You ain't gonna keep her from us no more."

She stands up and leads me out the door. "Let's get a cup of coffee and chat."

We walk to the surgery waitin' room. She gets a coffee outta the vending machine and I get a bottle of water. We sit across from each other on padded vinyl chairs.

She spills her guts. "I'm sorry to say, I let pride get in the way of common sense. Jake left without a word. He never called when his tour was over and he got back in town. I assumed that if he didn't want me, he wouldn't want our child. And I wasn't going to beg. I was determined to do it on my own."

I get that. Pride's what damn near sunk my family. Momma was too proud to let anyone know what the hell was happenin' in our lives or that we needed help. And she raised us up expectin' the same toughness from us. Turns out it ain't tough at all. It's fear.

I smile. "You did all right. She's a good kid."

She looks like a proud momma. "She is. She's the most amazing thing I've ever done with my life. And you're absolutely correct, it was completely unfair of me to keep her from Jake and you, and the rest of his family."

"Well, she got us now."

"She was chattering a mile a minute to fill me in on all of you, and how wonderfully welcoming you've been without even knowing she's half Swann."

"She fits right in. Took to tendin' the pens like a duck takes to water. Just like her daddy."

"She's been meticulously planning this trip for two years. I knew where Jake was from, so when Rock Narrows made national news, I paid attention. When I read about your mother's passing it hit me—because of me, because of my stubbornness—Tierney would never meet her grandmother."

She gets choked up and pulls a Kleenex outta her purse to blow her nose. "That's how I told her. I showed her the paper and explained how it connected to her. She was furious with me. Wouldn't speak for over a week and then she demanded to meet her dad."

I'm pissed too, but I'm sorry for Julia. My gut is too full up with feelin's. Between what's going on with Mitch and this. I can't make heads or tails of 'em.

Julia stuffs the used tissue in her pocket. "I told her I would make that happen, but she had to wait until she was eighteen."

"Why? That was just more wasted time."

"Well, I didn't think it would be fair to Jake to have another bombshell dropped on him right after losing his mom. But honestly, it was mostly because I was afraid Jake would reject her. I wanted the time to prepare her if he did. I wanted to be sure she could withstand it. Plus, I had no idea what type of man Jake had turned out to be. Maybe she wouldn't want him to know he's her father. Maybe she wouldn't want him in her life."

Mom's do a lot of twisted shit in the name of protecting their kids. It's probably a good thing I ain't never had a kid.

Julia picks at her fingernail. "Again, I was wrong. On all counts. All I can say is I'm sorry."

She's waiting for me to forgive her, but really, she gotta forgive herself.

"Look Julia, you did the best you could. And you know better now. Can't change the past, so don't beat yourself up with it. You gotta move on from here."

My phone chirps telling me I got a text. It's from Mitch. *He's gone.*

I stand up. "It's all gonna work out in the wash. But I gotta go now. My—" I stop 'cause I don't know what to call him. "My man's dad just died."

She hugs me quick before I can escape. "Go. And thanks."

JAKE—July 11

Yesterday kicked my ass and I don't want to get outta bed. Sydney's clanging around in the kitchen. Last night she was tight-lipped, only sayin' she needed time to "process." So, I know there's more we gotta talk about.

By the time I drag myself to the kitchen, Syd's on the front porch. I pour myself a cup of coffee and grab the baby monitor. She ain't brushed her hair and is still in her pj's. She got a baby blanket wrapped around her shoulders, sippin' coffee. It's cold for a summer morning.

"Hey." I bend down to kiss her.

"Hey yourself." She kisses me back.

She sits cross-legged on the rocker and stares out at the crick.

I rub the back of her neck. "You tossed and turned all night."

She nods and rubs her puffy eyes. "Yeah, yesterday was a lot. Maggie texted around five. Jed died."

"Good riddance."

"Agreed. But Mitch is torn up. Maggie's going to stay with him today; maybe a few days."

"Maggie got a good heart. Can't say I'd stay with Mitch after all he done—or didn't do."

Sydney gets snippy with me. "I think Mitch proved to be a stand-up guy."

Ain't worth a fight, so I back down. "Yeah, I guess. I guess you shouldn't punish a man for being a dumbass teenager. Especially knowing what a piece of shit his old man was."

"Yeah, the sins of the father . . ." She trails off.

"Talkin' about fathers . . . I hope you know I wasn't keepin' anything from you. I had no fucking idea I'm Tierney's dad."

"That's obvious by the way your dick responded to her," she snaps.

Damn. She went for the jugular. I swallow the puke that comes up every time I think about that.

"Sorry. That was a low blow. I've still got some anger to work through."

"I deserved it. I still ain't forgave myself, so I know it'll take time."

She nods and drinks her coffee.

I rest my foot on my knee and lean back in the chair. "Tierney's mom is taking her home when she's discharged."

Syd sits up tall and whips her head around to stare at me. "What? But she's supposed to help with the crabs when you're gone."

That gives me hope. Syd still wants her help. I really think we can be one big, happy family.

"Oh, she's comin' back. She told her mom she ain't going if she don't bring her back in time to help 'cause she promised you."

It's funny, but I feel pride at how responsible Tierney is.

"Okay. Good." Syd leans back in the rocker and zones out.

After a few minutes of quiet, I ask, "Well, whaddya think?"

"Think about what?"

"Tierney. About Helly having a big sister. About being a step-mom."

"What's there to think? It is what it is."

"Well, are you happy about it?"

"Jeez Jake, give me a break. I'm still in shock. I like Tierney quite a bit. She reminds me of a young me. She's great with Helly, and she even charmed Maggie. But finding out she's your daughter is a lot to take in. Are you happy about it?"

I can't hold back my smile. "I am. I think she's great! She's smart and nice, and I love that Helly's gonna have a big sis. I only wish my mom and pop had gotten to meet her."

"Or Helly," she says.

"Yeah, of course, I wish they could've met Helly too. It sucks Tierney leaves for college at the end of summer. I want more time with her."

Syd pulls the blanket tighter and takes another swallow of coffee.

"I told Tierney and her mom that I'm gonna help with the money for school."

At first Syd raises her eyebrows, and I think she's gonna balk, but then she gets a great big smile. "Obviously, we'll help her with college. William & Mary is quite prestigious. Tierney has a bright future ahead of her.

DEENA—July 12

Sydney invited me to lunch. After what happened to Tierney, I'm scared but I can't falter. It's unlikely, but still possible Sydney moved the trunk without opening it and doesn't know I was snooping. I'm going to assume she does know, and I've got to make her believe nothing I found made me suspicious. If she doesn't feel threatened, I may be able to buy myself some time, and time is what I need.

I take a deep breath, wipe my sweaty palms on my shirt, and slide into my car. Ten minutes early, I pull into Millie's parking lot. It's full. The Jed Donnelly scandal's been packing the place. Everyone wants to hear the latest gossip. I lift Davey out of his seat and take him by the hand. He toddles into the diner.

Millie waves from behind the counter. There's one empty booth. Grabbing a high chair, I tuck it at the end of the table, and strap Davey in it. I plop a container of cheerios and a sippy cup of milk in front of him, and he's happy.

Sydney rolls in a few minutes later. She slides Helly's car seat onto the bench seat and sits beside her.

"Hey," she says.

She's twitchy and her eyes are almost solid black. My shoulders tense.

"Well look at these two cuties," Millie says, coming over to take our orders. "These kids get cuter every day. Wish I could say the same for me. What can I get ya?"

I want soup, but that's too easy to poison. "A Reuben for me and a bowl of applesauce for Davey."

"The usual," Sydney says.

"Drinks?" Millie asks.

I already moved my pre-poured glass of water well out of Sydney's reach. "Water's good for me."

"I know," Millie says to Sydney. "Unsweetened tea." She hurries off to place our orders and keep the rest of the customers happy.

We sit in awkward silence until Millie brings the tea.

Sydney grabs Millie's arm before she can rush off. "Millie, wait, I have some big news to share with you and Deena. There's a new Swann."

Both Millie and I cover our mouths with our hands.

"Oh my God! You're pregnant. Congratulations!" I say, louder than I should have.

Every head in the diner turns to look at Sydney. She's beaming.

"No, no." She laughs and waves her hands in front of her. "At least not yet." She sits up a little taller in her seat, and increases her volume. "Jake found out he has a daughter. We are absolutely thrilled that Helly has a big sister."

There's silence in the diner. All ears strain to hear more.

"Oh wow!" I say. "That *is* big news! When will we meet her?"

"You already have. It's Tierney."

Sweat pops out on my chest and hands, and my stomach rolls at the news. Did Sydney know Tierney was Jake's daughter before or after she arranged her fall? Could that be why she did it?

And, what about Jake? Bile burns my throat. He's got to be totally disgusted with himself for lusting after his own daughter.

"Tierney, the girl that rented the boat in the marina?" Ned pipes in from the counter.

Sydney nods. "Yep."

"I shoulda guessed that. She looks just like a young Swannee. Who's the mom?" Millie blurts out the question that's on everyone's mind.

"Well, I haven't met her yet, but we're throwing a family picnic before Jake leaves for the boat show to welcome them both to the family. Her name is Julia Burke. Jake dated her when he was stationed in Norfolk."

There's a ripple of chatter. I catch a few sentences. *Girl in every port . . . How's he sure it's his? How many more kids'll pop up? Damn if I'd take her in.* By the tightness of Sydney's jaw, I suspect she heard them too.

"How do you feel about all this?" I ask, hoping to get a clue to what's going on in her mind.

She takes a sip of water and waits for everyone to quiet before answering. "Well, of course it was a shock, but now I'm excited. You know Tierney's been babysitting for me and helping with the pens. She's a lovely girl and really smart. She adores Helly and will be an awesome big sister. She's a great addition to our family."

She rehearsed that little speech. I'm sure of it. In fact, this whole lunch has seemed like a pre-planned show to announce her news. When you want something to spread through town you say it at Millie's.

Doris comes over to our booth. She's wearing a bright purple suit with a butterfly brooch. "It's big of you to welcome her mother."

Sydney bats her eyes innocently. "Why do you say that, Doris?"

"Well because, you know, she used to . . . to be with Jake."

Sydney waves her hand. "Oh Doris, that's ancient history. Jake and I are happily married. I have nothing to worry about."

I choke on my water. It wasn't that long ago Sydney was shooting daggers at Jake for hanging over Tierney.

"Why don't you bring her to the fish fry so we can all meet her?" Doris suggests.

"No, remember, Jake'll be at the boat show and Tierney will be helping me with the pens and Helly."

"Well how about church the following Sunday?" Doris presses.

"Yeah, that might work. I'll check with Tierney and Jake."

Sydney is awfully quick to agree. I know how she feels about church and Doris.

Doris claps her hands together. "Good! I'll start planning. We'll have a little reception after the service to welcome her to the community."

Doris's matching purple heels clack on the floor as she leaves.

I tilt my head and look at Sydney. "I'm surprised you said yes."

"Oh, I just didn't want to hassle with her. You know how pushy she can be. It was easier to say yes. Besides, who knows what will happen by then."

Millie brings our food. Davey's getting restless, so I start feeding him his applesauce.

"I bet Jake's happier than a clam," Millie says. "He's always wanted a bunch of kids. And then Cammie . . . well, you know."

"He is happy. Tierney starts college in Virginia in August so he's a little disappointed that he won't get to see her much—"

Millie interrupts. "Oh, I bet he'll be driving down there every weekend. He's gotta make up for lost time."

I'm sure I see anger flash in Sydney's eyes, but she covers it with a big smile. "True, it's not that far. It'll be good for them to get to know each other."

Millie grins. "I guess I got another girl to grandmother."

Sydney's nostrils flare. "Sure do."

"Well dig in," Millie says. "I got to get back to work or Harry'll be yelling."

To me, it's clear Sydney is not happy about her family's new addition."

"That's big news. Skip told me about her accident at the marina. Is Tierney recovering okay?"

"Yeah, the poor kid. She went home with her mom for a few days, but they'll come back here for the family picnic on the eighteenth."

She's painting a rosy picture, but I'm not buying it.

"You really are handling this good. I think I'd be a little jealous. Or at least annoyed to go from one kid to two with no warning. And then be expected to welcome her with open arms."

"Nope." she says. Her eyes are wide and she's got a creepy smile on her face. "I'm not either of those things. Like I said to Doris, I have nothing to worry about."
No, but I'm terrified Tierney does.

MAGGIE—July 12

My two-day old clothes stink like ass and I been using my finger to brush my teeth. While Mitch picks out a casket and plans a funeral, I run home to work a few hours, then get cleaned up and grab some fresh clothes before I head back to his place. I turn in the driveway. Jake's on his way to work.

He pulls up beside me and rolls down his window. "Hey, you all right?"

"Why wouldn't I be? Wasn't my old man. You tell Syd about Tierney?"

"I did."

"And?"

"And she's okay with it. Agreed we oughta help with her college."

I hope he's right but it seems too easy.

He points at my bateau. "You going out?"

"Yeah, for a few hours. Need the dough, taxes is due soon. Then I'm going back to Mitch's."

"Is he okay?"

"As good as you'd expect after killin' your old man."

Jake shakes his head. "Yeah, that's some shit, but I'm glad the bastard's dead."

"Yeah. I'll be happy as shit once he's buried and we can forget about him."

Jake looks at his watch. "Shit, I gotta roll. Gonna be late for work. Hey ask Syd about Thursday night. She's plannin' something for all of us."

"Yeah okay. And I'll be home before sun-up tomorrow to get a full day's work in."

Jake takes off out the road. I park in front of the house and hop outta the truck. Ruby runs full speed and damn near knocks me on my ass.

Sydney hears her bark and comes out of her house with Helly on her hip. She walks over and hugs me. I take Helly and tuck her little head into my neck.

"You okay?" Syd asks.

I don't gotta pretend with her. "Yeah, I'm good, real good."

"I take it you and Mitch reconciled?"

I nod. "He's a good man. Hardest part right now is workin' up some sympathy over his old man. Truth be told, I hope Jed Donnelly's walkin' through Hell's gates right about now. I just couldn't go with Mitch to pick out the son-of-a-bitch's coffin."

She looks surprised. "Did Mitch expect you to?"

"Didn't expect, but I bet he woulda liked it. I feel bad I ain't there with him."

Helly squirms and Syd takes her from me. I head towards the dock. I gotta get a move on if I wanna catch enough to make it worth going out.

Syd grabs my shoulder and looks at me all serious. "Don't beat yourself up. You've forgiven Mitch, and you're supporting him. That's enough."

"Well, it's all I got to give, so it gotta be enough."

"Look at you working the program!" Sydney raises her hand for a high five.

I roll my eyes and leave her hangin'. "Hey, Jake said something 'bout Thursday. What's up?"

"I'm going to have a cookout for everyone. Don't worry I won't be cooking. I'll order from Millie." She laughs.

"Who's everyone?"

"You, Mitch, Me, Jake, Tierney, and her mom and of course this bundle of cuteness." She rubs Helly's toes.

"So, you really is okay with everything?"

She gets a big smile on her face. So big it kinda looks fake. "Of course I am. Helly's going to love having a big sister and I have a built in baby sitter." She holds Helly over her head and makes her giggle. "I know you've already had lunch with Tierney, and you seemed to like her." Syd's voice is tight and high-pitched, and she talks fast. "Jake seems thrilled to have her in his life. I haven't met Julia, but I assume she is perfectly lovely. And now that Mitch and you have reconciled, we'll all just make the perfect family."

The black in her eyes is bigger than saucers, and the white part's silvery. Her cheeks are red. I get a flashback to the night she came home from Dollie's all revved up—the night Eddie died.

I push the memory away. "Whoa! Take a breath."

"Sorry. I'm just excited to have everyone together. So anyway, you'll invite Mitch?"

"I'll ask him. I think he's gonna bury Jed on Wednesday, so we'll see if he's up to it."

"Well sure, I understand if he declines. Are you attending the funeral?"

"Hell no! It'd be damn hard to keep from spittin' on his grave. Best I steer clear."

Helly fusses to be changed and fed.

"The princess needs care," Sydney says.

"I gotta get to work anyhow. Could really use a quick, good haul today."

"Good luck!" she calls over her shoulder.

Me and Ruby head down the wharf and hop in the bateau. When my feet hit the floor of the boat, my shoulders ease up. I throw the lines onto the dock and putter out the crick. I let all the shit go and run my line.

JAKE—July 18

Life is good.

Tierney's stretched out beside Helly on a big fluffy quilt, with Daisy at their feet. Helly looks up at her big sister with love, and Tierney gives it right back. Maggie leans against Mitch, relaxed and open. Nothin' like the Nails from two years ago. Sydney and Julia are yukkin' it up over mommy stories.

My only sadness is my mom ain't here to see her two beautiful granddaughters. Saturday will be two years since she died. She would have loved this day.

I sit down on the quilt beside my girls.

"Tierney," Julia says. "I can't believe how much you look like the Swann side of your family. I see lots of Maggie and your dad in you."

Maggie pipes up. "She got my older brother's eyes. He had those grey speckles."

"Yeah, I noticed that in the photo Tierney texted me," Julia agrees. She looks at Sydney and asks, "Do you think our girls will look like sisters?"

"Only time will tell," Sydney answers.

Time. I already missed so much of it with Tierney. I hate that I have to go to another damn boat show. When I get back, I'm going to spend every free minute with my daughters.

Tierney lays her head beside Helly's "I know we will. See, we already have the same mouth and nose."

I look at my girls—Sydney, Helly and Tierney. How could a man get any luckier? I've had some dark times in my life—real dark. Sydney changed all that, but I still never thought I could have it this good.

Helly leaves out a slobbery burp. We all laugh and I'm so damn happy I could cry. I give Helly a little peck on her chubby cheeks, and squeeze Tierney's shoulder.

Tierney smiles up at me. "Dad, this is the absolute best day I've ever had."

"Me too," I say, and mean it with all my heart.

SYDNEY—July 19

It's 2 a.m. Jake's at the boat show and, because of my special sleeping-pill-and-beer cocktail, I'm sure Maggie is dead asleep. Tonight is the night.

I fidget in bed, watching the eerie glow of moonlight wax and wane through my window. Finally, I hear it. The sound I've been waiting for.

The door clicks as Tierney goes out to check the pens. I ease out of bed and peek into Helly's room. She's sound asleep in her crib and Daisy snores from her bed on the floor beside her. I quietly shut her door, then walk into the main room.

It's dark except for a tiny night light. The sheets on the couch are rumpled from Tierney's naps between checks; the chenille blanket puddles on the floor.

I peer out the front window. The porch light is on and I can see Tierney walking to the pens. Her blonde ponytail sways side to side. Tierney strolls to the end of the dock, throws her head back, and raises her arms in the air, like she's thanking the universe for her good fortune. I see her shoulders rise and fall with her deep breaths.

Although I can't turn off the porch light without drawing Tierney's attention, I'm unconcerned. Ever adaptable, I slip out the back door and pad, bare-footed behind Maggie's house, sneak around the side, and crouch down behind a hydrangea bush to watch Tierney undetected. She turns back towards the pens and walks up the dock with a contented smile on her face. The spotlights caress her cheeks like a mother's hands. She really is beautiful.

She pulls the half-full tray of softshells out of the dock refrigerator, and sets it on the counter behind the pens. A few strands of hair slip from her ponytail and she tucks them behind her ear. I edge closer and stand behind the locust tree in Maggie's yard. I hear Tierney humming *This Little Light of Mine*. A bug grazes her face. She crinkles her nose and shoos it away. Now that I know she's Jake's daughter, I see him and Helly in her every gesture and expression. My eyes soften and I smile at her loveliness.

She slips the gloves on her hands and peers into the water of the pen, looking for sloughs. Her hands glide elegantly into the water, wooing the crabs. She has Jake's calm energy.

I sneak closer still, hiding behind the sheets I left hanging on the wash line. I check behind me. Maggie's and Rhonda's houses are dark. Tierney's humming changes to soft singing. Her voice is angelic. I wonder if Helly will have her singing voice.

Tierney's lost in her song, and the meditative motion of her hands. She doesn't notice me creep behind her. Like Jake, she unknowingly sways her head in rhythm with her sweeping hands.

I saw Jake's eyes when he looked at her; he's head over heels for his newfound daughter. He will want to spend every waking moment making up for his absence in Tierney's life. And Helly and Maggie already adore Tierney, too. Inwardly, I sigh. It's really such a shame that Tierney won't see Helly grow up, but I can't let her take what's mine.

I check to be certain the stool is on the mark and silently climb the two steps. As I reach for the clamp light, I hear Maggie scream, "NO!"

DEENA—July 19

It hits me like a thunderbolt. Jake's at the boat show and Sydney is alone with Tierney. I shoot straight up in bed, scaring Skip.

He's groggy. "What's wrong?"

My gut is telling at me to move. "No time."

I throw shoes on and sprint to my car. I gun it, speeding down route 409. The one light in Rock Narrows is red, but I don't stop. I'm dead certain I've got to get there quick.

Sydney's words are alarms blaring in my head. *"Who knows what will happen by then?" "I have nothing to worry about."*

I pray to God I'm wrong. I pray I'm overreacting. But if I'm right, Sydney said yes to church because, by then, Tierney won't be alive.

I tear into Sydney's driveway, kicking up oyster shell dust. Slamming the car into park, I run into Sydney's house. I hear Daisy bark behind the closed door of Helly's room. Otherwise, it's quiet. I fling open the door to Sydney's bedroom. The bed is empty. I check the closet—nothing. Next, I check the nursery. Helly's in her crib asleep. I scan the kitchen and living room area. There are rumpled sheets on the couch, but no bodies.

I run into the bathroom. The shower curtain is closed. My hands shake uncontrollably, but I swallow and rip open the curtain. Empty. I look in the mudroom—no one.

Grabbing a cleaver from the kitchen, I open the basement door. It's dark and I'm scared. I ease myself down the narrow steps, holding the knife in the air, ready for attack. I reach the bottom and search around. Empty. No one's in the house. Oh my God! Where are they? I take the basement steps two at a time and fly back out the front door.

I'm sprinting to Nails's house when I hear a groan from behind the wash line full of sheets. I tear past them, falling when one pulls free from the line and tangles around my legs. Another moan. I turn towards the sound and cry out in horror. I don't know who to help first.

Struggling to get free from the sheet, I half crawl, half lunge towards Nails. She's on the ground at the top of the dock. Her leg's twisted in a way legs don't go. It's got to be broken. She's unconscious, but moaning.

I kneel down beside her and gently shake her shoulder. "Nails. Nails. Are you okay?"

Her eyes flutter open and she grimaces in pain. "Save her."

She lifts her hand and points at the crab pens. I see a nightmare.

Tierney's hands and arms are in the pen water. Her body is jerking. Smoke rises from burn marks on her arm. Beside her, Sydney's back and head are in the water. Her legs are sticking straight out from her body, twitching.

Oh my God! They're being electrocuted.

Finally free of the sheet, I run to the dock, but am afraid to get too close. There's an overturned stool and a puddle of water on the dock that might have current running to it. One of the clamp lights lays in the eight inches of pen water, still plugged in. I dart up to Nails's porch and grab her broom. Once I'm back at the dock, I use the broom handle to pull the cord out of the plug.

Tierney's body slumps to the ground in a smoking heap. Sydney's legs fall and dangle lifelessly from the pen. I uncurl Tierney and check to see if she's breathing. She's not. I don't know CPR, but I try anyway.

Nails drags herself towards me to help. Her mangled leg bumps against a line barrel and she passes out from pain.

Tears stream down my cheeks. My chest tightens and I'm panting, but I keep pushing on Tierney's chest, over and over, begging her to breathe. She's not responding.

There's no one to help me deal with this. I slide my fingers in my hair and pull, trying to clear my head. I don't know what to do. I clench my jaw and stand up. I have to get a grip. I have to handle this.

Tierney's gone. Maybe I can save Sydney.

For a second I hesitate. Aren't we all better off if she's dead?

No! That's not me thinking—that's fear. I can't just stand here and let a person die.

I twist Sydney's head towards me, so when I pull her out of the pen her head doesn't hit the dock. Using all my strength, I yank her head and upper back against my chest at the same time I pull her out of the pen. Pain shoots up my spine when my tailbone hits the dock with Sydney's body on top of me. I roll her off me and check if she's breathing. She's not. I give her chest a thump with my fist, and another, and another. Nothing changes.

I slump back, resting on my heels between two bodies. I'm in a silent, slow-motion horror movie. The summer breeze inches Tierney's hair across her face. Drops of water, falling from the pens, take a minute to reach the dock. My head floats so slowly side to side the movement is indetectable. Nails comes to. Her mouth is moving, but I hear no sound, and then suddenly, I'm slammed with noise.

The water circulating into the pen sounds like a roaring waterfall. The croak of bullfrogs batters my head, and Nails's ragged breathing is like fingernails on a chalkboard.

"Is she dead?" Her words finally reach me.

"They both are."

She blacks out again. I need to call 911. I reach for my phone. It's gone. It must have fallen out of my back pocket. I step over Sydney's body, then Nails's body, and search the yard where I fell. It's there.

Shaking too much to stand, I sit in the grass and call 911.

"This is 911. What's your emergency?"

I look at the three bodies sprawled on the dock—Jake's sister, Jake's daughter, and Jake's wife. I think I know what happened. I think Sydney killed Tierney, and in the struggle when Nails tried to save her, Sydney ended up in the pen beside her. But do I know? Will it help Jake to know?

I see Jake's easy-going smile. I relive the relief I felt when he gave us the money to pay for Davey's medicine. I think of his motherless infant asleep in her crib. I remember tomorrow is the anniversary of his mom's murder. I choke on my sobs. His loss is too great. There is no need to destroy him with the truth of his wife's cruelty.

"Hello? Hello? What's your emergency?"

"There's been a horrible accident. An electrocution. Send three ambulances to Hall's Creek."

MAGGIE—July 19

My bone's broke and stickin' outta my leg. I need surgery. They called a surgeon in from Annapolis. He should be here in a coupla hours.

"Should I call Jake?" Deena asks.

After gettin' Helly, Deena followed my ambulance to the hospital. She ain't left my side.

I shake my head. I wanna tell him face to face. Not on a fucking phone.

The nurse messes with the IV that's got the pain killers. I need 'em. Hurts like a motherfucker. But I guess the medicine's making me sick 'cause I feel like I gotta puke. The nurse gets me a baggy thing and the call button, and leaves me and Deena alone.

"They're both dead, right?" I ask Deena.

She nods and snuggles Helly closer. "What happened?"

I swallow down puke that's coming up. "You ever wake up scared?"

"Yeah."

"That's what happened. I woke up about two, sweatin' like a pig. I don't know if I heard something or what, but my gut was tellin' me I hadda get up. I was groggy as shit, like I was drunk, but I wasn't. I still had half a beer sittin' on the counter. I kinda staggered out the porch door."

I hurl into the baggy. Deena rings the call bell and hands me a tissue and I wipe my mouth.

I run up the steps to the ICU. Mitch is still in the room. His head's on his dad's chest and he's crying. The nurses let me in and I hug Mitch's back while he hugs his dad.

I look into Jed's dead eyes. I didn't think it'd go down this way, but I ain't sorry he's gone. He was a mean son-of-a-bitch.

The nurse comes in. "You okay?"

I nod.

The nurse takes the puke filled baggy and gives me a clean one. "The combination of pain and pain meds is making you nauseous."

"Ya think?" What a dumb-ass statement.

Deena pats my hand and says to the nurse, "It's been a really rough night."

The nurse checks my IV and my vitals and leaves.

Deena wipes leftover puke off the corner of my mouth. "What happened once you were on the porch?"

"At first my eyes is fuzzy, and I can't see nothin' but the light shining on the dock. When I get closer, I hear Tierney singing. She got a pretty voice, like my momma." My voice cracks.

Deena pats my hand. "It's okay. You don't have to tell me."

"No, I want to. I . . . it's . . ." I take a deep breath and try to get my shit together. "When I walk around the wash line, I can see the pens plain as day. Tierney's hands are in the water to lift out the softshells. Sydney's behind her and looks crazy. Her eyes are like black saucers. I swear to God they were glowing. I ain't never seen nothin' like it."

I shake my head to get her face outta my brain. Helly gurgles. Her little blue eyes look all around. So sweet and innocent. Tears come when I think about her havin' no momma. I wipe them away. I gotta be strong for her, and Jake.

I suck in a breath and tell Deena the rest of the story. "Sydney steps onto a stool and reaches for the clamp light. It slams me like a mule-kick what she's gonna do. I yell, 'NO!' and run to the pens, but before I can get there, Sydney drops the light into the water."

Deena don't seem surprised at what Syd done. That's when it hits me.

"You knew, didn't you? You knew what Syd was gonna do. That's why you came down to the house. To stop her. That's why you told me that shit about Eddie and Shelby. You think she done all that too?"

Deena takes a big, sad breath. "I'm sorry, but yes. I think she did all of that too. And probably Whitey. And maybe more."

A chill shivers me and my throat feels like it's closing. "I need water."

Deena gets a cup and fills it from the pitcher.

I take a swallow. "Why didn't you call the cops before this all happened?"

"I had no proof, but there's a trunk—"

A nurse swishes in the room, and interrupts Deena. "Okay, in about thirty minutes, the anesthesiologist will come in to give you a pre-op checkup and then we'll prep you for surgery. You'll meet the surgeon right before we take you to the OR."

I lift the cup to take another gulp, but nurse grabs it out of my hand. "No, no. You can't have that before surgery. Sorry, that pitcher shouldn't be in here." She leaves and takes the water with her.

I try to work up some spit and swallow. "Tell me about the trunk."

"Sydney has a trunk packed full of stuff that's pretty damning, but . . ."

"But what?" I ask.

"But I was thinking maybe we should just get rid of it. We're the only ones who really know what happened. If we wanted to, we could make Tierney's and Sydney's death seem like an accident. I'm just wondering if it wouldn't be easier on Jake—and Helly—if we report it as an awful accident." She kisses the top of Helly's head. "I mean do we really want Helly to grow up knowing her mom is a killer?"

My neck gets hot and I'm mad. "And let that bitch off the hook?"

"She's dead. Nothing's going to hurt her. The only people who'll be hurt by the truth are Jake and Helly."

The thought of keepin' another fucking secret makes my chest heavy. "I dunno. I don't think I can keep it all to myself. I just got rid of all the shit weighin' me down. I don't need no new secrets eatin' me alive."

"When it gets too heavy, we've got each other."

She got a point. The truth will fuck Jake up. He's already gonna be a basket case. If we tell him that his wife killed his daughter, and his sister killed his wife, he might pull a Swannee on me.

"I'll think about it."

Deena squeezes my shoulder. "Okay. Tell me the rest. Tell me how you ended up with a bone sticking out of your leg and Sydney ended up in the pen."

I nod and finish the godawful story. "When Sydney drops the light in the water, Tierney's body tenses and jerks. I dive for the outlet to pull the plug, but Sydney body-slams me. She grabs my shoulders and tries to push me off the side of the dock into the water."

My heart pounds fast and my chest hurts.

"You okay?" Deena asks.

"I guess. It feels like I'm right there again." I take a big breath and keep talkin', hopin' like hell I'll feel better when I get the whole story out. "Syd yells, 'Stop fighting me. Let her go. It's best this way.'

"I punch Syd in the gut and grab her hair. She tackles me onto the dock. We roll around, and knock shit everywhere. I use all my strength and heave her off me. She grabs me and I push her backwards, tryin' to get to the plug before it's too late, but she twists and throws me to the ground. She falls on my leg. When I'm goin' down, it snaps."

Deena winces. "It almost makes me sick thinking about how much that must have hurt."

"Yeah." I shake my head. "I ain't never felt pain that bad. It made me dizzy. I knew I was gonna black out, so I used every bit of what I had left to lunge for her. I caught her leg and she tripped over the stool. Her arms flapped around to find her balance, but it didn't work. Her feet lifted up in the air, and she fell back, head first into the electrified water."

"Oh, that explains why she was backwards in the pen."

"Is that how the paramedics found her?"

Deena shakes her head. "No. When I pulled the plug Tierney fell to the dock. I drug Sydney out of the pen to see if I could save her. It was too late for both of them."

This is too fucking heavy. Tears fill up my eyes. "I tried. I really did. I crawled towards the plug to pull it out, but I kept blackin' out."

"Nails, you did everything you could. It's not your fault."

I swallow tears and nod my head.

"I'm here for you—now, tomorrow, next year. We're all going to get through this." Deena squeezes my hand.

The nurse comes in my room. "Are you ready for the anesthesiologist?"

I lift one finger. "Give us a minute."

The nurse ducks out.

"Call Mitch, okay?" I say to Deena.

"Sure, but what should I tell him?"

"Tell him you ain't sure what went down, but I need surgery. And then you take Helly and go home. Try to steer clear of the cops. If you gotta talk to them, just tell them what you saw when you got to the house. Nothing else. Okay?"

Deena nods.

I give her a weak smile. "I know I'm puttin' you in a bad spot, but I need time to figure shit out. I'll call you when I decide."

She nods. "Yeah, okay. I can do that, but I don't want to leave you alone. I'll stay until Mitch gets here."

"No."

The nurse comes in."This is Dr. Abbingdon. He's going to handle your anesthesia."

"Go," I say to Deena. "I'm fine. I'll be out like a light. Do what I told ya, okay?"

"Okay." She leans Helly in for me to kiss her. Her tiny little fingers wrap around mine.

"It'll be okay," I whisper to her.

*****

295

I wake up from surgery. Mitch smiles down at me. "Hi beautiful."

My first clear thought is *I love him*. My second clear thought is *Jake and Helly can never know.*

ACKNOWLEDGMENTS

As always, thanks to my supportive family for your tireless patience with endless rounds of "Can you just take a look at this?"

I am grateful to have found a top-notch critique group. Your insightful comments have improved my craft and your help has been invaluable.

Huge appreciation to Meri Freedman for her excellent proofreading.

And a heartfelt thanks to the awesome online writers' community. Your posts are a source of daily encouragement. A special shout-out to Darin Miller, author of *The Dwayne Morrow Mysteries*, for his much-appreciated support of my work!

A Letter To My Readers

Dear Readers,

The Eastern Shore of Maryland is a unique and vibrant place, ripe with characters and stories. It was my privilege to have lived there for several years. And it was a joy creating the Rock Narrows Suspense Series.

The Swanns' story doesn't end with the last pages of GREEN PEELER. I'll bring you more tales of Maggie, Jake, and little Helly. And Sydney, pre-Rock Narrows. Sign up to receive email updates about upcoming releases at lizzieQnert.com.

With the millions of great books available, I am humbled you chose to read mine! Thank you so much. I truly hope you enjoyed it!

It makes my day to hear from readers! Connect with me on FB, IG, or my website lizzieQnert.com.

And please, write a review. Your words have power. Reviews are the very best way to support authors!

Gratefully yours,

~ lizzie

Have you read?
More from lizzie Qnert

POWER SURGE

52-year-old CC Crane is no stranger to sexual harassment. For years, she rallied against the turn-a-blind-eye mentality. And still—even after #MeToo—sexual misconduct continues.

No more!

She won't stand by while women are being traumatized. Shameless men will no longer get away with bad behavior. CC issues the consequences she believes they deserve—humiliation, or for the worst offenders, death.

Her victims, however, are a bigger threat to women than she realizes. Many belong to the male supremacist hate group, Men R.O.A.R. (Reclaim Our Authority and Rights). When the hate group targets her daughter for working against sexual violence, CC's mama-bear ferocity kicks in, and she creates a hit list of local members.

Her activities are discovered by a R.O.A.R. member, and the tables turn. She becomes the hunted. Despite her best efforts, nothing happens as planned, and her vigilantism exacts a devastating price.

www.ingramcontent.com/pod-product-compliance
Lightning Source LLC
Chambersburg PA
CBHW022022240626
47154CB00007B/2221